KT-527-672

00401138282

Northamptonshire

DISCARDED

Libraries

RITA® Award finalist and Kindle bestselling author **Michelle Willingham** has written over forty historical romances, novellas and short stories. Currently she lives in south-eastern Virginia, USA, with her family and her beloved pets. When she's not writing Michelle enjoys reading, baking and avoiding exercise at all costs. Visit her website at: michellewillingham.com.

Also by Michelle Willingham

Forbidden Vikings miniseries

To Sin with a Viking
To Tempt a Viking

Warriors of Ireland miniseries

Warrior of Ice
Warrior of Fire

Warriors of the Night miniseries

Forbidden Night with the Warrior
Forbidden Night with the Highlander
Forbidden Night with the Prince

Untamed Highlanders miniseries

The Highlander and the Governess

Sons of Sigurd collection

Stolen by the Viking

Discover more at millsandboon.co.uk.

STOLEN BY THE VIKING

Michelle Willingham

MILLS & BOON

All rights reserved including the right of reproduction in whole or in part in any form. This edition is published by arrangement with Harlequin Books S.A.

This is a work of fiction. Names, characters, places, locations and incidents are purely fictional and bear no relationship to any real life individuals, living or dead, or to any actual places, business establishments, locations, events or incidents. Any resemblance is entirely coincidental.

This book is sold subject to the condition that it shall not, by way of trade or otherwise, be lent, resold, hired out or otherwise circulated without the prior consent of the publisher in any form of binding or cover other than that in which it is published and without a similar condition including this condition being imposed on the subsequent purchaser.

® and TM are trademarks owned and used by the trademark owner and/or its licensee. Trademarks marked with ® are registered with the United Kingdom Patent Office and/or the Office for Harmonisation in the Internal Market and in other countries.

First published in Great Britain 2020
by Mills & Boon, an imprint of HarperCollins*Publishers*
1 London Bridge Street, London, SE1 9GF

Large Print edition 2020

© 2020 Michelle Willingham

ISBN: 978-0-263-08635-5

Northamptonshire Libraries

MIX
Paper from
responsible sources
FSC C007454

This book is produced from independently certified FSC™ paper to ensure responsible forest management. For more information visit www.harpercollins.co.uk/green.

Printed and bound in Great Britain
by CPI Group (UK) Ltd, Croydon, CR0 4YY

To Kat Schniepp, for your daily encouragement, words of wisdom, and for being my friend all these years. You have walked a difficult road and come out stronger. And, with your help, so have I.

Prologue

The kingdom of Maerr, Norway—ad 874

It was the morning of his wedding. Although most men would have welcomed the day, Alarr Sigurdsson had the sense that something was not right. The shadowed harvest moon last night had promised an ill omen, and the wise woman had cautioned him to delay the marriage.

Alarr had ignored the *volva*, for he was not a man who believed in curses or evil omens. The union would bring a strong alliance for his tribe. He had known Gilla Vigmarrsdottir since they were children, and she always had a smile and was even-tempered. She was not beautiful in the traditional way, but that didn't matter. Her kindness made him amenable to the match. His father, Sigurd, had negotiated for her bride price, and the *mundr* was high, demonstrating their family's wealth.

'Are you ready to be chained into the bonds of marriage?' his half-brother Danr teased. 'Or do you think Gilla has fled?'

He didn't rise to Danr's bait. 'She will be there.'

Alarr had worn his best tunic, adorned with silver-braided trim along the hem, and dark hose. His black cloak hung over his shoulders, but it was the absence of his weapons that bothered him most. His mother had asked him to leave them behind, claiming that they would only offend the gods. It was an unusual request, and one that made him uneasy, given all the foreign guests.

Her beliefs did not mean he intended to remain defenceless, however. During the wedding, he would receive a ceremonial sword from Gilla as a gift, and at least he would have that. Weapons were a part of him, and he took comfort in a balanced blade. He felt more comfortable fighting than joining in a conversation.

It was strange being the centre of attention, for he had two brothers and two half-brothers. As the second-born, Alarr was accustomed to being overlooked and ignored, a fact that usually allowed him to retreat into solitude and train for warfare. The intense physical exertion brought a strange sense of peace within him. While he practised with a blade, he didn't have to compete with anyone, save himself. And now that he had earned his status as a fighter, the men respected him. No one challenged him, and he had confidence that he could win any battle he fought.

Not that Sigurd had ever noticed.

Although his father tried to behave as if they had no enemies, Alarr was no fool. There was an air of restlessness brewing among the tribes. He had visited several neighbouring *jarls* and had overheard the whispers of rebellion. Yet, his father did not want to believe it.

Danr shot him a sidelong grin. 'Are you afraid of losing your innocence this night?' With that, Alarr swung his fist, and Danr ducked, laughing. 'I hope she is gentle with you, Brother.'

'Be silent, unless you want me to cut out your tongue,' he threatened. But both knew it was an idle threat. His half-brother was never serious, and he often made jests. Fair-haired and blue-eyed, all the women were fascinated by the man, and Danr was only too willing to accept their offerings. Alarr knew that his half-brother would find his way into a woman's bed this night.

The scent of roasting meat lingered in the air, and both cattle and sheep had been slaughtered for the wedding feast. Sigurd had invited the leaders of neighbouring tribes, as well as their daughters. Undoubtedly, he would be trying to arrange future weddings to advance his own position. Although Sigurd was a petty king, it was never enough for him. He hungered for more status and greater power.

Alarr walked towards his father's longhouse and found Sigurd waiting there. The older man had a satisfied expression on his face, though he was wearing only a simple woollen tunic and hose. His hair was greying, with threads of white mingled in his beard and hair. Even so, there was not a trace of weakness upon the man. His body was a warrior's, lean and strong. Sigurd had bested many men in combat, even at his advanced age. 'Are you ready?'

Alarr nodded, and they walked alongside one another in silence. Outside their settlement, his ancestors were buried within the Barrow. The graves of former warriors—his grandsire and those who had died before him—were waiting. There, Alarr would dig up a sword from one of the burial mounds. The weapon would become his, forged with the knowledge of his forebears, to be given to his firstborn son.

* * *

After a quarter-hour of walking in silence, Sigurd paused at the base of the Barrow and gestured for Alarr to choose. He was glad of it, for he already knew whose sword he wanted.

He climbed to the top of the Barrow and stopped in front of the grave that belonged to his uncle, who had died only a year ago, in battle. Hafr had trained him in sword fighting from the moment Alarr was strong enough to lift a weapon. There was no one else whose sword he wanted more.

He and his father dug alongside one another until they reached the possessions belonging to Hafr. Alarr tried to dispel the sense of foreboding that lingered while he respected the ashes of his uncle. The sword had been carefully wrapped in leather, and Alarr took it, uncovering the weapon. The iron glinted in the morning light, but it would need to be cleaned and sharpened.

'Do you wish to take the sword?' Sigurd asked quietly.

'I do.'

His father then reached out to seize the weapon. Once he had given it over, Sigurd regarded him. 'Much is expected of you with this marriage. Our kingdom of Maerr has risen to great power, and we need to strengthen our ties with the other *jarls*. You must conceive a son with Gilla immediately and ensure that our alliance is strong.' He wrapped the sword in the leather once more and set it aside. 'Perhaps my brother's wisdom and strength will be yours, now that you have his sword.'

Alarr gave a nod, though he didn't believe it. He wanted the sword because it gave him a tangible memory of his uncle. Hafr had been more of a father to him than Sigurd, whether he'd known it or not. Alarr had spent most of his life trying to gain Sigurd's approval, to little avail.

They reburied the ashes of his uncle, along with Hafr's worldly possessions, before returning to the settlement. Alarr walked towards the bathhouse, for it was time for the purification ritual. He had not seen Gilla since her arrival, but he had seen several of her kinsmen and a few others he didn't recognise.

When he entered the bathhouse, the heat struck him instantly. Steam rose up within the air from heated stones set inside basins of water. Wooden benches were placed at intervals, along with several drying cloths.

Alarr stripped off his clothing and saw that

three of his brothers were waiting. His youngest brother Sandulf was there, along with his older brother, Brandt, and their half-brother Rurik, Danr's twin. Unlike Danr, Rurik was dark-haired and quiet. In many ways, Alarr found it easier to talk with Rurik. They trained together often, and he considered the man a close friend, as well as a brother. Their youngest brother, Sandulf, had a thirst to prove himself. He had dark-blond hair and blue eyes and had nearly put adolescence behind him. Even so, Alarr didn't like the thought of his brother fighting in battle. Sandulf lacked the reflexes, though he'd trained hard. He feared that only experience would help the young man gain the knowledge he needed now.

'Whose sword did you choose?' Sandulf asked.

'Hafr's,' Alarr answered. At his answer, Rurik met his gaze and gave a silent nod of approval. His brother had also been close to Hafr, since Sigurd had distanced himself from his bastard sons.

Alarr strode towards the wooden trough containing heated water. He began the purification ritual, pouring the warmed water over his body with a wooden bowl and scrubbing off the dirt with soap. As he did, Brandt remarked in a low voice, 'There are many strangers among the guests. Did you notice?'

'I did,' Alarr answered. 'But then, our tribe is well known across the North. It's not uncommon. And we know that Sigurd wants to make other marriage alliances.' He sent a pointed look towards Rurik, which his half-brother ignored.

Even so, Brandt looked uneasy. 'He's endangering our tribe by bringing in warriors we don't know. Some were from Éireann.'

The island was several days' journey across the sea. Sigurd had travelled there, years ago, and had brought back a concubine. She had given birth to Rurik and Danr a few months after her arrival and had never returned home, even after Sigurd set her aside. Although Saorla had died years ago, this was the first time any visitors had come from Éireann. Alarr wondered if there was some connection between the visitors and his half-brothers.

Regardless, he saw little choice but to let the foreigners witness the marriage. 'They are already here now. We cannot deny them our hospitality.' With a shrug, he added, 'Sigurd likely invited them in the hopes of wedding one of their daughters to Rurik or Danr.'

'Possibly.' Brandt thought a moment. 'We cannot deny them a place to stay, but we can deny them the right to bring in weapons. We will say it is to abide by our mother's wishes.'

It was a reasonable request, and Alarr answered, 'I will see to it.' He reached for his clothing and got dressed.

'Wait a moment.' Brandt approached and held out a leather pouch. 'A gift for your wedding.' Alarr opened it and found a bronze necklace threaded with small pendants shaped like hammers. It was a visible reminder of Thor, a blessing from his older brother.

He stood so Brandt could help him put it on. Then Alarr looked back at his brothers, unable to cast off the sense that something was not right at all. Perhaps it was the unknown warriors, or perhaps it was the knowledge that he would be married this day.

A sudden premonition pricked at him, that he would not marry Gilla, as they had planned. Alarr knew not why, but the hair on the back of his arms stood up, and he could not set aside his uncertainty. He tried to dispel the restlessness in anticipation of the wedding. Like as not, every bridegroom had those feelings.

Sandulf trailed behind him. 'May I join you, Alarr?'

He shrugged. 'If you wish. But we are only exchanging the *mundr* and Gilla's dowry. You may want to wait.' The wedding activities would last most of the day, and there were enough witnesses without needing Sandulf there. 'You could return when we make the sacrifices to the gods. That part is more interesting.'

His brother nodded. 'All right. And in the meantime, I can watch over our guests and learn if any of them are a threat.'

'Good.' He understood his youngest brother's desire to be useful, and it might be a wise idea to keep a close watch over the visitors.

Alarr departed the bathhouse and watched as his brothers went on their way. Brandt joined him as he approached the centre of the settlement. His older brother said little, but his face transformed when he spied his heavily pregnant wife, Ingrid. There was a moment of understanding that passed between them, along with joy. Alarr wondered if he would ever look upon Gilla's face in that way when she was about to bear a child.

'It won't be long now,' he said to Brandt. 'You'll be a father.'

Brandt nodded, and there was no denying his

happiness. 'Ingrid thinks it's a boy from what the *volva* told her. I hope they are right.'

Alarr walked alongside his brother until he reached Sigurd and Gilla's father. It was time to discuss the bride price and dowry. But before they could begin, they were interrupted by his mother. She hurried forward and whispered quietly to Brandt, whose face tightened. Then he gave a nod.

'I must go,' he said to Alarr. 'There is a disturbance with tribes gathering to the north. I should be back later tonight for the wedding feast, but I've been asked to intervene and prevent bloodshed, if possible. I am sorry, but it cannot wait.'

Alarr inclined his head, wondering if this was the ill omen the *volva* had spoken of. It also struck him that his mother had spoken to Brandt and not to him or to her husband. She did not like Sigurd, but then again, it was possible that the king already knew and had ordered Brandt to go in his stead. Sigurd's presence at the wedding was necessary.

'Do not go alone,' Alarr warned his brother.

'Rurik will accompany me, along with a few other men,' Brandt promised. His gaze fixed upon his wife, who was walking towards the other women, and his features softened. 'I will return as soon as I can.'

'Go then,' Alarr said. 'And return this night for the feasting.' He clapped Brandt on the back before turning his attention back to the negotiations.

Sigurd was already bargaining with Vigmarr as the two exchanged the dowry and *mundr*. Since they had already agreed upon the bride price, it was hardly more than a symbol of the union to come.

Alarr saw Gilla standing behind her father. She wore a green woollen gown with golden brooches at her shoulders. Her dark hair hung below her shoulders, and upon her head, she wore a bridal crown made of woven straw, intertwined with flowers. Her smile was warm and welcoming, though she appeared slightly nervous.

Beside her, the *volva* was preparing the ritual sacrifice to the gods. The wise woman began chanting in the old language, supplications for blessings. Several of the guests began to draw closer to bear witness, and the scent of smoke mingled with the fresh tang of blood. The slain boar was offered up to Freyr, and the *volva* took a fir branch and dipped it into the boar's blood.

She then made the sign of the hammer, blessing them with the sacrificial blood, as well as the other wedding guests.

Although Gilla appeared amused by the ritual, the sight of sprinkled blood upon her face and hair made Alarr uneasy. He watched as the wise woman then sprinkled the boar's blood on each of the guests. But instead of the guests revering the offering, there seemed to be an unspoken message passing among several of the warriors. Alarr could not shake the feeling that this was an omen of bloodshed to come.

Let my brothers be safe, he prayed to the gods. *Let them come back alive.*

Alarr watched the men, his attention caught by the tall Irish king. He didn't know if Feann MacPherson had come as an invited guest, or whether he had arrived of his own choice. It might be that he wanted an alliance or a wedding for his daughter, if he had one. The king wore a woollen cloak, and there were no visible weapons. Yet the man had a thin scar along his cheek, evidence of an earlier battle. His dark hair was threaded with grey, but there was a lean strength to him.

When he saw Alarr staring, his expression tightened before it fixed upon Sigurd. The hard look was not of a man who wanted an alliance—it was of a man itching for a fight.

Someone needed to alert the guards, but Alarr could not leave in the midst of the ceremony. He searched for a glimpse of Danr or Sandulf, but they were nowhere to be found. He only saw his aunt nearby, and she could do nothing.

You're overreacting, he tried to tell himself. But no matter how he tried to dismiss his suspicions, his instincts remained on alert. He could not interrupt the ceremony, for it would only humiliate his bride. This was meant to be a day of celebration, and Gilla's smile was bright as she looked at him.

She was a kind woman, and as he returned her smile, he forced his thoughts back to the wedding. Friendship was a solid foundation for their union, and he inwardly vowed that he would try to make this marriage a good one.

He stood before her, and Sigurd brought the sword of Hafr that they had dug from his uncle's grave. Alarr presented it to Gilla, saying, 'Take this sword as a gift from my ancestors. It shall become the sword of our firstborn son.'

She accepted the weapon and then turned to her father to present their own gift of another sword. 'Take this sword for your own.'

The blade had good balance, and he tested the edge, noting its sharpness. Gilla knew of his love for sword-fighting, and she had chosen a weapon of quality. It was a good exchange, and he approved of her choice.

Alarr placed the ring for Gilla upon the hilt of the sword, and was about to offer it, when he caught a sudden movement among the guests. Feann cast off his dark cloak and unsheathed a sword from where it had been strapped between his shoulder blades. His men joined him, their own weapons revealed. The visible threat made their intentions clear.

Sigurd's face turned thunderous at the insult, and he started to reach for Alarr's sword.

He handed the weapon to his father and commanded, 'Take Gilla to the longhouse and guard her.' The last thing they needed was his father's hot-headed fighting. 'Vigmarr and I will settle this.'

He took back his uncle's sword from Gilla, and her face turned stricken when she murmured, 'Be safe.'

His father heeded his instructions and took Gilla with him, along with a few other men. His aunt joined them, running with her skirts clenched in her hands. He heard his mother scream as she fled towards another longhouse in the opposite direction. Only when the women were gone did Alarr breathe easier.

It was a mistake. Chaos erupted among the guests as his men hurried towards the longhouse where they had stored their weapons. King Feann uttered a command in Irish, and his men surged forward, cutting down anyone in their path.

Alarr ran hard, and iron struck iron as his weapon met an enemy's blade. He let the familiar battle rage flow through him, and his uncle's sword bit through flesh, striking down his attacker. The weapon was strong, imbued with the spirt of his ancestor. Alarr swung at another man, and he glimpsed another warrior behind him. He sidestepped and caught the man in the throat before he slashed the stomach of his other assailant.

The volva *was right*, he thought. *It was an ill omen.*

Already, he could see the slain bodies of his kinsmen as more men charged forward in the fight. Alarr searched for his brothers, but there was no sign of Sandulf or Danr. By the gods, he hoped they were safe. If only Brandt and Rurik had been here, they could have driven off their enemies. He caught one of his kinsmen and ordered, 'Take a horse and ride north as hard as you can. Find Brandt and Rurik and bring them back.' The man obeyed, running hard towards the stables.

A strange calm passed over him with the knowledge that he would likely die this day. The shouts of kinsmen echoed amid the clang of weapons, only to be cut short when they died. The Irish king started to run towards the longhouse, but Alarr cut him off, swinging his sword hard. The older man caught his balance and held his weapon against the iron.

Feann paused a moment. 'Stay out of this, boy. The fight isn't yours. Sigurd has gone too far, and he will pay for his crimes.'

'This is my wedding, so the fight *is* mine,' Alarr countered. He swung his weapon, and the king blocked his blow. 'And I am not a boy.' He was beginning to realise that Feann had travelled seeking vengeance, and his intent was to slaughter Sigurd. But what crimes was he talking about?

They sparred against one another, the king toying with him. Alarr struck hard, intending to stop the man. But with every blow, he grew aware that Feann was stalling, drawing out the fight. It was then that he saw men surrounding the longhouse where his father was protecting his bride. Gilla's father, Vigmarr, was fighting back, trying to defend them.

And then Alarr caught the unmistakable scent of smoke and fire.

He renewed his attack, slashing with his sword as he fought to find a weakness. Feann parried each blow, and when the screams of the women broke through, Alarr jerked his attention back to the longhouse.

A slashing pain struck him in the calves, and he saw the king withdraw a bloody blade, just before his legs collapsed beneath him. Alarr met the man's gaze, waiting for the killing blow. Instead, Feann's expression remained grim as he wiped his blade. 'If you're wise, boy, you'll stay on the ground.' Then he strode towards the longhouse.

Alarr tried to rise, but the agonizing pain kept his legs from supporting him. He called out to his men to attack and defend the longhouse. But a moment later, he watched in horror as the fire raged hotter. Someone threw open the doors, and Sandulf staggered out. Four other men emerged from a different door, and Alarr struggled to his

knees. He spied the slain bodies of his father…
Gilla… Vigmarr and his wife…

His stomach lurched, and Alarr turned his gaze back to the sky, hating the gods for what they had done. A lone raven circled the clouds, and he could only lie in his own blood while his enemies cut down the remaining wedding guests and returned to their ships.

In the dirt beside him, he saw the familiar glint of a golden brooch.

Chapter One

Ireland—ad 876

The heavy slave collar hung around Breanne Ó Callahan's throat. Her mouth was dry from thirst, and she could hardly remember how long it had been since she was taken captive. The days blurred into one another, for she had been stolen from her foster home and sold into slavery. The trader had locked her in chains, and she had travelled for days in a wagon with the other women. She knew that he intended to sell her in the marketplace at Áth Cliath, for he could get a higher price for her there.

Exhaustion weighed upon her, and her body ached from bruises where she'd been beaten. It had been especially humiliating when they had taken her to the healer. Although it had been a woman who had touched her, her cheeks still burned at the memory. The healer had verified her virginity, and Breanne knew it was the only reason she had not yet been raped. The slaver knew that he could command a higher price for her innocence. She tried to clear her mind of the terrors rising and the fear of being held down and claimed by a stranger this night.

Breanne clenched her hands together in a vain attempt to keep them from shaking. Thus far, no one had come for her. She had searched in vain for any sign that her foster father had sent men to save her. They might not know where she was being held captive. With each day that had passed, her hope had begun to fade.

Do not surrender, she warned herself. *Not yet.*

There might be a chance at escape with so many people in the marketplace. She held fast to the frail hope, even as they dragged the first woman to the auction block. Breanne did not know her name, but the girl began to sob at her fate.

The trader called out the woman's value and stripped her naked in the marketplace. The girl whimpered when he extolled the virtue of her slender body and soft breasts. He turned her around, and there was no denying the lustful gazes of the men.

Breanne turned her attention to the crowd of

people, searching for a way out. There were a dozen wooden carts rolling through the streets, and if she could only get to one of them without being noticed, she might hide herself among the barrels or beneath the straw. She would have only precious seconds to act, and only then if she could break free. Her wrists and ankles were chained together, but if she shortened her stride, she could still run. All she had to do was wait until the woman before her was sold. She was last among the women, a lucky place, for soon there would be no one chained to her and she might be able to flee.

Her brain warned that it would be nearly impossible to escape notice. Not if she was running with an armful of chains. But even so, she tried to keep hope. If she imagined the alternative, the panic would rise up and overpower what little courage she had left.

The first woman was sold to a fat merchant, and he seized her hair as he pulled her forward. He groped her bare breast, laughing before he covered her body with a rough shift. Breanne suppressed a shudder. During the auction, her gaze fixed upon a row of three carts. One of them might serve as a place to hide—but first, she needed to create a distraction.

An outdoor peat fire burned nearby, and she spied another cart filled with straw. A fire, she decided. It would allow her to flee unnoticed while the others attempted to put out the blaze.

The second woman was sold, then the third. But before the fourth climbed up to the block, Breanne saw a taller man drawing near. His dark hair hung to his shoulders, and his piercing blue eyes stared at her. He appeared to be one of the *Lochlannach*, a fierce warrior from across the sea. His skin held a darker tone, and an iron chain containing three hammers encircled his throat. He looked like a man who had spent the entire summer upon the waters.

Breanne lifted her chin and stared back, refusing to let him intimidate her. A hint of a smile lifted his mouth, as if he had accepted her challenge. *Danu,* what if he attempted to buy her? It was clear that she had caught his interest. He appeared to be a man accustomed to getting his own way.

She noticed his strong hands and the way his shoulders filled his tunic. Unlike the fat merchant, there was no trace of weakness in his body. A vision flared in her mind, of being stripped naked before this man. Her body flushed at the thought. His blue eyes never left hers, and she felt a strange pull within her, as if he had somehow caressed her flesh without a single touch.

The warrior took another step closer, and this time, she noticed his slight limp. He wore armour, and a sword hung from his side. Who was he?

Her heartbeat pounded, and she had no more time to wonder, when the slaver dragged her up the stairs towards the block. He held the length of chain in his arms, and Breanne locked her gaze with the *Lochlannach*, wondering about his intentions. It would not matter. She would be no man's possession.

She feigned weakness, reluctantly drawing close to the block. Though she continued to walk forward, she waited until she could feel her captor's grip on the chain going slack as he prepared to strip her naked.

Now.

Breanne dived forward, leaping from the block towards the crowd. As she'd predicted, the unexpected motion jerked the chain from the slaver's hands. She lunged through the crowd of onlookers, making her way towards the wooden carts ahead.

Many tried to stop her, but she shoved her way

past them. The weight of the manacles on her wrists and ankles impeded her movement, but she would do anything to escape.

But a moment later, a hand caught her chains and dragged her backwards. Breanne fought to free herself, but the chains held fast.

'Let me go,' she gritted out, but she could not move. When she turned around, she saw the face of the *Lochlannach*. His expression was unyielding, like iron.

He wrapped the chain around his arm, making it impossible for her to escape him. His blue eyes were chips of ice, with no pity in them. Her heartbeat quickened, for she knew he would never release her.

'Please,' she begged.

He ignored her, holding the chains with one hand as she struggled to free herself. The slaver approached and raised his hand to strike her. Before his fist could make contact, the *Lochlannach* caught the man's wrist and held it. He spoke in a foreign tongue she did not understand, but his tone brooked no argument. The slaver started to argue, but the man ignored him. Instead, he reached into a pouch at his waist and withdrew a handful of coins. He placed them in the slaver's palm, and the man's protests were silenced.

And so, it was done. She had been bought by this *Lochlannach*. Hatred rose up within her at the thought of being this man's slave or worse, his concubine. She struggled again to free herself, but it was no use. He kept the chain tight, securing her firmly at his side until he reached his horse. In one motion, he lifted her up, before he swung up behind her.

He spurred the animal and rode towards the outer edges of Áth Cliath. Throughout the short journey, he said nothing at all. She almost wondered if he was even capable of speaking her language. Her only consolation was that he had not attempted to touch her...yet.

The uneasiness inside her intensified, doubling her fears. He was a raider and a Norseman, one who would take whatever he wanted. Why had he bought her? She wanted to believe that it was only a moment of chance, a sudden whim.

But he had been watching her and waiting. He had stopped her from fleeing the slave market, and now, he had claimed her. Gods be merciful.

They reached the river, and he dismounted from his horse, lifting her down. Breanne wondered if she could dive into the water, but he dispelled any thoughts of escape by keeping her chains tight. Inwardly, she cursed the man for taking her. She wanted to return home to Killcobar, and now she might never see Feann again. He and her foster brothers were the only family she remembered, since her parents had died years ago. Was Feann even looking for her? Or worse, had he given her up for dead?

Her heart ached at the loss of her home and family. The pain welled up inside her, mingled with loneliness and fear. She knew not what would happen to her any more. It seemed as if her life had crumbled into pieces, scattering to the wind.

The *Lochlannach* led her towards the docks until they reached a small boat where another man waited for them. The vessel was not large, and the sail was tied up against the mast. Her captor lifted her inside, and she glanced down at the dark water, wondering if she had the courage to jump. The other man seemed to guess her thoughts, for he shook his head in warning.

The Norseman spoke to the other man in the language she did not know. Another flare of anxiety caught her, for she feared they might take her to their country. She might never see Éireann again, and the thought terrified her.

'Who are you?' she asked, even knowing that they might not understand her. The men lifted the anchor and began to row out to the open water. As she'd predicted, they did not answer her question. Once again, she eyed the water, wondering if she dared to jump. But then, the chains would only drag her down to the bottom of the river and cause her to drown.

Though it was still morning, the sky was dark and heavy with moisture. Clouds obscured the sun, and soon, fat raindrops splattered upon her. Breanne welcomed the water, trying to quench her thirst by opening her mouth. The Norseman seemed to notice, and he held out a drinking skin, tipping it against her lips. She took a sip, and the water was stale but welcome. When she had finished, he took it back. Then he reached inside a wooden container and pulled out a heavy fur of seal skin. He lifted it over her, and she realised that it would shield her from the rain.

She was taken aback by the gesture. Why should he care if she were drenched from the rain? It poured over him and his shipmate, soaking through his dark hair. Though he rowed steadily, he kept his gaze fixed upon her.

His attention unnerved her, reaching deep within. Though he had bought her as his slave, she could not deny that he had shown kindness.

And it was difficult to reconcile the two parts of this man. What did he want from her?

She remained still while the rain fell steadily. Both men were soaked now, but they appeared indifferent to the elements. When she eyed the other man, she saw that he was watching her with interest. There was no sense of surprise, as if he had expected to have a female slave aboard the ship. It made her question what else he knew.

Breanne huddled beneath the seal skin, and they continued to row until the river met the edge of the sea. Áth Cliath was now behind her, and she could see only a light fog and the water surrounding them everywhere. Once they were further out to sea, the Norseman gestured for her to put out her chained wrists. He withdrew an awl and a small hammer, and she understood his intention. Within moments, he had hammered out the pin and her chains fell to the bottom of the boat. Next, he removed her neck collar, and she rubbed at the chafed skin, feeling relief from the weight. Last, she extended her ankles, and he removed the chains there, as well.

Her wrists were raw, and she tried to ease the soreness. She didn't quite know what to think of this man. True, there was nowhere she could run, now that they were nearing the open sea.

Perhaps he'd meant to offer her comfort, and for that, she was grateful.

Even so, she could not dispel her suspicions. She was his captive, and he had no intention of freeing her. Was he trying to soften her distrust? Or perhaps he did not want her to fight him when he forced her to share his bed. Breanne swallowed hard, trying not to think of it.

During the journey to *Áth Cliath*, countless hands had groped her, and she had fought to protect herself. They had laughed at her, and she'd received a few bruises when she had struck back.

Breanne gripped the edges of the seal cloak, shutting her eyes to try to blot out what was to come. Though this journey would grant her somewhat of a reprieve from his attentions tonight, she did not doubt that the *Lochlannach* meant to use her for his own pleasure. His blue eyes stared upon her with interest, and her body prickled at the thought of his hands upon her bare flesh. She tried to dispel the thought, but the more he stared at her, the more she sensed that he would not be a brutal lover. Instead, she imagined those rough palms caressing her skin, arousing her. Without warning, her breasts tightened against the thin fabric of her shift and she caught her breath. He was handsome and stoic, a fierce warrior with undeniable strength. At the thought of him pressing her back against the sleeping furs, she could not suppress the unexpected response from her body.

And by the gods, she knew not what he would do to her.

Alarr sailed with Rurik, grateful that his brother had maintained the silence. He didn't know if his captive knew any of their language, and he didn't want to take the risk. For that reason, he had spoken little on the journey, until it was in the early hours of the next morning.

He'd been tracking King Feann's foster daughter for the past sennight, fully intending to use her as a hostage. He had paid a soldier to take Breanne and bring her to him, with the understanding that she would remain unharmed. Instead, the man had betrayed him, selling her to a slaver who had taken a shipment of women along the coast. It had taken several days to track her to Áth Cliath, and Alarr was irritated by the delay. But now, he realised that there was an unexpected advantage, for she would know nothing of his connection to Feann. He could learn more about her foster father's weaknesses if he could coax her to talk.

Although Feann had not been the one to plunge the blade into his father's heart, Alarr knew the Irish king had been involved in the plot. There was no question that the man had travelled across the sea, seeking the death of his enemy…but why? What had Sigurd ever done to Feann that would cause such a response? He needed to uncover the secrets that veiled his father's death.

After the wedding massacre, his brothers had taken him into hiding to recover from his wounds. They had burned the bodies of Gilla and her family before burying their ashes. Alarr had kept Hafr's sword as a reminder of the tragedy. King Harald Finehair had stripped his brother Brandt of his claim to Maerr, giving it to his aunt's husband, Thorfinn. Thorfinn had declared them outlaws, and Alarr and his brothers had no choice but to leave Maerr. But not before they had all sworn a blood vow of vengeance. Every man who had played a part in the wedding slaughter would face justice for what he had done.

Alarr had asked Rurik to accompany him to Éireann, while there were rumours that others had gone to Alba and even to Constantinople. Within a year, Alarr hoped to scatter the ashes of their enemies so that they would find no place in Valhalla.

And Breanne, foster daughter of King Feann, would be used to gain the information he needed. Although his knowledge of the Irish language was not strong, Alarr had learned enough to understand it during the past year. Rurik's grasp was better, since his mother had been Irish.

He'd understood every question Breanne had voiced, along with her frustration when he'd refused to answer. But he had given her a crust of bread and some dried meat, which she had devoured. He and Rurik took turns keeping guard until at long last, she had succumbed to sleep, curled up against the seal fur he had given her.

Breanne Ó Callahan was a beautiful woman with hair the colour of a sunset—gleaming red and gold in the light. Her green eyes reminded him of the hills in Maerr, and there was no doubting her courage. She had a strong will, and he admired her refusal to weep or yield. There were bruises on her face, neck, and arms, as well as the raw flesh at her wrists and ankles, but she had not complained of pain even once.

* * *

They had sailed through the afternoon and night, using the stars to mark their path. Rurik slept for a time, and Alarr caught an hour of rest before dawn broke across the sky, revealing the southern coast of Éireann. They would reach the Hook Peninsula soon, and Alarr intended to shelter there and rest for a few days. His father had spoken of Styr Hardrata and his wife Caragh, who had formed their own settlement near the coast. The thought of a true bed with furs and a fire were a welcome respite from the miserable rain that had not once relented. Even in morning, the clouded sky offered very little light.

'What will you do with her?' Rurik asked quietly.

'She will give us the information we seek about Feann, and we will use her to get inside the gates of Killcobar. After that, I care not.'

Rurik adjusted one of the sails, and in the distance, they could see the flare of torches from the harbour. 'Do not get too close to her, Alarr. Question Breanne if you must, but do not soften.'

He understood his brother's warning. When it came to women, he found it difficult to remain harsh. His mother had taught him to be kind to maidens, and he could not cast off his upbringing so easily. And there was no doubting that Breanne was a temptation.

A darker voice within him whispered that he could claim her as his concubine. It would be another act of retribution against King Feann to dishonour his foster daughter in such a way. He imagined this beautiful woman curled up against him, her bare skin warming his. Her reddish-gold hair was tangled against her face as she slept, and he wondered what it would be like to have that silken length against him.

'She will tell us everything,' he said. 'But only if we let her believe that we mean her no harm. We will say that we are taking her home in the hopes of a ransom.'

'You're going to betray her,' Rurik said quietly.

It was unavoidable, and Alarr refused to feel any guilt. He had journeyed across the sea for many days, keeping his rage at the forefront of his mind. 'I will do what I must. The woman should believe that we are helping her. Afterwards, I will kill Feann for what he did to our father and me.'

Alarr adjusted the sails as they neared land, and he centred his mind upon the settlement ahead. Absently, he rubbed at the scars on his calves. It was nothing short of a miracle that he'd managed to walk again. The healer had treated his wounds, wrapping them tightly so the muscles could heal. For the next year, he had struggled with every step, and even now, he had a limp. No one spoke of his fighting skills any more. They knew, as he did, that his days of being a warrior were over. He could barely keep his balance, much less defeat an enemy. It ground at his pride, a festering resentment that would never fade.

The dark memory of his wedding day lingered within him, an ever-constant reminder of what he'd lost. Alarr wanted to avenge his family's honour, and the surest way to reach Feann was through his foster daughter. He would revel in the moment when he could avenge his family, watching the life fade from Feann's eyes. And after he'd killed his enemy, the ghosts of his past would be silenced at last. If he lost his own life, he cared not. He was no longer the warrior he had once been, and he would rather die than be less of a man. All that mattered now was vengeance.

When they drew closer to the pier, Alarr took a length of rope. Breanne stirred from sleep the moment he touched her. 'Where are we?' she asked.

He didn't answer but bound her hands tightly in front of her. Annoyance flared in her eyes, but he would not risk losing such a valuable prisoner.

'Of course, you're not going to answer,' she responded. 'You probably don't understand a word I'm saying.'

Alarr helped Rurik tie off the longboat, and when Breanne tried to climb into the water, he jerked the rope binding her hands and pulled her back. She cursed at him, but he ignored her.

Once the longboat was secure, he stepped into the hip-deep water and reached for his captive. She fought him, but he held her tightly and strode through the waves until they reached the shore. The settlement lay a short distance from the water's edge, closer to the river. Alarr lowered her to the sand but kept her rope in his hands, forcing her to walk alongside him.

'If you think I am going to remain your slave, you are mistaken,' Breanne muttered. 'The moment you try to sleep, I will disappear. And may the gods curse you if you dare to lay a hand on me. I will cut it off first.'

She continued to voice her frustration, cursing them with every step. They walked from the water's edge, up the sandy hillside, to the open meadows. A few sheep grazed nearby, and they continued their path towards the fortress in the distance. Only when they had reached the gates did she stop her endless words. The settlement was newly built, and even beyond the walls, Alarr could see that construction of several longhouses had recently begun.

Four warriors guarded the gates with long spears, and there was no sense of welcome in their demeanour. Alarr approached with Rurik and greeted them. 'Tell Styr Hardrata that Alarr and Rurik, sons of King Sigurd of Maerr, have come to seek shelter.'

One of the men inclined his head and departed, but they were forced to wait until he returned with Styr's permission to enter. Only then did the guards allow them inside the settlement.

By now, the inhabitants had begun to stir. The guard led them towards one of the longhouses near the centre, and they passed by men carrying peat for the outdoor fires. An old woman stirred a pot, adding raw meat to the stew as she stared at them.

Weariness made his vision blur, but Alarr

continued walking with Breanne's ropes in one hand and Rurik at his side. Although he had never met the Norse leader, he hoped to learn if the man had any connections to King Feann or if he had any knowledge to share.

They followed the guard inside and passed by several tables as they approached the dais. Styr Hardrata rose from his chair and came to greet them. The leader was tall, with dark-blond hair and a light beard. His brown eyes held a welcome, but there was also a sense of caution, as if he would not hesitate to strike them down if they were a threat.

'We bid you welcome, Alarr and Rurik, sons of King Sigurd.' His gaze narrowed upon Breanne, and he exchanged a glance with his wife. 'Who is your hostage?'

Alarr jerked the ropes forward. 'She is a concubine I bought from Áth Cliath. I intend to ransom her to her foster father, King Feann of Killcobar.'

Styr's wife appeared unsettled by their captive. Her long brown hair was braided and bound at the nape of her neck, and she wore a cap. Her violet eyes softened with sympathy. 'Let me take her, Alarr. She is hurt. I will see to her needs and talk with her.'

The leader introduced her, saying, 'This is my wife, Caragh. Will you allow her to tend your hostage?'

Alarr considered it a moment. 'As long as she is not permitted to leave the settlement.'

Styr gave the orders to his men and nodded. 'If she tries, they will bring her back again.'

'Untie her,' Caragh ordered. 'She will come with me. You may speak with Styr a while, and I will make a place for all of you in one of our longhouses. I know you will be wanting to rest after your journey.'

Alarr could hardly suppress his yawn, and the young woman smiled. 'Perhaps on the morrow, you can help our men with the harvest. We would welcome your assistance.' There was no doubting that this was how she intended them to repay their debt, by offering labour in exchange.

Even so, Alarr was uneasy about letting Caragh take Breanne with her. He didn't trust his slave not to flee, but neither could he insult his hosts by implying that they could not keep her hostage.

'Bring her to me as soon as you can,' he agreed. It was the only thing he could say without offending Styr's wife. He could only hope that allowing Breanne some small measure of comfort would be the first step towards earning her trust.

'You must be weary,' the woman said. Breanne was startled to hear the Irish language flowing so easily from her. Her expression must have revealed her shock, for the woman introduced herself. 'I am Caragh, formerly of the Ó Brannon tribe. My husband is Styr Hardrata.'

'I am Breanne Ó Callahan.'

'And your foster father is King Feann, is he not?'

She nodded, wondering if Caragh could help her. 'He is. I am trying to get home again. I was taken captive and sold into slavery.'

'These men are taking you home,' Caragh said. 'Did you not realise?'

No, she hadn't. But then, the men had told her nothing at all—not even their names. 'I cannot speak their language. They have said nothing to me.'

The young woman's eyes turned sympathetic. 'Well, I would not say that they are bringing you home out of kindness. More that they intend to ransom you.'

That sounded more realistic. But even so, Breanne could hardly believe what she was hearing. She had tried to escape, and the *Lochlannach* had bought her. 'Why would they do this? They don't even know me.'

'They are mercenaries. And you're wrong— they know exactly who you are.'

Now, it made more sense why the *Lochlannach* had taken her captive, if he had known that she was the foster daughter of a king. But how? She had never journeyed to Áth Cliath, nor had she seen this man before.

Perhaps they had overheard something in the marketplace. Someone else might have recognised her, or he might have heard a rumour. There was no way to truly know. But the realisation that they were bringing her home—even for a ransom—caused such a wave of gratitude, she could barely suppress her smile of relief.

'Who are they?' she questioned. 'They have not even told me their names.'

'The older man is Alarr and the younger is Rurik. Both are from the kingdom of Maerr.'

She had never heard of it, but then, she had never left her homeland or travelled anywhere outside of Éireann.

'Would you care to bathe and change into a clean gown?' Caragh offered.

'I would be so grateful.' Breanne had only the rough shift that the slavers had forced her to wear and the seal fur that the men had given her to keep warm.

'I will take you to one of the longhouses. I fear we have only begun building our settlement, and there are many shelters that are still unfinished. We hope to have them completed before winter, but we need the help of every man.' She offered a slight smile. 'I had thought, for a time, that Styr and I might travel across the seas. But now we decided to stay here for the winter…' She rested her hand upon her stomach, and Breanne understood her unspoken blessing of a child to come.

Caragh led her back towards a small partitioned room that contained a wooden trunk. She opened it and sorted through garments until she chose a green gown. 'Here. This might fit you.' She held it out, but Breanne was reluctant to take it.

'It's too fine,' she argued. 'I cannot accept something so beautiful.'

'You may wear it until you are home again,' Caragh said. 'And then send it back to me.' There was no other choice, so Breanne accepted the woollen gown. The stitching was delicate, and she had no doubt it would be warm and comfortable.

Caragh led her back outside towards a different longhouse that was partially finished. On the way, she caught the attention of a young man and gave him orders in the Norse language. Then she took the gown from Breanne. 'I will send you a maidservant to tend your bath. I will give her the gown, and she can help you dress afterwards.'

Breanne thanked her, and Caragh brought her towards the far end of the longhouse. Another partition hid the wooden tub from public view. It was not large, but the idea of warmed water was a luxury that she welcomed.

While they waited for the servants to fill the tub with the hot water, she told Caragh of her foster father's ringfort where she had grown up. A hollow feeling seized her inside. Had anyone searched for her? Or had they given up, believing she was dead or ruined? It hurt to imagine that Feann had turned his back on her and discarded her as a foster daughter. But it was a real possibility, one she had to accept. She was not of his bloodline. An ache settled within her heart at the thought of being forgotten and alone.

After the tub was filled with hot water, Caragh

added scented oil to the bath. A young maidservant joined them, and Breanne allowed them to strip off her garments before she settled into the steaming tub.

The warm water consoled her, and she kept her knees drawn up, sinking down as low as she could to immerse herself. She leaned back, dipping her hair into the water, and the maid gave her soap for washing. She scrubbed away the dirt, wishing she could scrub away the memories of captivity so easily. Her wrists and ankles burned from the sores made by the manacles and the ropes. The maidservant brought a linen drying cloth, but before she could help her out of the tub, the *Lochlannach* returned.

She covered herself and glared at him. If he had come here intending to glimpse her naked body, it would not happen. 'Get out,' she ordered.

His blue eyes stared at her, but instead of leaving, he turned around. 'If you want to return home, you must learn to obey.'

It was the first time she had heard him speak her language. The sound of his words had a foreign cast to them, and she suddenly realised that he had kept silent on purpose. She motioned for the drying cloth and the maid brought it to her.

In a swift motion, Breanne shielded her body and wrapped the drying cloth around herself, before she stepped out of the tub.

'I have no reason to obey,' she countered. 'And I am not afraid of you.' It was a lie, but she spoke the words with mock confidence, hoping he would believe them. It unnerved her to realise that he had understood every word she had spoken.

'What is your name?' she demanded, wanting to hear it for herself.

'Alarr Sigurdsson,' he answered. 'Of the kingdom of Maerr.'

'I am Breanne Ó Callahan,' she answered. 'My foster father is King Feann MacPherson of Killcobar.'

'I know who he is.' He turned at that moment, and his gaze fixed upon her. 'I recognised you the moment I saw you. And you are worth more than a slave.'

'How could you possibly know me?' she demanded. 'I would have remembered you.' Heat flared in her cheeks when she realised what she'd said. But it was too late to take back the words. Breanne tightened her grip upon the drying cloth, and in that heated moment, she grew aware of his interest. He studied her face, his gaze drifting downward to linger upon her body. There was no denying that he wanted her.

But worse was her own response. She was caught up in his blue eyes and the dark hair that framed a strong, lean face. There was a slight scar on his chin, but it did nothing to diminish his looks. The *Lochlannach* warrior was tall and imposing, his physical strength evident. Only the slight limp revealed any weakness.

'What do you want from me? A ransom?'

He reached out and cupped the back of her neck. It was an act of possession, but instead of feeling furious, his sudden dominance made her flesh warm to the touch. His blue eyes stared into hers as if he desired her, and she was startled by the unbidden response. Though she tried to meet his gaze with resentment, her imagination conjured up the vision of his mouth descending upon hers in a kiss. This warrior would not be gentle…no, he would claim what he wanted from her. Heat roared through her, and she thought of his hands moving down to pull her hips against his.

That might be what he wanted from her, after all. She was well aware of how female slaves were used as concubines. The thought shamed her, but another part of her was intrigued by this man. She could not deny the forbidden attraction, and she had the strange sensation that his touch would not be unwelcome.

As if to make his point, Alarr stroked the nape of her neck before releasing her. 'You will remain with me at all times, obeying everything I ask. If you do this, then I will remove your bindings.'

'When?' she demanded.

'When you have earned my trust. Not before.'

His arrogance irritated her. Was he expecting her to become a slave in truth, subservient to every demand? Never. She could not pretend to be someone she was not. The instinct arose, to tell him that he would be waiting an eternity. Then again, if there was any truth to his words, she would be hurting her own chances of getting home.

'You ask a great deal of me,' Breanne said at last. 'I do not know you, and I do not trust you at all.' He was no better than a mercenary, and she had no doubt that there was a great deal he had not revealed. But then, what choice did she have? She needed an escort to bring her home.

'I have not forced myself upon you,' he pointed out. 'This, I could have done many times. I could also have given you to my brother.'

She reddened at his words, for they were true. He *had* treated her with honour, though he had kept her bound. She would not have trusted him either, were their situations reversed.

'I am grateful,' she said honestly.

'If you do not run away, we will take you home to your father. But if you defy me, you will face consequences.'

She stiffened at the overt threat. 'If you beat me, he will know of it. And you will not be rewarded.'

'I never said I would harm you.' His voice had gone deep, almost seductive. She took a step back, fully aware of her nakedness beneath the drying cloth. Never had a man looked at her in this way, and she could hardly breathe. His hand moved to her face, drawing an invisible line down her jaw. Beneath the drying cloth, her breasts rose up, almost aching to be touched.

And suddenly, she realised that this man was dangerous in ways she'd never even imagined.

Chapter Two

It took an effort not to react to Breanne after her bath. Her skin was rosy from the heat, and damp tendrils of hair framed her face. He had watched as a droplet of water had spilled down her throat to the shadowed hollow between her breasts. He'd wanted nothing more than to push the drying cloth away, revealing her body. *She is the foster daughter of your enemy*, he'd reminded himself. He needed to gain her trust, and leaving her untouched was necessary.

Alarr had turned his back to allow her a measure of privacy while the maid dressed her in Caragh's gown. While they were occupied, he ordered another servant to bring him a length of silk. After Breanne was dressed, Alarr bound her wrist to his with the silk, ensuring that she could go nowhere.

'Is that truly necessary?' she asked. 'I cannot leave the fortress.'

'It is. You have not yet earned my trust.' He did not want her to even imagine thoughts of escape. Her hair was wet and combed back, dampening the edges of the green gown. It fit her waist perfectly and clung to her curves. There was no denying the beauty of Breanne Ó Callahan. Her gown brought out the green in her eyes, and the soft rose of her mouth. He wanted to taste her lips, to make her understand how badly he wanted her. Having her hand bound to his only tempted him more.

As they passed among the others to walk outside, he saw the men glancing at her with interest. He glared in response, warning them not to look, and most turned away. She was not theirs to admire.

Alarr led Breanne to the longhouse where Caragh had offered them a place to stay. Inside, there was a sleeping pallet and a long curtain that could be drawn across the space. Breanne appeared uneasy about the private space and tried to step back from it. He took her hand and drew it closer to his. With her wrist bound in silk, she could pull back a short distance, but nothing more.

'We have journeyed for over a day without stopping,' he said to her. 'I intend to rest with you at my side.'

'I am not tired,' she started to protest, but he pulled her closer.

'You will lie beside me.' He didn't trust her not to run, and he was weary from lack of sleep.

The fear on her face revealed her suspicions, but he added, 'Have I not said it is not my intention to claim your innocence? If I give you back to your foster father untouched, it is worth more to me.'

She still appeared uneasy, but he pulled her near and forced her to lie down on the pallet. He curled his body against hers, and her hair was wet and cold against his face.

'Sleep,' he ordered. He only intended to rest for an hour or so—long enough to get through the day.

But with her body nestled close, he grew aware of her light scent. She tried to keep her distance, but he saw that her skin was prickled with gooseflesh. Despite her words, she was not immune to his presence. But perhaps that was only her fear, not an answering desire.

Beside him, he could feel her tension. She was

not about to fall asleep, no matter how much he might want her to.

'What is it?' he demanded. 'I have said I will not harm you.'

She hesitated for a time. The silence stretched out until at last she whispered, 'You knew who I was in the slave market. How is that possible? I've never seen you before.'

He wasn't about to give her the truth. 'It does not matter.'

She refused to relent and continued her questions. 'Aye, it does. I want to know your purpose.'

He gave her no answer, for he owed her nothing. And still, she remained persistent. 'What of my foster father? Do you know him?'

Never would he forget the man who had cut him down, causing his limp. Nor the man who had plotted to murder his father. The taste of vengeance was bitter upon his tongue, but Alarr held no pity towards the man. Even after over a year, his leg often ached from the phantom pain of the blade. There were days when he felt like an old man with ancient bones, especially after a hard rain.

But at last, he answered, 'I have seen King Feann before.'

'How?'

This time, he reached over and touched her lips. 'Sleep. Unless you want me to bind your mouth closed.'

She grew quiet at that, but he realised that Breanne Ó Callahan was not a woman who would obey meekly. Nor would she submit to his commands. Were she not the daughter of his enemy, he might have admired her spirit.

As it was, he intended to heed his brother Rurik's advice to not grow attached to this woman. Breanne was beautiful, and there was no doubt that his body craved hers. But she was a means to an end, and he had to somehow force her to lower her barriers and give him the information he sought. He needed to know everything about the fortress—the number of guards, the weapons, every door and every threat. And the only way he could gain such information was by winning her trust.

Yet Alarr had to maintain his distance, as well. He could not let temptation interfere with his plans. He was prepared to risk his life for revenge, and he did not expect to survive the battle, given his physical weakness. But at least he could claim Feann's life even as he surrendered his own.

Beside him, he could feel her attempting to loosen the length of silk, to free herself. In silent answer, he drew the silk tighter around his arm and gripped her body close. She would never escape him—not while she held the answers he sought.

'I don't like you,' she informed him.

'I don't like you either,' he lied. 'But you are worth a great deal of silver. And in the end, both of us will get what we want.'

'My foster father will have you killed,' she said. 'If you believe he will pay a ransom for me, you are mistaken.'

'Because he does not want you back?'

'Because he has a strong army, and they will cut you down and take me back.'

Alarr tightened his grip around her and began fishing for information. 'Feann is a petty king. He has no more than a dozen men.'

'You are wrong,' she countered. 'He has at least fifty men. Perhaps more.'

It was likely an exaggeration, but he didn't doubt that the Irish king had fifty men who were loyal to him, even if they weren't soldiers. Yet, Breanne had revealed possible numbers, which was useful. He knew if he simply rode into Killcobar, they would slaughter him where he stood.

He needed his own warriors to cause a distraction, men who would fight while he avenged Sigurd's death. His brother Rurik would join him, but it would be more difficult to get others to endanger their lives. He could ask Styr for men, but the *jarl* would not grant fighters unless Alarr gave something in return. He would have to think upon it.

After some time, Breanne stopped fighting him. She softened as she slipped into sleep, and her body relaxed against his. It was strange to hold a sleeping woman in his arms, but the sensation was not unwelcome. The scent of her hair and skin sent a bolt of arousal through him. He could imagine leaning down to kiss her throat, cupping her breasts and stroking them until she gasped from her own desire. The image made him grow hard, and he gritted his teeth.

Breanne snuggled against him in her sleep, and the motion deepened his discomfort. He wanted her badly, and now, he was starting to understand that returning her untouched might be more difficult than he'd imagined. It was not only her beauty that attracted him—it was her fiery spirit of rebellion.

Now was not the time to seduce this woman, for he had to remain fixed upon his goal. Breanne was a distraction, and there was no honour in pursuing her when it could come to naught. It took every ounce of control he had, but he refused to touch her. Instead, he closed his eyes, knowing that sleep would be an impossible feat.

It was early evening when Breanne awakened, after Alarr touched her shoulder. She rose from the pallet, her wrist still tied to his.

'We will eat now,' he said and led her from the sleeping space. She was starving, so she made no protest when he led her to another longhouse where men and women were gathering. Already she could smell the roasted meat and fish, and the yeasty scent of bread nearly brought tears to her eyes. Although Alarr had given her travelling food, it had been nearly a fortnight since she'd had a proper meal.

Alarr opened the door and guided her inside. Long trestle tables were set up with benches, and the people gathered together as one tribe to eat. Children sat upon their mother's laps, while others teased one another as they fought over better seats. She was overwhelmed by the number of people, but Styr and his wife Caragh welcomed them and guided them to their places near the dais.

It made her self-conscious being bound to Alarr. Though she understood that she was his prisoner, it made her uneasy for everyone to see it. He led her to sit down and then regarded her. 'If I remove your bindings, will you vow to stay and eat?'

Her heart pounded at the thought of precious freedom. A part of her longed to seize the moment, to flee and hope that she could escape. But the logical part of her brain warned that this was a chance to earn his trust. She could not simply run; she had to make her plans carefully.

'I swear it.' She looked him in the eyes as she made the promise.

He stared as if he didn't quite believe her, yet there were so many people inside, it would be nearly impossible to go. Finally, he gave a nod and untied the silk binding, unwrapping it. 'You will remain at my side at all times. Do not go anywhere without my permission.'

She inclined her head to agree and rubbed at her wrist. Alarr gave her a trencher, and upon the bread was roasted mutton with carrots and a thick sauce. She was so hungry it took an effort to eat with good manners when she wanted to stuff it into her mouth as quickly as possible. The meat was warm and savoury, and she had never tasted anything so good. Alarr ate beside her, but she noticed that he never took his eyes off his companions. He was alert to his surroundings, fully aware of everything.

Though she'd believed he was friends with Styr and Caragh, it appeared that he could not ever be at ease. Like a man on guard, his gaze focused upon the doorway when each man entered. His body remained tense, his hand near his weapon.

The other man he'd travelled with, his brother Rurik, was dining with some of the younger warriors. Although he listened to the tales of the other men, he said nothing. Once or twice, she caught him looking at his brother, but he appeared ill at ease, even among other *Lochlannach*.

As she sated her hunger, Breanne followed Alarr's example and studied each of the men and women. They were very similar to her own people, telling stories, laughing, and sharing in food. Caragh, doted upon her husband, and she reached over to touch him in small ways. There was nothing but love in every gesture, and Breanne found herself feeling envious.

No man had ever looked upon her in the same way Styr looked at Caragh. Or even with desire, as Alarr had looked at her when she'd emerged from bathing. Her skin tightened at the memory. But she could not stop the worry that no one would come for her. It had been weeks, and the isolation caused an ache deep inside her.

She had grown up among the MacPherson tribe and had believed that she was like a daughter to Feann. He had allowed her to sit beside him on the dais after his wife had died. She had cared for his sons as if they were her brothers, and now all were being fostered with other family members to strengthen tribal bonds. But now she wondered if her presence had been a burden after the death of her parents. It might be that Feann had only intended to marry her off to further his own alliances.

They don't want you, a voice inside murmured.

She tried to push back the doubts, but it was hard to believe that anyone cared about her now. A coldness gripped her inside, the loneliness and fear taking root.

'What is it?' Alarr asked from beside her.

'It's nothing.' She didn't want to tell him anything, though he did appear concerned.

'You look pale.' He eyed her, and she met his expression without offering any answers. There was no reason for her to reveal the truth to this man. They were strangers, and she owed him nothing at all.

'I am fine,' she repeated.

'No, you're not.' He tore off a piece of bread, still waiting.

He could wait a very long time, as far as she was concerned. Breanne glared at him. 'If I'm not, it's only because I am your captive. And even if you do intend to bring me home, I despise being a prisoner.'

'I removed your bindings, did I not?'

She flushed, not really knowing how to reply. It was easier to shrug than to say anything.

'You have nothing to fear from me, so long as you obey,' he said.

She bristled at his command and sighed. 'Obedience is all men ever want.'

'For your protection,' he said softly. But then a moment later, his gaze narrowed as if he'd just thought of something else. 'Or is there another reason you are afraid? Was there someone you left behind who is searching for you? A husband, perhaps?'

She sobered, feeling embarrassed by his questioning. Though she hadn't planned on saying anything, she blurted out, 'Feann *was* planning to choose a husband for me. Until I was taken.'

At the time, she had been eager to wed, wanting a family and a home of her own. A true home— not a foster home where she felt like an outsider. But now, that dream had burned into ashes.

'Was he planning to wed you to another king?' Alarr demanded. He appeared almost displeased by the news, and beneath his tone there was a hint of jealousy. She didn't want to imagine why. Though she had tried to remain shielded from his interest, there was no denying the heat that had sparked between them.

'I don't know which suitors Feann was considering.' She took a sip of the mead and found it sweet. 'Possibly someone favoured by King Cerball. It matters not now. No man will have me to wife anymore.' There was no self-pity in her words—they were fact. What man would wed her after she had been held captive by a *Lochlannach* warrior? No one would believe her if she claimed she was untouched.

'Was there a man you had hoped to marry?' He tore off a piece of bread, not making eye contact with her. Instead, his gaze was fixed upon Rurik.

She could hardly believe they were conversing about her future, as if he were a friend. And yet, it was almost too easy to confess her thoughts to a stranger. What did it matter if he knew her innermost feelings? After he returned her to Feann, they would never see each other again.

And so, she admitted, 'I was hoping for a kind man, one who has all his teeth.' She suppressed a grimace at the thought, for it was not uncommon for young noblewomen to be married to older kings.

'What of your parents? Wouldn't they arrange the match instead of Feann?'

She shook her head. 'My parents have been dead for years. Feann has been my foster father since I was two years of age. He allowed me to stay, since I have no living family.' At least, none that she had ever met. Given a choice, she preferred to remain with the man who had cared for her all these years, rather than strangers. Once or twice, she had asked him about who was governing her homeland, but Feann had been vague about the answers, saying only that her lands at Clonagh had been claimed by King Cerball and were under his protection. Whenever she had asked about them, Feann had warned her to put those thoughts far from her mind. Her father had been executed as a traitor and his lands were forfeit. She didn't know how her mother had died, but Feann had refused to speak of it.

The truth was, she felt no connection to Clonagh, since she had never visited the lands. It wasn't difficult to set aside her legacy and look towards a different future. She had always believed she would live with her husband.

Alarr poured more mead for her. 'Do you remember your family at all?'

Breanne shook her head. 'Feann was more of a father to me than anyone else.' She said nothing of her father's betrayal, for she had been warned never to speak of it, and Feann believed it was dangerous.

'Do you think he claimed your parents' lands upon their death?'

Breanne shook her head. Her suspicions rose up at so many questions, but she finished by saying, 'Feann is not a conqueror. He's a good man.'

A sudden darkness came over Alarr's face, as if he did not care for the king. Breanne ventured, 'You don't agree with me, do you?'

He masked his emotions immediately. 'I hardly know him.'

But somehow, she didn't fully believe him. Alarr stood, and the sudden motion made him catch the edge of the table for balance. He reached for her hand and led her towards the dais. As they walked, she noticed his limp was more pronounced than usual. Perhaps his scowl was from pain instead of something her foster father had done.

When they reached the table where Styr and Caragh were dining, the young woman smiled at her in friendship. Alarr spoke with Styr in their native language, which Breanne could not understand. Instead, she drew closer to Caragh and asked in a low voice, 'What are they saying?'

Caragh answered, 'Alarr has asked us for men to accompany you to Killcobar. In return, he is offering his services to us.'

'What services?'

'It is time to harvest the grain, and we need many hands to accomplish the work. We are also trying to build the remaining longhouses before the winter sets in. Our people need shelter, and we cannot fit everyone here.'

'So he intends to bargain our labour in exchange for escorts?'

Caragh nodded. 'It is reasonable enough. But while Styr may send men to protect you, I do not think they will fight.'

Breanne nodded and lowered her voice so no one else could overhear her. 'It would be better if Alarr brought me home without asking for a ransom.' It was possible that Feann would grant him a reward if he asked for nothing. 'If he makes a demand for silver, I cannot say what my foster father will do.'

Caragh's face turned grave and she spoke quietly to her husband in the Norse language before she turned back to Breanne. 'We have come to an agreement. You will stay with us for the next fortnight, and afterwards, Styr will send a dozen men to guard you on your journey to Killcobar. But they will remain outside the gates.' It was clear that they would not allow their own men to face any threats.

A fortnight was far too long. Breanne shook her head. 'I cannot remain here for longer than a few days.'

'It will take more time than that to harvest the grain,' Caragh argued. 'My men cannot leave until it has been stored for the winter.'

Breanne understood the woman's dilemma and tried to find a compromise. Alarr and Styr were engaged in their own conversation, but she still kept her voice low. 'Will you allow me to send word to my foster father? It might put his mind at rest if I tell him I am staying here by choice.'

'Feann would send only men to fetch you,'

Caragh predicted. 'And I don't believe Alarr would let you leave with them.'

Breanne sobered, knowing that she was right, 'No. He wouldn't.' Although he had unbound her wrist to allow her to eat, she had no doubt that he would bind her again this night. His behaviour was possessive, almost overprotective.

Alarr stood with Styr, and he sent her a warning look to stay with Caragh. The two men walked down from the dais to speak with Rurik, giving them a measure of privacy.

Caragh eyed her with sincerity. 'You must understand why we will not risk a fight within our gates between Feann and Alarr. We will not allow the king's men inside our settlement. Else it would bring harm to our own people.'

Frustration blossomed within Breanne when she realised there was no choice but to back down. 'I can stay for a sennight, but no longer. Afterwards, if you have finished harvesting your grain for the winter, will you send your men to accompany us?'

Caragh nodded. 'We will. Or you can leave beforehand, if you believe Alarr and Rurik would provide adequate protection.'

She hesitated. Although both men were *Lochlannach* fighters, there was no denying that there were dangers in travelling with such a small group. Two arrows could bring them down, leaving her unprotected.

'You are right,' she admitted. 'It would be safer to travel with more men.'

Caragh brightened. 'Good. We will be going out to work in the fields in the morning, and we would welcome your help.'

Breanne was embarrassed to admit the truth. 'I have never harvested grain before. I know very little about it.'

'The men will cut the stalks, and we will collect the grain and shake the kernels free.' Caragh said. 'The women will show you how.' She stood from her chair and offered, 'On the morrow, I will show you how to bind back your hair and use the folds of your gown as an apron.'

Breanne followed her, and as they neared the men, she cast a look at Alarr, waiting for permission. He inclined his head and said, 'You may go with her.' Then he added, 'But do not run away.'

His warning irritated her, for she did possess honour. Caragh and Styr had offered their hospitality, food, and shelter. She would not try to run—not when she now knew Alarr's intent was to ransom her. If she bided her time, she would reach home once again. The thought brought an aching within her, the fervent desire to be back at Killcobar.

And yet, she somehow sensed that it would not be the same again.

Alarr rose at dawn to work alongside the men. Although the morning air was cool, they had stripped off their tunics, wearing only hose. Each man had a scythe for cutting the wheat, and Styr divided the fields so that the men were spread out over different sections. The sun had just risen, and the scent of ripened grain filled the air.

Alarr welcomed the physical activity, for it gave him time to think. The motion of swinging the scythe caught him in a rhythm, and he allowed his mind to drift. It was backbreaking work, but he found satisfaction in watching the stalks fall to the ground.

Behind the men, the women gathered the fallen stalks. He kept a close eye on Breanne to ensure that she had no intention of escaping. She had bound her hair beneath a length of cloth like the other women, and she wore a gown with a wide apron. The women followed behind the men, gathering the stalks of wheat in their aprons, before they returned to place the grain in large baskets. Some of the older women and children were seated with large baskets, running the stalks through their fingers to harvest the wheat berries.

Alarr turned back to the field, slicing through the grain in a steady motion. He kept his steps slow, to disguise his limp. As he worked, he tried to piece together the faces of the men who had come to his wedding. But the only face that remained constant in his memory was Feann. The king's men had surrounded the longhouse and set it on fire, slaughtering those inside. The wedding celebration had transformed into a horrifying vision of blood and death. The images were burned into his memory, and he would never forget. Nor could he ever imagine another marriage, if he happened to survive the fight with Feann. The ceremony was tainted with bloodshed for ever.

He glanced back at Breanne. Her steady look held curiosity, but now that she knew he was taking her home, she seemed content to wait. At least, for a time.

They worked from morning until early afternoon, when Styr called a halt to their harvesting. Caragh arranged for the women to bring meat, cheese, and bread to the labourers, along with pitchers of cold water from the stream. Alarr's arms were aching, and although it was not warm, he was sweating from the hard work.

He saw Breanne joining the other women near a large stretch of cloth. They had gathered baskets of wheat berries atop it, and the women each held on to an edge of the cloth, lifting it into the air. They shook the wheat to separate the chaff, and one of the women began singing. Though she did not know their language, he saw Breanne learning the song, and she joined in. The sunlight shone against her face, and she smiled at the other women as she worked and sang.

For a time, Alarr watched her. Strands of reddish-gold hair framed her cheeks, and she was flushed from the warmth of the sun. Rurik came up beside him and saw the direction of his gaze. 'Don't,' he warned.

'Don't what?' Alarr feigned ignorance, though he knew full well what his brother meant. Against his better judgement, he glanced back at Breanne and saw her watching him. Her expression was not one of disinterest, and she flushed before looking away. Alarr turned back, feeling a sense of satisfaction.

'You have to take her back to Killcobar. She's not yours to keep as a concubine,' Rurik warned. 'No matter how fair she is.'

'I know that.' Even so, it didn't mean he couldn't admire what he saw. Alarr walked alongside his brother to a different part of the field and picked up his scythe again. He cut a pathway through the grain, slicing the wheat. Rurik joined him in silence. The exertion felt good, and he was able to hide his limp as he moved slowly. Behind him, the women began gathering sheaves again, and several children helped them. He spied a young girl with dark hair, laughing as she picked up the grain. The sight of the child filled him with a sense of remorse. Had Gilla lived, he might have sired a child by now. But it was more likely that he would never have children.

He sobered at the thought and glanced at the horizon ahead. One fortnight from now, he would face Feann and gain the answers he sought.

The desire for revenge had kept him from falling into despair. During the nights of agony while his flesh had knit itself together last year, he had envisioned Feann falling beneath his blade. It had given him a reason to live, for the gods knew he was now worthless as a fighter. The image of Feann's death was branded in his mind, an inevitable task that he intended to fulfil.

'Alarr,' his brother interrupted his thoughts, nodding towards the other men. 'What are your plans to get us inside Killcobar?'

'We will use Breanne's knowledge of the structure and its defences.' He needed to know all about the interior of Killcobar, and she would give him the information without even knowing what she'd done.

'She will not tell us anything,' Rurik predicted. 'She won't risk her family for our sake.'

'She won't know our intentions,' he answered. 'I will converse with her about her home and she will not suspect my purpose.' By the time she learned the truth, it would be too late. She would despise him, but that hardly mattered.

'And once we get inside the fortress?' Rurik prompted. 'What then?'

'We will give Breanne back to her father and pretend to leave. I will avenge our father's death, as we planned.'

'And how will we escape Killcobar? What is your plan to get out?'

'You will already be gone,' he answered. 'Feann will want us to leave, and I will ensure that he believes we obeyed.'

His brother stopped cold and stared at him. 'Are you *trying* to die? You'll be killed the moment you get close to him.'

He faced his brother. 'Do not doubt that I can kill him. I am not that weak.'

'You've gone weak in the head!' Rurik exploded. 'I know you are capable of murdering our enemy, but what I doubt is your ability to survive the fight.'

Alarr only stared at his brother, saying nothing at all. He had never expected to live through the battle. He would do whatever was necessary to gain his vengeance—even if it meant sacrificing his life in return.

His brother let out a low curse. 'Why would you do this, Alarr? I won't allow it.'

He picked up his scythe and began walking back towards the others. 'Because you have no choice.' He was weary of living his life as less than a man, a broken warrior. Why would it matter if he lost his life? Every man wanted his place in Valhalla, through an honourable death in battle. This was the way, and in surrendering himself, he would avenge those he'd loved.

And Rurik could do nothing to stop him.

Breanne was finding it difficult to concentrate. Although the women had showed her how to strip away the wheat berries and separate the chaff, she was distracted by the sight of Alarr cutting the grain. With each slice of his blade, his shoulders flexed, revealing his strength. His muscles were thick and hardened from years of training. A few scars revealed tests of battle, and she found herself spellbound by his sunwarmed skin. She could almost imagine him drawing near, a walking temptation. There was no denying her fascination with his body, and it annoyed her. He was her captor. He had bound her in ropes and taken her away as his slave.

But he never treated you as a slave, her conscience reminded her. *He is bringing you home.*

For ransom. It was about silver, she knew. And the sooner her traitorous body accepted it, the better. But she could hardly tear her gaze away from him.

When the afternoon waned, the men put away their scythes and went to the stream to bathe.

Caragh helped her gather up a basket of wheat berries, and they walked alongside one another. 'Thank you for your help,' the young woman said. 'Many hands make the task easier.'

Breanne nodded, noticing that Caragh was walking closer to the stream. It fed into a small lake, and the men had stripped naked and were swimming. She forced herself to look away, but Caragh paused a moment.

'I have spoken to Styr, and we have decided to offer you another choice.'

She didn't understand what the woman meant. 'A choice in what?' When there came no answer, Breanne glanced up.

Caragh studied the men, fixing her attention upon her husband before she looked back at her. 'You could leave on the morrow with a small escort of my husband's men,' she offered. 'They would take you within a mile of the gates, and you could return home without Alarr.'

The offer was tempting, but she pointed out, 'We both know he would never allow me to go.'

'We believe he has another reason for escorting you home,' Caragh ventured. 'One that has little to do with a ransom.'

She frowned, waiting for the woman to continue. 'What do you mean?'

'The kingdom of Maerr is very powerful. Alarr's family has no need of silver. Their wealth far surpasses ours.'

A coldness caught Breanne's spine, and she stared back at Caragh. 'What are you suggesting?'

The woman shook her head. 'I don't know. But there is another reason why Alarr wants to bring you to Killcobar. And ransom is not a part of it—of that I am certain.'

Breanne didn't know what to believe. 'I know that he wants your men to accompany him,' she said slowly, 'but I thought it was for our protection. It's not safe for only three of us to approach Feann's stronghold.'

'That might be true,' Caragh said. 'But were it me, I would try to find out more.'

She didn't understand what the woman was implying. What else was there? He had purchased her and intended to sell her back to her foster father. 'Alarr will not tell me anything,' Breanne argued. 'I am his slave, not his friend. Or, his hostage, I suppose.'

Caragh only smiled. 'I have seen the way he looks at you. He desires you, Breanne. And a man's desire is a good way to get the answers you seek, when his guard is lowered.'

Breanne faltered at the words. Even now, she was aware of Alarr's constant attention. He never took his gaze from her for a single moment. When she turned back towards the lake, she saw him watching her. His body gleamed with water droplets, and his hair was wet. He pushed back the water from his face, and his gaze fixed upon hers. She felt a sudden tautness in her body, a yearning she did not expect. 'I don't know.'

'Come with me,' Caragh told her. 'We will store the grain below ground.' She led Breanne to a smaller shelter. Inside, a ladder was set inside the earth, revealing an underground storage cairn. Caragh climbed down the ladder and Breanne passed her the basket of wheat berries. Then she joined the young woman below ground. The walls were lined with stone, and the air was cool below. There were dozens of baskets of grain, and on the far wall, she spied barrels and other wooden storage containers. The *Lochlannach* tribe had begun collecting food for the winter, but it would not yet be enough to feed everyone.

When they returned to the ladder, Caragh paused. 'If you want to go home without Alarr, Breanne, we can find another way.'

Breanne hesitated, knowing that Alarr would fight back against anyone who tried to take her. But despite his possessive demeanour, he had never mistreated her. With each passing day, he granted her a little more freedom. She had revealed more about her life than she had intended, but it was strange to realise that it had lifted the burden. Nearly a fortnight had passed, and no one had come for her, save Alarr. To a certain extent, the ground between them was shifting. It was not yet friendship…but she did not consider him an enemy, either. If her father's men tried to harm Alarr, it would bother her.

And she didn't know what to think of that.

Caragh paused a moment, resting her hand upon the ladder. 'What do you want to do, Breanne?'

'I'm not certain,' she confessed. 'Alarr did save me from the slave market when no one else did.' The bitterness returned, even though she realised it was difficult for anyone to track her by sea. 'I feel as if I owe him the chance to take me home,' she admitted.

And yet, she knew so little about the man. It was far too soon to trust him. In the end, she said, 'I will think upon it and let you know.'

'As you will. But be careful.' Caragh met her

gaze for a long moment before she led the way up the ladder.

The air was warmer above ground, and once they returned to the centre of the settlement, the scent of stew and fish kindled her hunger. The older women had remained behind with the younger babies, and the waiting food was a welcome sight. Breanne searched for Alarr, and when at last he caught her gaze, there was no denying the heat within it. His tunic was damp with sweat, and his eyes drank in the sight of her. He looked as if he wanted to take her hand and drag her into a darkened corner. Her heartbeat quickened at the thought. She felt a sense of guilt about her attraction, but then Caragh's words came back to her. *He desires you.*

Her flush went all the way to her toes. She wasn't accustomed to attention, for she preferred to remain apart from others. Men usually ignored her, except when King Feann had forced her to stand before them. Or when he had seated her beside him on the dais at the queen's place. It made her feel uncomfortable to have so many people watching her. She had only agreed because she knew there was no one else.

She wondered if Caragh's words were true, that Alarr's family had great wealth. Why then, would he go to such a pretence? Or why would he journey so far?

Breanne couldn't imagine any reason at all. If she asked him, he would never admit the truth. She would have to gain his trust, possibly even his interest. He might be more willing to speak if she behaved in a softer manner towards him. She was unaccustomed to using feminine wiles upon a man, but she needed to know if Alarr posed a threat to her foster father.

He joined the other men, lining up for food. She held back, waiting her own turn, but to her surprise, he crossed the space and stood before her. 'You need to eat,' he said, offering her the wooden plate of food.

'But that's yours,' she protested.

She saw that he was about to argue, and instead suggested, 'Why don't we share? If we are still hungry, we can get more.'

At that, he relented. Breanne led him towards one of the outdoor hearth fires and sat upon a log nearby. He joined her and offered her the first choice of the fish. She broke off a piece of trout, but instead of holding it out, she brought it to his mouth. Her fingertips grazed his lips, and Alarr caught her hand. 'What are you doing,

Breanne?' His gaze narrowed upon her clumsy attempt to gain his notice.

'Offering you food.' She feigned innocence, but he would have none of it. She realised then, that she had been too obvious. Instantly, she dropped the fish back on the plate. 'If you don't want it, fine.' She picked up the bread and tore it in half, eating her portion without looking at him.

Only then did he take his own bread. She felt her cheeks burning, for he was already mistrustful of her. She should have known that he would suspect any kindness she showed to him.

He offered her the plate again, but this time she took her fish and left him half of it. He ate part of it, but then asked, 'Do you want any more?'

'I've had my fill.' She remained seated beside him, while he finished the remainder.

An awkward silence descended between them, and he said at last, 'If we bring in the harvest sooner, Styr will grant us the escorts. It may not take long.'

She nodded but said nothing. Eventually, Alarr rose from the log and brought the wooden plate to one of the older women, who took it from him. He brought back a cup of ale and handed it to Breanne.

She took a sip and then gave the cup to him. Alarr drained the ale and stood watching her for a moment. She felt the intensity of his gaze warming her skin, and at last, she lifted her chin to stare back. She was caught up in his handsome face, and then his mouth tilted in a slight smile. Breanne felt unnerved by the attention and finally asked, 'What is it you want?'

He studied her and shrugged. 'I need nothing.'

And yet, he continued to stare. His demeanour utterly disarmed her, though she tried to remind herself that it was only an unwanted flare of interest, one that would go away soon. She knew better than to let her wayward thoughts become something more. If his interest was real, then it was only a physical attraction. Alarr would bring her home to her foster father and then leave her behind. She would never see him again.

She was interrupted by Caragh who said, 'Breanne, we have need of your help, if you can join us.'

'Go with her,' Alarr commanded. Without waiting for her answer, he went back to join his brother and the other men.

Caragh took her by the hand and led her towards an outdoor table laden with apples. 'Some of the apples have ripened, and we are drying them for the winter.' On another table, there was a heavy length of wool set out with apple slices to be dried in the sun. She offered Breanne a small knife and bade her join the others at the table.

She began slicing the fruit, grateful for the distraction. Her failed attempts at attracting Alarr's interest embarrassed her, and she inwardly chided herself. She'd never been very good at flirting with a man. Why should today have been any different?

An old woman nudged her and spoke in the Norse language, laughing as she nodded towards Alarr. Breanne had no idea what she'd said, but she flushed at the teasing.

'She offered to make you a love charm,' Caragh said. 'That is, if you're wanting one.'

'No,' she blurted out. 'That's the last thing I need.' She was Alarr's captive, and she did not want to be too close to him. His focused attention already made her ill at ease.

'Oh, I don't know,' Caragh said. 'There are advantages to love.' A soft smile stole over her face, and she lowered her hands to her abdomen. Breanne answered her smile.

'When will your baby come?' she asked.

'In the spring.' The young woman's expression brightened at the thought. Caragh glanced towards the men where she spied her husband. A soft smile came over her face. Then she rose from the pile of apples and left Breanne among the other women.

The old woman nudged her again as she glanced over at Alarr. Then she cackled and passed her another apple. Breanne saw the other women suppressing their laughter, but she stiffened and turned her attention to cutting the fruit. In time, they stopped their teasing.

After a few hours, it was growing dark. Her neck and shoulders ached, but all the apples had been peeled, sliced, and laid out to dry. She stood from the table, rubbing her sore neck. The women went back to the longhouse where they had dined the previous night, and Breanne joined them. She did not see Alarr or Rurik, and she took a bit of meat and cheese for a light meal. It was already dark outside, and she was weary from the work.

She decided to return to the sleeping space, and when she arrived, she saw Alarr seated on the pallet. Her first instinct was to back away, but then, that would accomplish nothing.

'Come here,' he ordered. 'I have need of your help.'

She obeyed, not understanding what he wanted. When she drew closer, she saw that he was holding a small wooden box that contained an herbal salve. She couldn't quite make out all the scents, but one of them was strong, like mint.

'What is it?' she asked.

He handed her the box. 'I want you to rub this into my scars.' Alarr lifted the edge of his hose and showed her an angry red scar just below his knees. It appeared that someone had tried to cut off his legs, and she was shocked at the evidence of such a violent injury.

'What happened to you?'

'I was badly wounded in battle,' he answered. 'The healer thought I might never walk again.'

'You proved her wrong,' Breanne said. She didn't pry, realising that this was what had caused his limp. He disguised it well, and now that she had seen the scars, it made her sympathise with him.

He added, 'The pain plagues me when I stand for too long. This medicine helps.'

She opened the box and the scent of mint grew

stronger. 'You are very fortunate to have survived.' Then she knelt down beside the pallet. 'Turn over.'

He obeyed, and she dipped her hands in the salve. She put a generous amount on his right calf, rubbing it into his skin. The red scar left an indentation in his flesh, and she moved her hands over his legs. His calves and thighs were large, revealing the muscled strength of a warrior. She had never touched a man like this before, and she moved her palms over him in a circular motion. He flinched at her touch, but she gentled it, feeling the knotted muscles beneath her fingertips. 'Are you in pain?'

'Yes,' he gritted out.

She used her fingers to massage his calf muscle, being more careful when she reached the deep scars. Slowly, she rubbed the salve into his skin, pressing gently against the muscles. It was strangely intimate, caring for him in this way. And yet, she recognised the pain he was in. With every touch of her hands, she saw his knuckles clench against the fur coverlet.

For the next few minutes, she tried to soothe the aches, sliding her hands over his skin. Though she supposed she should feel uncomfortable touching him in such a way, the truth was, she found satisfaction in working out the knots. She could tell when she had eased his pain from the way he relaxed beneath her hands. And when he no longer flinched at her touch, she drew back.

'Is that better?'

He rolled over, and the flare of heat in his eyes caught her by surprise. Without warning, Alarr pulled her atop him. Her legs straddled him, and she could feel the hard length of his arousal. 'No,' he murmured softly. 'It's not better.'

Breanne gasped when he sat up, drawing her to him. Her heart thundered, for she had never been so close to a man before. Her softness embraced his rigid body, and she went utterly still.

Alarr hesitated a moment, his gaze burning into hers with a silent question. When she did not struggle, he cupped the back of her head and dragged her into a fierce kiss. She could hardly catch her breath as he devoured her with his hot mouth and tongue. Shock and desire poured through her, and she clung to his shoulders, hardly knowing what was happening. Never in her life had she been kissed like this. He plundered her mouth, claiming her in a way that provoked a strong desire. Between her legs, she felt her own arousal deepening, and her breasts tightened. God help her, she could not push him away. And she didn't want to.

Instead, she found herself kissing him back, giving in to her own needs. A rough growl came from his throat, and Alarr rolled her on to her back, still lying atop her. He continued to kiss her until her mouth was swollen, her lips bruised. But she hardly cared at all. She was lost in this forbidden moment, unable to think clearly.

The voice of reason tried to intrude, but she silenced it, revelling in the dark feelings. Her body delighted in his touch, and thoughts of surrender spun through her mind. She could give in to his seduction, allowing him to claim her. Everyone would believe that was what had already happened, since he had bought her as his slave. No one would believe that she was still a virgin.

Yet, she hardly knew this man. How could she succumb to these feelings when she knew not his true purpose? She could not trust him, nor could she surrender her innocence.

With reluctance, she broke the kiss and turned her face to the side. Alarr did not release her, but instead, he rolled to his side, pulling her back against his chest. She was cradled against him, and he kept both arms around her.

'Sleep,' he commanded.

Sleep? How could she possibly close her eyes now? Her body was alive with hunger, craving something she did not understand. He was still heavily aroused, and she doubted he could sleep either. But perhaps he recognised the danger and was putting an end to it before it went too far.

Breanne stared at the partition, feeling as if she could hardly bear to be in Alarr's arms. This was not what she had intended at all, not when she had planned to win his trust. Instead, she felt confused and uncertain, almost afraid to move.

She was playing a dangerous game, and he had won the first round. Her heart pounded, and it took a while for her breathing to calm down. It embarrassed her to remember how she had behaved. She had mistakenly believed that she could soften Alarr, gaining the answers to her questions. Instead, he had aroused her so deeply, she was embarrassed at her own reaction. She was allowing herself to weaken, to fall prey to his touch.

Worst of all, she had enjoyed it.

He doesn't truly want you, Breanne warned herself. *He is using you for ransom. You mean nothing to him, and he will leave you.*

She knew this, beyond all doubt. It was foolish to let down her guard for the sake of physical touch. Until now, she hadn't realised how truly lonely she was. Feann had been kind to her, but he was not her true father. Nor had his wife ever been a mother to her. She had always felt isolated and awkward at Killcobar, never knowing why. She was not a MacPherson, but rather, an Ó Callahan. Perhaps that was why she'd never felt at home among them.

She could not let herself fall prey to Alarr's advances, nor could she risk her own desires. For he would only abandon her, just like everyone else.

Chapter Three

Over the next few days, Alarr was torn between keeping his distance and sleeping with Breanne in his arms at night. Something about her presence brought him into a deeper slumber. She made the nights more bearable, and despite the physical frustration, he would not allow her to sleep elsewhere. Sometimes in the morning when he awakened, he watched her sleeping. Her mouth was softened, her fair lashes resting against her cheeks. Though she often braided her hair before she went to sleep, sometimes the reddish-gold strands slipped free, resting against the curve of her face. There was no denying her beauty, and Alarr suspected that any man would be furious at the loss of her.

If Gilla had been taken before their wedding, he would have raised an army of men to find her. Why, then, had no one done the same for Breanne?

It made him wonder if there was another danger he had not considered. He had travelled with the intention of avenging his father's death… but what if Feann was gone from Killcobar? If they attempted an attack, the king's men would slaughter him where he stood.

No, it was better to learn where his enemy was before he made a decision.

This morn, he intended to speak with Styr and begin making his plans. They had harvested nearly all the grain now, and the men had turned their attention towards building more longhouses.

He found Styr upon a ladder, hammering nails into one of the unfinished dwellings. The air was cooler this morn, and Alarr picked up his own hammer and a pouch of iron nails. In truth, he welcomed the constant activity to take his mind off Breanne. Being unable to touch her was its own torment.

He worked alongside Styr for a time, waiting for the right moment to speak. 'Has Breanne's foster father gone in search of her? Or is he still at Killcobar?'

'I've not heard,' Styr answered. He pounded another nail into the wood.

'Did anyone send word that Breanne was taken?'

The leader shook his head slowly. 'There was no news until you arrived.'

Then that meant Feann was trying to keep Breanne's fate quiet. Perhaps to protect her status, Alarr decided. He met Styr's gaze and informed the man, 'I will be taking her back to Killcobar in a few days, if your men can be ready.'

Styr struck another nail into the wood with a mallet. 'They can, so long as the grain is stored. But they will not fight, unless I command it of them.'

'It is not my intent to provoke a fight,' Alarr answered, 'but neither will I be Feann's target.'

'Why do you not send Breanne back to him without a ransom?' Styr asked. 'We both know you have no need of the silver.'

Alarr eyed the *jarl* and hesitated, wondering if he should admit the truth. He decided against it, for Styr would not want to endanger his men. Thus far, he intended to use Breanne as a distraction. After he brought her back, he would pretend to leave with the others. And that night, he would confront Feann alone and gain his vengeance.

The thought of facing the man brought about the dark memory of his battle injury. His calves had a phantom ache, even now, from Feann's sword.

'I believe Breanne was betrayed by some of her foster father's men,' he said at last. 'If they were the ones to sell her into slavery, then it is not safe for her to go alone.'

That seemed to satisfy Styr, and he thought a moment. 'I understand. I will ask our men this night who would like to accompany you.'

'My thanks.'

A sense of guilt slid through him at the half-truth. One of Feann's men *had* taken Breanne and accepted payment for her—but after Alarr had hired him. He had fully intended to steal her away, only to be betrayed when she was sold into slavery. That same man might be there still, and if he were, Alarr intended to seek his own justice.

Yet, it still bothered him that no one had come to search for her. Dozens of men should have tried to find her, and he couldn't understand why they hadn't. It felt as if he were missing information that could later become a threat.

Alarr returned to his work and saw Breanne joining the women. They had gathering baskets and were talking to one another as they walked. Caragh was beside her, and the woman smiled at him when they passed. Breanne's cheeks flushed when she risked a glance.

As Alarr continued to work on the longhouse with the other men, he let himself fall into the steady rhythm of the work. It felt good to labour while his mind drifted to his plans. Yet even as he worked, he couldn't stop looking back at Breanne. Her red-gold hair was bound back into a long braid, and while she spoke with Caragh, she was smiling.

Alarr thought of last night when Breanne had massaged the medicine into his aching limbs. Her touch had aroused him deeply, and he had wanted nothing more than to spend the night pleasuring her. She allured him like no other, and when he'd kissed her, she had kissed him back. He didn't know what was happening between them, but he knew it was wrong. She was an innocent, and he had taken advantage of her. Breanne had succumbed to temptation, but there could never be anything permanent between them. After he took her to Killcobar, she would never see him again. He was prepared to face his own death—but he didn't want her involved. His honour was weary and worn, but in this, he would stand firm. She deserved a man who would be there for her, who would care for her.

As for himself, he was a broken shell of a man. Because of Feann's sword, he'd lost his ability to fight. Even now, running was difficult without a hard limp. He felt like a cripple at times, and the truth was, he'd avoided any raids or skirmishes since he'd been wounded.

It was like a splinter in his soul, degrading him as a warrior. His need for vengeance wasn't only about his father's death…it was for himself. He despised Feann for what he had done, and he would never stand back and abandon the matter—even if that meant using Breanne and betraying her trust. He could not let himself soften towards her. There could be no emotion to threaten his resolve. He would kill her foster father, and he cared not what happened afterwards. He tightened the invisible bonds around his conscience, refusing to even consider mercy. Mercy was not shown to his father or to him. And Feann would pay the price for murder.

* * *

Morning shifted into afternoon, and eventually, Styr called a halt to their work. They climbed down from the ladders and began to walk towards the centre of the settlement, when suddenly, Alarr saw the women returning near the gates. Several were carrying baskets of apples, but Breanne was not among them.

Caragh came running towards her husband, and there was a stricken expression on her pale face. Styr caught her in his arms, and they spoke together in private. The leader glanced at several of his fighters, and his expression was grim. Then he fixed his gaze upon Alarr, motioning him to come closer.

'We need men to help us search,' he said. 'Breanne has gone missing.'

The words took him aback, and for a moment, Alarr was torn between fear and wondering if she had taken the opportunity to escape. He had let down his guard too soon and had allowed her too much freedom. He had trusted that she would not leave, believing she would wait until he brought her home.

Yet, after he'd kissed her, he might have frightened her into thinking he intended to claim her body. He had wanted to, but he'd kept his restraint. Did she somehow believe he would force himself upon her? Never would he claim a woman without her consent.

But she might not know that.

He had become too complacent. In the end, she was his slave—and she had likely seized the chance for her freedom. He could not allow her to destroy his plans for vengeance. Not after he'd come this far. He turned to Styr. 'I need a horse.'

Styr barked a command to one of his men, and soon, one returned with a gelding. 'Alarr.'

He turned back and met the leader's gaze. 'What is it?'

'Caragh doesn't think she ran away. She believes Breanne was taken.'

He stilled at that, and his anger hardened into resolve. If another man had dared to take her away, Alarr would bury his blade into the man's heart. Instinct roared within him that she belonged to him.

And yet, she didn't. She had never been his, though he had bought her. Breanne had remained fiercely independent, and he had been attracted to her proud spirit. But if someone had dared to take her, Alarr would not ignore the threat. He would track down her assailant and punish him for what he'd done.

Styr added, 'It happened so fast, Caragh didn't see them. One moment Breanne was helping them with the apples, and then the next, she wasn't there.'

Who could have taken her? Was it one of Feann's men? Or had his earlier instincts been correct, that she had run away? It hardly mattered now—the only thing of importance was getting her back again.

Alarr mounted the animal and rode hard towards the gates. Within seconds, four other men joined him, Styr among them. He realised, too late, that he should have questioned Caragh further about what she had seen. Instead, they would have to track Breanne, hoping that there was some trace left behind. Though she was his hostage, he could not stop the flare of worry. An unprotected woman could easily become another man's prey.

Alarr rode hard towards the small grove of apple trees further inland. The trees grew in a clearing surrounded by a deeper forest that stretched across the western side of the peninsula. His emotions knotted, but he shut them down, focusing all his efforts on finding Breanne. When he reached the trees, he dismounted and searched for signs that she had separated from the group of women. He examined the grasses, even the slightest bent twig for a clue to discover where she'd gone.

There. He saw a footprint on the edge of the clearing, close to the stream. It disappeared, and he guessed that she had crossed the water and gone into the wood. Though he would have preferred to go on horseback, the woods were so thick, it was not possible. He turned back to the other men. 'Will you take the opposite side and search for her? I will look among the trees.'

Styr gave the orders to split up, and it was then that Alarr realised his brother Rurik was not among the men. He frowned, trying to think when he had seen Rurik last. Yestereve, possibly. Had Rurik gone in search of Breanne?

He tried to hasten his step, but his right leg was unsteady as he tried to run. His left leg was more stable, since the blade had not cut as deeply. But as he continued to limp through the woods, it soon became clear that no one had come this way. He returned to his horse, frustrated that there was no sign of either Breanne or his brother.

Alarr continued to search all afternoon but came up with nothing. He expelled a curse, wondering how he would ever find them.

* * *

Breanne glared at her captor, seething at this turn of events. 'Let me go,' she demanded.

'No.' Rurik led her deep into the woods, and branches scratched at her arms as it grew darker. 'Let him believe you ran away.'

'You were supposed to take me home,' she insisted. 'It's why I *didn't* run away.' She jerked back from him and spat. 'At least I showed honour. You have none.' It infuriated her that Rurik would do something like this. She wasn't afraid of him, and yet, she knew not what his intentions were.

'My brother is going to get himself killed. And you're not worth the cost of his life,' Rurik said. He seized the ropes and pulled hard. 'I am taking you back before he begins a war.'

What did he mean by that? 'Alarr isn't starting any kind of war,' she muttered. 'He wants a ransom, that's all.'

Rurik's face twisted. 'Is that what you think?' He let out a sound of exasperation and forced her to continue walking.

Breanne recalled Caragh's warning that Alarr had no need of silver. It sounded as if it were true, now. 'Well, what else am I to think? It's all he's ever told me.'

'And why would he tell you the truth?' Rurik continued his dogged path, and his words cut her down. She had the sense that he was hiding a great deal, and she pressed the point.

'Then what *is* the truth, Rurik?'

He would not say but forced her to duck beneath a thick oak branch. 'Keep walking, Breanne.'

Did he truly believe she would stay silent and obey? Her own frustration mounted higher. 'And what if I don't want to? I know you even less than I know Alarr. What if you are lying and your intention is to sell me back into slavery?'

At that, he shoved her back against a tree. His blue eyes gleamed with fury. 'My intention is to save his miserable life. And yours.'

'I don't trust you,' she shot back. 'You've dragged me out into the middle of nowhere, and everyone is searching for us. And you can only claim that you're trying to save him.' She raised her chin. 'Why would you need to save him? Why would you think Alarr is going to do something foolish?'

He stared hard at her, as if trying to decide what to say. She saw the indecision in his eyes, and finally he came to his own conclusion. 'Because Feann is the reason why Alarr has those scars. He cut him down, and now my brother cannot fight any more.'

'What do you mean?' An invisible frost seemed to slide within her veins. There was no doubting the seriousness of his words. She had touched the scars, and she knew how much Alarr suffered when he overexerted himself.

But Rurik refused to answer. Instead, he seized her ropes and demanded, 'Walk.'

Numbly, she obeyed. Though she ought to be somewhat grateful that he was taking her home, it was a day's journey from here, perhaps longer. They had no horse, no shelter, and no food. It was clear that Rurik had acted on impulse, and she wondered if he even knew where he was going.

Strange that she should now be wondering how to return to the *Lochlannach* settlement, instead of being eager to go home. Alarr had made her feel safe, whereas she didn't trust Rurik to protect her. He was only one man.

She thought about his claim, that Feann had caused Alarr's wounds. How could that be true? Her foster father had never gone to Maerr, to her knowledge. He had only ever travelled to Britain two summers ago. Surely Rurik was mistaken.

Or had Feann lied?

She decided to try another tactic. 'I need a moment to catch my breath.'

'We have no time. Else they will find us.' The determination on Rurik's face revealed that he was not going to let her ruin his plans. She weighed her options, wondering who she trusted more. Rurik claimed that he was trying to avoid a war…but she was more concerned about Alarr. She believed in her heart that he was a man of honour, for he had never forced her or claimed her as his concubine. Even when he had kissed her, tempting her into surrender, he had not demanded her body. He had treated her as a woman of worth, and that meant something.

She preferred to travel with Alarr, and though he would be angry at his brother, she wanted no part in this escape. Seeing no other choice, Breanne let her body fall slack to the ground, making herself into dead weight.

'I am not going,' she said. 'If you intend to take me, you'll have to carry me.'

The black rage on Rurik's face frightened her, but she forced herself to stare back. Once, Alarr had told her that his brother was known as Rurik the Dark at home. Though it had been a name describing his dark hair, she saw that it also implied a darkness to his mood.

'Get up,' he demanded. There was no mercy in his voice, only a quiet rage.

Breanne drew her knees up, shielding herself in case he decided to hit her. But she did not rise from the ground.

With a grunt of annoyance, Rurik lifted her up and slung her over his shoulder. 'Stubborn woman.'

'I could say the same of you. This isn't safe, and you know it. Alarr will be furious with you.'

'It was my only chance to stop him.'

He strode through the trees as if she weighed nothing, but after a time, he shifted her to the opposite shoulder. She didn't know how to talk her way out of this, but the trees were thinner in this part of the forest. Ahead, she spied a clearing. At least she could gain a sense of where she was.

Rurik slowed his pace and set her down as soon as they reached the edge of the trees. He took her bound hands and pulled her forward. 'I do not want my brother to die. And if Alarr brings you back, Feann will not hesitate to slit his throat.'

'My foster father has never seen him before.'

Rurik shook his head. 'Ask Feann yourself.

He will tell you of the raid in Maerr and what happened on Alarr's wedding day.'

She stared back at him. Alarr had never once spoken of a wife. If anything, she had believed he was a lonely man from the way he'd held her at night. 'His wedding?'

'Ask him what happened to Alarr's bride.' His voice was like stone, hard and unyielding.

'Tell me,' she whispered, though she suspected the truth already. From the harsh look on Rurik's face, the woman must be dead. And if he was somehow right about Feann's misdeeds, then Alarr had a very different reason for wanting to see her foster father.

She started to take a step forward, outside the trees. But a moment later, Rurik jerked her back. 'Wait.'

She didn't understand why he held her, until a few moments later when she heard the sound of a horse approaching. If it was Styr's men searching, she wanted to be found. Before he could stop her, she screamed for help.

Rurik clamped his hand over her mouth and let out a foul curse. 'Be silent.'

She could feel his anger from the way his thumbs dug into her jaw, but what choice did she have? The rider was her only hope.

When she caught sight of them, she saw four men, with only one on horseback. Rurik picked her up, running through the trees. Breanne nearly struck her head against a low branch, but within moments, the rider caught up to them. He reached for the rope binding her hands and pulled it hard. Breanne lost her balance and fell to the ground, and Rurik stumbled backwards since he had tied one end to his arm.

'What do we have here?' the man asked. Breanne kept her head down but recognised him as Oisin MacLogan. Her foster father had welcomed him once, and Oisin had wanted to court her as his bride. Something about the man had made her skin crawl. His words were kind, but she had sensed the insincerity beneath them. She had refused him as a husband, and after she'd turned him down, Oisin had been furious.

Breanne prayed he would not recognise her and kept her face hidden beneath her hair. She was angry with herself for alerting Oisin to their presence before she'd known who it was. Rurik had been right about wanting to remain hidden. It was her fault that they'd been found.

'Such fiery gold hair,' Oisin said, dismounting from his horse. 'I know who *you* are.' The other three men joined him, and they formed a circle around Breanne and Rurik, making it impossible to escape.

Her pulse quickened, but she could do nothing when he jerked her to her feet.

'Hello, Breanne. Such a pleasure to see you again.' A thin smile spread over his face. 'Now why would the foster daughter of King Feann be a captive? Did you try to refuse this man as your husband?'

She sensed his unspoken words: *The way you refused me.*

Breanne didn't answer, keeping her gaze fixed upon the ground. She didn't dare look at him, for Oisin was a dangerous man. *Danu*, why had she screamed before she'd seen who it was? She'd been so foolish, and now they would both pay the price. Oisin believed he was above everyone else, and he still resented her for not choosing him as her husband.

He reached out and smoothed her tangled hair. 'Not so highborn now, are you, Breanne?' With a nod to his kinsman, he said, 'Kill her captor.'

Horror washed over her, and Breanne screamed again as loudly as she could, hoping someone else would hear. When one of the men approached Rurik with a blade, he answered the threat by unsheathing a pair of daggers from his waist. The blades were short, and he would have to move in close to strike a deadly blow.

Breanne picked up the slack in the ropes binding them together. She needed to free herself before the restraints were used against him. She moved in closer, holding the rope so Oisin could not seize it. When his companion lunged towards her, she dodged behind Rurik. He shielded her, but they were easily outnumbered. She needed a weapon of her own. Behind her, she spied a broken branch lying on the ground. It would have to do.

Breanne dropped the rope for a moment and reached for the branch. Though she didn't truly know how to fight with it, she was only trying to keep the men away. She called out once again for help, even knowing that it was futile. A rush of fear filled her as she held on to the length of oak.

The last time she had tried to show courage in the slave market, her escape attempt had ended within moments. She had tried to fight back, only to fail. How could she dare to try again?

Her mind was racing with thoughts of death or being defiled by these men. Oisin would be delighted by the idea of claiming her innocence. He would punish her for daring to refuse him.

Nausea roiled within her, and she hated the feeling of being so powerless to fight back.

The other man reached for her, and Breanne reacted on instinct, striking his head hard with the branch. He stumbled backwards, but it did not diminish her fears. Her hands were shaking as she gripped the branch, trying to defend herself. Although she knew she was no match for these men physically, she had to push them back or die trying.

Over and over, she called out for help, hoping someone would hear them. Their greatest weakness was being tied together. It limited Rurik's movements, and she could not run. 'Give me one of the daggers,' she muttered underneath her breath. 'I'll give you this branch. I need to cut us free.'

He gave no sign that he'd heard her, but when he drove back one of the other assailants, he handed her the blade and she exchanged it for the branch. While he kept the men back, she sawed at the ropes binding them. Within moments, she was free. Rurik fought with renewed vigour, now that they were separated. She tried to give him back the blade, but he would not take it.

'Keep the dagger and run,' Rurik ordered. 'I'll hold them off.'

'If I do that, we're both dead,' she insisted. Their only hope of survival was to fight together. If they separated, it would be too easy for the men to overpower him.

Inwardly, she gave up a fervent hope, *Alarr, we need you.*

If he and the other *Lochlannach* could only find them, there was a grain of hope. Her stomach twisted with fear as she stood at his side. She prayed that the gods would have mercy upon them.

Oisin smirked and eyed his companions. 'When I've finished with her, you can have her next.' He reached for her fallen rope, but Breanne jerked back, keeping away from him. He only laughed, and she realised they were toying with her.

'You need to get help,' Rurik uttered. 'We don't have a choice.'

'I can't leave.'

In answer, he gave her a hard shove. 'We will die if you don't. Take my blade and go!'

Breanne seized her skirts and ran towards the thickest part of the woods, back in the direction of the settlement. Both Oisin and another man pursued her, which was likely why Rurik had demanded it. He had a better chance of surviving against two enemies than four. But she couldn't get caught.

Breanne ran as fast as she could, towards the densest part of the forest. She dodged in between saplings, knowing it would slow Oisin down when he could no longer ride his horse. The men were closing the distance, and she gripped the dagger Rurik had given her.

Over her shoulder, she saw Oisin riding hard towards her while the first man pursued her on foot. Without warning, her foot caught at a hidden root and she went sprawling to the ground. Her wrists ached from landing on them, and she forced herself to grab the dagger and flee. Another tree branch scratched her face, but she barely felt the cut.

Within moments, Oisin caught up to her. He grabbed her arm, twisting her wrist until she cried out and the dagger fell from her grasp. Pain radiated through her as he pulled her atop his horse. He gripped her hair and used it to push her down, so that her head hung over one side of the horse in front of him on the saddle. She could not tell where the other man had gone.

'Did you think I would let you go?' He drew

the horse into a walk, guiding the animal back towards the place where they had left Rurik. 'You belong to me, Breanne. You always have.' His voice was silken, and it made her skin crawl.

She tried to remain calm, but inwardly, she was trembling. Was Rurik still alive? Would anyone come for her? The blood rushed to her face, and she felt a wave of dizziness.

You need to think clearly, her brain warned. *Find a way to escape.*

But a sudden noise caught Breanne's attention. Oisin would not let her raise her head, but she heard him grunt as a man dropped down from the trees and pulled Oisin from the saddle. She lost her balance and landed hard on the ground, the wind knocked out of her.

Though she could hardly breathe, her heart filled up with gratitude when she saw Alarr. His dark hair was pulled back with a cord, and his blue eyes burned with fury. He jerked Oisin to his feet and punched the man across the face, splitting his lip. He cursed at him in the *Lochlannach* tongue, and although Breanne could not understand a word of it, there was no denying Alarr's fury.

She tried to stay out of the way, and her lungs burned as she tried to calm herself and catch her breath. But then she caught the gleam of iron and saw Rurik's fallen blade at Oisin's feet. Her enemy feigned surrender and took another blow to the jaw before he dropped facedown to the ground.

Alarr reached towards the man, and Breanne warned, 'He has a blade.'

Just as she'd predicted, Oisin swung with the dagger in his grip. He barely missed Alarr, who stumbled backwards.

This time, she caught the sudden wariness from Alarr as he struggled with his balance. Although he had caught Oisin by surprise, their enemy took command of the fight. He charged forward and as Alarr tried to sidestep, his leg slipped, and he lost his footing again.

Oh, no.

Her courage faltered, replaced by sudden fear. She knew that Alarr had once been a powerful warrior. The heavy ridged muscles gave evidence to that. But for the first time, she saw him falter in battle. He had hidden his weaknesses so well, she'd never guessed how badly he'd been wounded until she'd seen the scars for herself.

'My brother cannot fight any more,' Rurik had said. And now she witnessed his struggle as he tried to defend himself. Oisin used the ad-

vantage and pinned him down. Fury blazed in Alarr's eyes, and he used brute strength to shove the man away. He rolled over to avoid the dagger and then stood—only to have his knee give out again.

We're going to die, Breanne thought. *Unless I do something.* She couldn't just stand back and watch this—not when she could help Alarr.

Oisin started to charge again, but this time, Breanne had no intention of letting this fight continue. She picked up a large stone and threw it at him as a distraction. He spun, and that gave Alarr the chance to take him down. He dragged his enemy against a fallen log and struck the man's face, beating him in a violent rage, as if to lash out at his own weakness. Breanne could hardly bring herself to watch, but before she could move, a second attacker came out of hiding. She called out a warning, and Alarr dodged the death blow, using the man's momentum to push him into Oisin. The man could not stop his motion, and his dagger sank into Oisin's shoulder. The Irishman roared with fury, and he tore the weapon free, slashing his own kinsman's throat.

By the gods, she'd never seen such savagery. If Oisin would kill his own kinsman, what would he have done to Alarr or to her? Breanne scrambled backwards, and Alarr helped her on to the horse. He was about to go after Oisin, but the man dropped to his knees, his face grey from blood loss.

'Leave him,' Breanne said. 'Rurik needs you now.' She didn't know what had happened, but they needed to find him.

Alarr claimed Oisin's mount and swung up behind her. She guided the horse back to where she had left his brother. Along the way, she tried to calm the tremor that held her emotions captive.

'Did you run away?' he demanded. 'Or did my brother take you?' In his voice, she caught the tone of accusation.

'I didn't run,' she insisted. 'This was Rurik's plan, not mine.' She wanted to tell him more, but they were nearing the place where she had left his brother.

Rurik sat on the ground, holding his bleeding arm. Two men were dead beside him, and Breanne breathed a sigh of relief that he'd survived. Thank the gods.

Alarr dismounted and she followed his example, tearing off a length of her skirt to use as a bandage. She went to Rurik and bound his arm for him, asking, 'Are you all right?'

He nodded. 'It's not deep.' For a moment, he spoke to his brother in their native language, and she caught the concern in Alarr's voice. He helped Rurik rise to his feet, and they argued for a moment.

'What's wrong?' she asked.

'I've told Rurik to take the horse, and he's being stubborn. He thinks I need to ride.' The dark look of frustration revealed Alarr's annoyance. His limp was more exaggerated than usual, and she knew that he was angry at himself for it. Rurik claimed that Feann had caused his limp…but it was more than that. The wounds had healed, but Alarr would never again be the same fighter. He had proven himself to be fierce and strong—but one misstep in battle could end his life.

'Were you hurt during the fight with Oisin?' she asked him quietly.

'It's always this way after I run,' he gritted out. 'Riding won't change it. It's not from exertion.' He pointed towards the trees and added, 'My horse isn't far from here.'

Breanne understood that he did not want to show any sign of weakness while his brother was wounded. To Rurik, she said, 'You should ride until we reach Alarr's horse. If you don't lose any more blood, your wounds will heal faster.' Then she turned back to Alarr. 'I will walk beside you until we reach your horse. Then we'll ride together.' She intended to keep her pace slow, for both their sakes.

Rurik didn't seem pleased, but his complexion had gone pale from blood loss. He had killed both men, but he appeared dizzy from the wounds. 'Fine,' he gritted out.

Alarr gave a single nod, but she could tell his pride was wounded. He tried to disguise his limp, but it was nearly impossible.

'How far is it to your horse?' she asked.

'I'm not going to fall over, if that's what you were wondering.' He pointed towards the clearing. 'My horse is just outside those trees.'

Again, she could hear the rigid pride in his voice. She wondered if he would want her to rub the medicine into his scars again, from the pain he was trying to mask. The thought of touching his bare skin made her breathless. After this day, she wanted to feel his body against hers, to fall into his kiss and forget about the danger they'd narrowly avoided. But she pushed away the idle daydreams. She knew it was foolish to imagine there would be anything between them.

'How did you find us?' she asked. 'I had hoped

someone would hear my screams, but the settlement is so far away.'

'I tracked you both and rode outside the forest for what I thought would be the right distance. Then I heard your scream.' As they walked alongside one another, his hand brushed against hers. 'I stayed hidden because of the other men.'

'I am so glad you came,' she murmured. 'If you hadn't been there...' She didn't want to imagine the outcome. Oisin would have taken her as his slave and concubine, punishing her for refusing his suit.

Rurik leaned against the horse, closing his eyes from the pain. Breanne watched him for a moment, but it seemed that he was managing to keep his balance on horseback.

'Why did my brother take you?' Alarr asked. 'It's not like him to do something like that. Did you try to coax him into bringing you home?'

'He didn't want you to confront Feann.' She knew there was far more to his accusation, but now was not the time to discuss it. 'We will speak more of it later.'

As they trudged towards the edge of the trees, Alarr struggled with his limp even more. She let him lean against her for balance, but she could tell from his expression that it embarrassed him.

His horse was hobbled and was grazing. Alarr untied the animal and helped her up before swinging up behind her. A light rain began to fall, and she shivered against the chill. He drew her against him, offering his own body heat.

They rode in silence with Rurik on the journey back to the settlement. Her emotions and thoughts were tangled up, for she was so grateful to him for the rescue, despite his struggle. Alarr was a complicated man, she realised. Although his fighting skills had suffered, there was no denying that he had managed to win the battle.

Yet, she believed Rurik's claim, that Alarr intended to confront her foster father. If the king had attacked during Alarr's wedding, then there was no doubt that he would demand vengeance. He had the demeanour of a man who had lost everything. Such a man was dangerous, for he cared naught for his own life. She didn't know what to think, but she needed to understand his intentions.

And somehow, she had to stop him from harming Feann.

When they arrived back at the settlement, rain had soaked them through to the skin. Alarr called for the healer to tend Rurik's wounds, and he was surprised that Breanne remained with them. She appeared worried for his brother, and only when the healer reassured them that Rurik would be fine, did her tension seem to dissipate.

Alarr limped back to their sleeping space, and she did not speak as they returned to the long-house. Once they were alone, she reached into a bundle for a dry gown. He stripped off his wet tunic, and when he turned to fetch another, he saw her staring at him. Her green eyes held interest, and he saw that she was clutching the gown to her breast. The linen of her underdress was nearly transparent, revealing the soft skin and curves of her body. Slowly, she dropped the sodden gown, exposing the curve of her breast and the rosy nipples through the sheer fabric of her shift.

He hardened at the sight of her and the arousal was a familiar frustration. He ached to touch her, and the memory of her kiss made it far worse. But now was not the time. There was fear in her eyes and the innocence of a maiden. She knew nothing of what she was offering. Not truly. It was only the instinctive desire to feel alive after such a close brush with death. His own body was coursing with the same needs, and his hon-our was slipping.

'Are you in pain?' she murmured. 'Do you need me to rub the medicine into your scars again?'

He should refuse, for it was unwise to have her hands upon him. The thought of her palms caressing his skin was a temptation he could not deny. His body was strung tight, desiring her with every breath that was in him.

But Breanne took his silence as assent. She went to fetch the box of salve, and he lay upon his stomach, trying to gather the remnants of his control. He focused on the pain in his muscles, of the never-ending ache in the scars. When she smoothed her hands over old wounds, he groaned. But it was not from pain—it was from desire.

As she touched him, he dug his hands into the furs. Breanne knew the right amount of pressure to ease the tightness in his flesh, followed by a gentle smoothing touch. He revelled in her hands upon him, until she revealed, 'Your brother said that your wounds were caused by Feann.'

Her statement was like a bucket of ice poured over his body. He rolled over and sat up. Her expression was guarded, a warning in her eyes. 'What else did Rurik tell you?'

'He told me that the attack happened on the

day you were supposed to be married. And your brother wanted to stop you from causing a war.'

Alarr wanted to curse, but he held back his anger. He didn't want to tell her any of it. The memories were too raw, and locking them away was the only way to bear the pain. Instead, he held a stoic silence, keeping his emotions in a block of invisible stone.

'Was Rurik telling the truth?' she ventured.

He gave a single nod. 'I couldn't walk for over a year. My brothers took me into hiding and I lived with the healers until I recovered.' The memory of that agony washed over him, along with the feeling of helplessness. He'd been unable to save his father or his wife. Alarr met her gaze and added, 'Feann killed my father, my bride…and my ability to fight. I won't forgive him for it.'

Her face appeared horrified by his confession. Regret and guilt transformed her expression, and she reached out to take his hand. 'I'm so sorry for what he did to you. I cannot change the past, but you saved my life today. And I am grateful for that.'

He sensed that she was nervous about something, but he could not guess what. Slowly, she unbraided her hair, letting it fall across her thin shift.

'I thought I was going to die.' She reached to touch his heart and murmured, 'But you found me when I was in danger. Not my foster father. Only you.'

The slight weight of her palm pressed down upon his guilt. Alarr seized her wrist and held it there. 'Don't pity me, Breanne.'

'It's not pity. You won that fight.' Her green eyes held sympathy, but he didn't believe her. He had barely managed to keep his balance. One wrong motion, and they both might have died.

'I'm not the man you think I am.' He leaned in close, meaning to intimidate her. 'I will have my vengeance against Feann for what he did. And I don't care who stands in my way.'

'And if I stand in your way?' she ventured.

He refused to let her make him into a hero, when he wasn't. 'Stay away from me, Breanne,' he warned. He could smell the aroma of her skin, and he gripped her hand, trying to maintain his control. 'I'm not safe right now.'

'I don't want you to be.' She wrapped her arms around his neck to embrace him, and the fragile hold he had upon his control shattered. He crushed her mouth to his, savouring the taste of her warm lips. She kissed him back, and he could not get enough. His hands moved over her shift, wishing he could tear it into pieces. Instinct claimed him now, and he pressed her back towards the furs, needing her body beneath his.

Alarr wanted to caress her bare skin, making her crave him as much as he desired her. He knew Breanne's virginity should belong to her husband. But when her hands slid beneath his tunic to his bare skin, he no longer cared about anything except touching her. He laid her back upon the pallet, kissing the soft skin of her throat. She gasped, digging her fingertips into his hair and arching her back.

'Alarr,' she whispered, moaning as he tasted her skin. Her eyes were closed, and she bit her lower lip as if she were trying to gather command of her feelings.

His brain warned him again to stop, but he was past the brink of control. He wanted her to fully understand what she was offering, to taste the danger. And if he could touch her intimately, it might frighten her enough to keep her distance.

He peeled back her damp shift, revealing her round breasts. Her nipples were pink, the tips erect and tempting. He gave in to his own desires and bent to taste one. Her shuddering gasp made him grow rock hard.

Never in his life had he needed anyone as much as he needed her.

Chapter Four

Breanne could hardly gather her thoughts as he suckled at her breast. Sensations flooded through her, and between her legs, she grew wet. No man had ever touched her like this, and she didn't know how to stop him.

Nor did she want him to stop.

Her emotions were tangled up in a knot, and she knew it was a mistake to start this. And yet, right now, she wanted to push away the fear of death and embrace life. She wanted to seize a moment of pleasure, knowing that it would fade away, come the dawn.

A part of her wanted to draw Alarr closer, to convince him to leave her father alone. If he cared for her, he might one day abandon his vengeance.

But for now, she surrendered to his touch, not knowing where it would lead. He feasted upon her, his hands moving lower as he laved one nipple and then the other. He caressed the tip, and she nearly sobbed with delight. It was an aching torment to have his hands upon her, and her brain fought for clarity.

The boundaries between them had lowered. She had to somehow gain Alarr's affection, if not his trust. He would use her to get close to Feann. She believed that, after what she'd learned of her father's misdeeds. But she couldn't grasp that her foster father would murder innocent women and men. She needed answers, but right now, every thought in her brain disappeared at the sensation of Alarr touching her.

He stripped her shift away until Breanne was naked beneath him. If she didn't speak, if she didn't stop him, he would claim her. And by the gods, she desired this man.

His hand moved between her legs, parting them. When he touched her intimately, fear shot through her, even as her body craved him. Panic rose within her, for she was losing control of herself. Now that she was facing the loss of her virginity, she wasn't certain it was the right choice.

She wanted to tell him to wait, but before she could speak, he slid a finger inside her. She was so wet, so deeply aroused, it made it hard to breathe. Intense pleasure flooded through her, and a moan broke forth from her lips as he used his touch to caress her. Her mind and heart warred with one another, and her fears transformed.

'Alarr,' she breathed. But it wasn't a plea to stop—it was a plea for more.

He misunderstood her and spoke against her lips. 'I warned you that this wasn't safe. When you offer yourself to me, I will take everything you give.' His mouth returned to her other breast, and as his tongue swirled over her nipple, he penetrated her with his finger. Slowly, he entered and withdrew, adding a second finger as he stroked.

The pleasure was blinding. He was taking her higher, and she felt her body straining for release. Before she could plead again, a shuddering wave broke over her, and she arched hard, trembling with a violent eruption. She was shaking so badly she could not gather a clear thought.

'You don't want a man like me inside you, Breanne.'

His claim held a darkness, and she was too weak to make a reply. Instead, she closed her eyes and looked away. She was not ready to offer herself—not even in exchange for her father's life.

A moment later, Alarr stood and straightened his clothing. And then he left without another word.

Alarr slept in another longhouse that night. He had given in to his desires, fully expecting Breanne to push him away. And yet, she had only welcomed him. She was on the brink of surrender, and the intimacy had only drawn them closer. Her body was made for his, and he had revelled in the delight of touching her, of bringing her to fulfilment.

But it was not at all what he'd intended. He had planned to take her to the brink of lovemaking, just far enough to frighten her into keeping her distance. But instead of refusing him, she had responded openly to his touch. By the gods, he'd had no choice but to leave. If he had dared to sleep beside Breanne, he would not have been able to stop himself from claiming her. She would have enjoyed it—of that he was certain. And so would he.

She is your hostage, his brain reminded him. *Yours to do with as you wish.*

And would it not be an even greater vengeance

against Feann, if Alarr claimed the virginity of his foster daughter? What if he became her lover, spending each night in her arms? The idea took root and grew. He was torn between the primal needs and his own sense of honour.

The morning sky was tinted rose and grey as he walked towards the healer's hut. Alarr went to visit with Rurik but found that his brother was still sleeping. The healer sat beside him, and she murmured, 'I gave him medicine last night and again this morn. The cut upon his arm was not the only wound.'

He saw that his brother's ribs were bound up and said to the old woman, 'My thanks for tending him.'

She smiled and stepped back from the herbs she had been crushing with a mortar and pestle. 'I will leave you alone with him for a moment. Though it is unlikely he will awaken after he drank the sleeping potion.'

Alarr was grateful for the privacy. In the dim light of the fire, he saw the profile of his sleeping brother. Regret filled up within him that Rurik had tried to stop him from his vengeance against Feann. Worse, he knew it was because his brother believed he would die. Rurik had no faith in his ability to fight—and was that any wonder? Even when he had tried to rescue Breanne, he had stumbled several times. Had she not intervened, he might not have won the fight.

That knowledge grated upon him still. It didn't matter that he had trained and struggled to improve his fighting abilities over the last year. His body was permanently maimed, and he would never again be the same.

When Breanne had thanked him for saving her, he had sensed her sympathy—but that wasn't what he'd wanted at all. He had welcomed her kiss, and nothing had pleased him more than to watch her come apart. In that moment, he had become a conqueror, wanting her to desire him as much as he craved her.

Not only was she a beautiful woman, but she had courage. When she had been attacked by Oisin, he'd been overcome by fury. He didn't want any man touching her. He had grown accustomed to waking beside her, and if their circumstances had been different, he might have considered keeping her with him as more than a hostage.

He could not stop thinking of her. What if he *did* seduce her into sharing his bed? She could remain with him for the next few days while he satiated his craving for her. The hunger for her body, the need to quench his desire, was a burning need. She had responded to his touch, her body rising to his call. Every sigh, every moan had only ensnared him more tightly.

But it was dangerous to form any attachment. He knew the risks of confronting Feann. It would likely mean his own death, but Alarr hardly cared. The only ones who mattered were his brothers—and they understood his need for vengeance. He couldn't allow anything to threaten his plans—especially Breanne.

Even more, he knew that once he had taken Feann's life, those green eyes would transform with hatred. And if he claimed her body or worse, filled her with a child, it would hurt her even more. Though he despised Feann, Breanne deserved better.

As he took his brother's hand, he realised that Rurik likely owed his life to Breanne. It unsettled him that she had woven herself into their lives. He had planned to use her for information, but guilt weighed upon him. Breanne would not tell him anything now—not after Rurik had revealed his hatred of Feann. Alarr was torn between the ruthless need for information…and his own regard for her. She was a woman of honour, and it bothered him that he had to betray her. He needed to push her away, to ensure that she despised him. Only then, he could he distance himself.

Alarr was glad his brother was sleeping, for it gave him time alone with his thoughts.

He closed his eyes, bringing back the darker memories of his wedding day. Never would he forget the faces of those who had fallen, of the blood that stained the earth. And of Gilla's sightless eyes staring back at him. The wrenching regret pulled within him, reminding him of his purpose. He could not be distracted by a beautiful slave.

When he strode outside, he tried to mask the limp, but it was impossible. His leg was aching from the exertion, and he made his way towards one of the unfinished longhouses. There, he picked up a saw, wanting to occupy his hands. He measured the correct length and sawed the wood, welcoming the familiar ache of physical effort. A few other men joined him, but as he worked, his mind turned over the problem of Feann. He still knew very little about the fortress, nor did he have a solid plan of how to infiltrate their defences long enough to kill the king.

Styr joined him and said quietly, 'I am glad of

your help, my friend. But I would like to have words with you and your brother about your journey to visit Feann.'

'Later,' he agreed. 'Rurik is recovering from his wounds. The healer gave him a sleeping potion.'

Styr paused, resting against the longhouse. 'As you will. But we must come to an agreement about your journey and my men as your escorts.'

He understood the man's unspoken words— that he would not endanger his kinsmen under any circumstances.

'I only want them as escorts to Killcobar,' he said. 'They may remain outside the gates when I speak with the king.'

Styr inclined his head. But then he narrowed his gaze. 'Rurik told me of Feann's role in your father's death.'

'His men slaughtered my father and my bride.' He made no effort to hide the cold fury.

Styr regarded him. 'While I understand your reasons, I cannot let my men be involved in this. If your intent is vengeance, you must go alone.'

'I am asking for your men to protect my brother and Breanne on the journey. I will act alone.'

'But if Feann survives, it will bring war between my tribe and his people.' Styr shook his head. 'This I cannot do.'

'He won't survive.' In this, he had complete faith. Though he knew not how, he was confident that Feann would die.

'And what of Breanne? You would kill her foster father?'

'She knows what Feann did to my family. And to me.' He climbed down from the ladder. 'When Rurik awakens, we will speak again.' He nodded to Styr before he turned back towards the longhouse where he'd been staying with Breanne. She was not there, and he saw her walking towards the healer's hut where he had left Rurik. A hard ache caught him in the gut that she was concerned about his brother's welfare.

He hurried towards her and stopped her before she could go inside. 'I must speak with you.'

He expression remained guarded, but she asked, 'How is your brother?'

'The healer gave him a sleeping potion,' he answered. 'And he had a few other minor injuries that she treated.'

'But he will recover?'

He nodded. 'In a few days, I think.' He reached

out to rest his palm against her spine, guiding her away. 'We need to talk about the fate of your foster father.'

Nerves gathered within her, but Breanne knew she had to choose her words carefully. Alarr had strong reasons for wanting vengeance against Feann, and she didn't delude herself into thinking she could change his mind. He led her towards the horses and asked, 'Do you want to ride?'

She glanced up at the sky which was turning amber, the sun rising higher. 'For a short time,' she agreed. There was no doubting that he intended to speak with her about his plans. And somehow, she had to talk him out of them.

He chose horses for them and helped her mount. Breanne followed him outside the gates and noticed that he was leading her south, towards the coast.

After half an hour of riding, she saw the gleam of the water and the reflection of the sun. The sky was a blend of fire and gold, beautiful in its wildness as it embraced the coming afternoon.

He paused when they were near the edge and guided her towards an outcropping of limestone. He helped her dismount, and she went to sit on the pile of limestone while he hobbled their horses, allowing them to graze.

The air was still cool outside, but she hardly felt the chill. Her heart was aching at the thought of what Feann had done and Alarr's need for vengeance. She knew not how to stop him. There was no trace of mercy upon his face, no sense of understanding.

But she knew that he desired her. It was the only weapon she had, and she wondered if she dared to use it. Could she convince him to let go of his anger and need for revenge? Was there any way to change his mind?

A voice inside warned that there was no means of stopping a warrior like Alarr. He would never forgive her foster father for killing his family.

She had so many questions rising up inside. Why would Feann do such a thing, if it were true? There had to be a strong reason. And if Alarr confronted him, he risked his own life. As she studied his profile, she wondered how she would feel if he were to die.

Alarr had rescued her, saving her life when she had needed him most. And beneath his fierce exterior, she sensed that he was a man of honour. He could have forced himself upon her at any moment; yet, he had not. He had awakened her own hunger with his touch, and she had only found pleasure in his arms. But would he listen to her pleas? Or would her feelings mean nothing at all to him? She needed to know more.

'Will you tell me what happened?' she asked quietly. 'On the day of your wedding.'

He came to sit beside her. Without answer, he countered, 'Will you tell me of Feann's defences or how to get close to him?'

'No.' Breanne drew her knees up, staring at the water. 'I cannot betray him. He is the only father I've ever known.'

'He is not the man you think he is,' Alarr said. 'He travelled across the sea with his men and attacked for no reason.'

'He would not have sailed such a distance, if it were not important. That is not his way. Perhaps he was seeking his own vengeance.'

'Sigurd did nothing to him. Their kingdoms are a great distance apart.'

She didn't know the reasons either, but she felt the need to voice another truth. 'Feann was not the man to murder your father. You know this.'

'I blame him, even so. It was his men who surrounded the longhouse and killed everyone inside, including my father and my bride.'

Her heart ached for him, and she fought back the tears that threatened. She couldn't understand how any of this could have happened.

His voice was heavy, laced with bitterness. 'Then they scattered and went to their ships. Any man who pursued them was cut down and left to die. I lost many kinsmen that day.'

She tightened her grasp around her knees, trying to sort out her foster father's actions. 'That doesn't sound like something Feann would do.'

'He did. And he will pay for the deaths he and his men caused. Whether he wielded the blade or not.'

Her heart was pounding, and she knew not what to say or how to stop him. Right now, he was only thinking of vengeance and not what would happen afterwards. She wanted to protect her foster father, but she knew that Alarr would never set aside his plans.

To stall him, she decided to ask more questions. 'How did they attack you?'

'They stood among the wedding guests. Our men were unarmed during the wedding. It was not a fair fight.'

'Why were they unarmed?' Breanne asked, frowning. 'They are *Lochlannach* warriors, are they not?'

Alarr stiffened at her question. 'My mother demanded it.'

'Now why would she do that?' It made no sense for warriors to be unable to protect themselves.

'She claimed it would anger the gods.' But as soon as he spoke the words, she could see the realisation dawning upon him. He knew, without her saying a word, what she was implying.

But Breanne questioned it, none the less. 'Did your mother have a reason to want your father dead?'

'I don't know.' There was so much anger rising within him, it seemed that his temper would burst forth at any moment. She didn't press further, but instead, touched his shoulder gently. His muscles were rigid beneath her hands. Without asking, she massaged the tension from him.

She didn't know why she was touching him. He was her enemy, a man who wanted her foster father dead. But the question now was whether she could turn him away from his desire for vengeance.

She slid her hands to his neck, gently stroking the knots. Instead of granting him relief from his pain, he caught her hands and held them.

'This wasn't why I brought you here,' he said. 'Much as I do want your hands upon me.'

She could hear the edge of pent-up desire in his voice, and the heat of his palms against hers only evoked her own interest. She could not stop thinking of last night, and her cheeks burned at the memory.

'Why did you bring me here?' she asked.

He released her hands and faced her. 'To give you a choice. You helped save my brother's life. If it is your wish not to be there when I face Feann, I could leave you behind.'

She frowned, not understanding his intention. 'Then how would they allow you inside the gates?'

'Rurik and I would break in, and I would challenge the king.'

She shook her head. 'There is no means of getting inside without me. There are no weaknesses in the fortress. The walls are guarded day and night to make sure of it.'

But his offer made her pause. If he intended to breach the walls alone, he would die. She had no doubt of it. 'Will you not hear what my foster father has to say?' she asked. 'It may be that there were other reasons for the attack.'

'Innocent men and women died that day. I will not forget their deaths or my vengeance.'

For a long moment, Breanne stared out at the sea, turning over the problem in her mind. Her foster father had caused Alarr's injuries and the loss of his loved ones. But the man who had cut Alarr down was the same man who had comforted her after the deaths of her parents. Feann had taken her into his home, raising her among his sons, and she loved him. He was the only father she had ever known.

And yet, he had abandoned her when she'd needed him most. It had been weeks since she'd been sold into slavery, and he had never tried to find her. Yet, Alarr had been there for her from the beginning. Even now, he was trying to find a compromise between them, despite his intentions of vengeance. She wanted to believe that she could change his mind.

Her feelings were a storm of confusion. To whom should she be loyal? To the man who had abandoned her or to the man who had saved her? She didn't know what the answer was, not when she was caught in the middle between them.

Alarr had offered her freedom, as if he no longer intended to use her. Did that mean he had come to care for her? He had touched her like a lover, awakening feelings she didn't understand. But if she allowed him to go alone, she sensed that her father would harm him. If Feann *had* gone to the wedding and was involved in the death of Alarr's father, he would recognise him and possibly kill Alarr. She couldn't allow that to happen.

'I will go with you to Killcobar,' Breanne said at last. Not only because she hoped to protect her father, but also because she didn't want Alarr to die. She couldn't put a name to her feelings, but she owed him her life. It wasn't right to turn away from him.

Breanne walked alongside Alarr towards the water's edge. The sun dusted the waves in a glittering haze of light. She removed her shoes and walked along the frigid sand. The icy water matched her mood, and she tried to think of what she could do. The truth was, she didn't want either of them to be hurt.

Alarr trailed behind, and she paused a moment, letting the waves pool around her ankles. But the cold brought a new clarity to her thoughts. There *was* something she could do to protect him and still grant him compensation for his loss, if he were to agree. Alarr might desire vengeance, but bloodshed could be avoided in a different way.

It was a means of putting herself between the two men, shielding them both through her actions. Her nerves gathered up inside her, for she didn't know if she dared to voice her suggestion. It was an unlikely choice, one he might reject.

She didn't even know if it was what she wanted. But if it meant protecting two men she cared about, perhaps it was the best solution.

Breanne turned back to him as she walked through the wet sand. 'This is not finished between us. I will not allow you to harm Feann. But I know of another way you can be compensated for your losses.'

Alarr met her gaze but was already shaking his head. 'There is nothing that would atone for what he has done.'

'Hear me out,' she continued. 'My foster father owes you for your injuries, and if he played any part in your father's death, he must pay the *corp-dire*. The *brehons* will see to it that justice is served.'

'He will never pay a single coin for my sake,' Alarr said.

Breanne steeled herself. 'He would if you become my husband.'

Alarr hadn't known how to answer her, but Breanne pressed her finger to his lips. 'Do not give me an answer yet. Only think about it. It may be a means of avoiding war.'

For her sake, he had held his silence.

After they returned to the fortress, Alarr spent the rest of the afternoon and evening working on one of the longhouses, turning over her suggestion in his mind. Why would Breanne suggest marriage between them? She knew his intentions towards her father. Did she believe that a union would bring peace? Never. He could not abandon his plans, even for her.

She had kept her distance from him for the remainder of the day until they returned to the shelter that night. Breanne turned away from him in their shared pallet, but he could tell from her uneven breathing that she was not asleep. Slowly, he drew her close until she was facing him. 'Why would you believe we should wed, Breanne? Is there not another man you would rather marry?'

In the faint light of the oil lamp, he could see the uncertainty in her expression. Her body was curled towards him, and her cheeks flushed. 'No one would have me to wife. Not after this.'

'You are still a maiden,' he felt compelled to remind her. Although he had touched her intimately, she was innocent in body.

'They never searched for me,' she said. 'Not in all these weeks. Believe me when I say that no man of Feann's kingdom wanted to wed me.' Sadness and humiliation weighted her words. 'I never understood why. Was I not good enough? Was there something I should have done differently?'

Alarr knew not what to say, for he didn't understand her people's reasons for abandoning her. Had Breanne been his betrothed bride, he would have torn the countryside apart to find her. 'You would never want to marry a man who blamed you for your own captivity,' Alarr said. 'It would not have been a good union.' He paused a moment and added, 'Just as we are not suited to one another.'

'My offer of marriage was about keeping the peace for the time being,' she argued. 'Not necessarily an alliance for the rest of our lives. Only until you are compensated for your losses.'

A temporary marriage, then. But he still believed that was unwise. For if he wedded Breanne, he suspected he could not let her remain a virgin.

He brought his hand to her waist, not really understanding why he had the need to touch her. 'I am prepared to face my own death for his, Breanne. It's why I travelled this far.'

He saw the uncertainty in her eyes and the fear. But he didn't want her to build him up as a hero. Feann deserved to die for what he'd done. There would be no mercy, no turning back now.

She studied him with a sombre gaze. 'If we are wedded, Feann will not harm you.'

Alarr didn't believe that for a moment. 'If Feann already slaughtered my family and my bride, he would not hesitate to have me killed.'

'He would protect you for my sake,' she said quietly. There was an edge of desperation in her tone. 'If we visit Killcobar together, I could talk to Feann. We could reach an agreement.'

He wanted to argue that Feann cared only for himself. Such a man would not listen to reason or agree to a *corp-dire* payment. The king hadn't even bothered to search for his foster daughter. But if Alarr revealed that, it would only hurt her feelings. Breanne held loyalty to a man who deserved none of it.

His mood hardened at the thought. Every time he thought of that day, of the blood and death, it ignited the fury inside him, stoking the flames of vengeance. 'I will never forget what he did.'

'I understand,' she murmured. 'But surely there is a way to compensate you for your loss. According to the law—'

'The law will not bring back my father. Or Gilla.' He pulled back from her and met her gaze squarely. He could never be swayed from this course. He needed her to understand that, but more than that, he needed distance between them. Her soft heart was weakening his resolve. The closer he grew to Breanne, the more he doubted his decisions. It was better to shut down any thoughts of marriage.

'There can be no wedding between us. Not now or ever.'

She closed her eyes as if his words were a physical blow. 'I know you do not want me as your bride. But so many lives could be saved. Including your own.'

He cared naught for his life. What good was he to anyone now? He could barely fight, and he never wanted to see a look of fear or loathing on Breanne's face if he was unable to defend her. He had barely managed to save her from Oisin the first time.

He could not allow her to sacrifice her own future for his, nor could he imagine another wedding—not even to a woman he desired so badly. The memories of bloodshed would never leave him, and he could not even consider marriage. He didn't deserve happiness after his first bride had died before he could save her. The gods had punished him by allowing him to live as less than a man with visible scars to remind him of his failure.

But he refused to accept that life. Better to die avenging those who had lost their lives than to go on with his.

Breanne was far too good for someone like him. He had to cut her off and make her despise him. It was the only way to protect her from being hurt. And so, he delivered the cutting blow.

'You are only a slave to me, Breanne. It's all you've ever been.' Alarr stood from the pallet, turning away so he would not see her reaction. 'I bought you to get close to Feann. And then, I always intended to kill him.'

He did not stay to hear her answer, nor did he want to see her face. He wanted to sever all ties between them and cause her to hate him. Only then, would it be easier to leave her behind and enact his plans for vengeance.

Outside, the night air was cool, a welcome contrast from the heat of his skin. Alarr strode across the fortress, the gates flanked by torches. Guards stood at intervals, and he nodded in greeting. He knew not where he was going— only that he needed to escape the confines of the longhouse.

You did what was necessary, his conscience reminded him. *You had to let her go.*

And yet, he loathed himself for what he'd said—even knowing that there was no other choice but to hurt her.

As he passed a shadowed corner, he heard a soft laugh. There, he spied Caragh seated upon a low stool, Styr kneeling before her. The leader was washing her feet, and the act grew intimate when his wife's laugh turned into a low intake of breath. Alarr kept walking, pretending as if he hadn't seen them. But the image struck hard within him, of what it would be like to spend each day with a woman he cared about...of what it would be like to touch her and hear her sigh with desire.

The closest he had ever come to it was when he'd touched Breanne.

Chapter Five

In the morning, Breanne awakened and stared at the partition, feeling humiliated and broken.

'You are only a slave to me, Breanne. It's all you've ever been.'

Alarr's words had cut her to the bone, reminding her that she was worth nothing to him. She wanted to weep, but there were no tears, only the aching anguish within her. Not only from his refusal, but it was also because she felt abandoned by everyone.

No one wanted her. Not her foster family, not her betrothed husband, and not the man who had saved her. The shame burned within her that she had dared to offer him marriage.

It didn't matter. Alarr had made his point clear. There would be nothing between them. His intent was to use her and discard her.

But that didn't mean she would stand aside

and let that happen. She had other ways of getting home, and she had no intention of becoming Alarr's pawn in a game of death.

She stood from her pallet and walked through the longhouse, searching for Caragh. The young woman was nowhere to be found, but she saw Styr instead. The leader was speaking with one of his men about building another longhouse, and she waited quietly until he had finished. After the other man had left, Styr motioned for her to come closer.

'Was there something you needed, Breanne?' he asked quietly.

She nodded. 'I have decided to accept your wife's offer. She told me you could send several of your men as my escorts and return me to Killcobar without Alarr.' Breanne could see no other alternative than to return home in secret, before he could stop her. Then she would play no part in his attack. The harsh ache in her stomach returned along with her shame.

Styr hesitated before saying, 'You've decided not to travel with him, then?'

Breanne shook her head. 'He intends to kill my foster father. So no, I will not let him use me in his vengeance.' If words would not convince Alarr, she had no choice but to use actions instead.

Styr motioned for her to walk with him. 'Are you certain this is what he intends?' Although the *jarl* kept his tone even, she suspected he was probing for more information.

Breanne gazed at him squarely. 'He wants no ransom. His purpose is revenge.' From the look in Styr's eyes, she realised that he did not appear at all surprised. It made her wonder what else he knew.

'What happened between Alarr and Feann?' Styr asked.

She chose her words carefully. 'Feann slaughtered Alarr's bride and father on his wedding day. Alarr wanted to use me as a means of getting close to him. He planned to avenge the deaths of his family.' She paused and added, 'Rurik wanted to stop him. He thought if he brought me home first, then it would stop Alarr from his plans. But then we were attacked.'

'One man cannot avenge the deaths of so many,' Styr argued. 'He would die in the attempt.'

The ache deepened inside her at the thought. 'He would. But Alarr has said that it does not matter to him.' Nor did *she* matter to him. She should have been more guarded with her feelings, but she had allowed him to cloud her sense of reason. 'I would rather go home by myself. But he cannot know of this.'

Styr's expression was stoic, and he said, 'Let us go and speak with Caragh.'

He led her outside, past the other longhouses, until they reached the stables. Inside, the air was pungent, and the animals grazed in their stalls. Caragh was brushing a mare, speaking softly to her. When she heard them enter, she turned and smiled. 'I could not resist the urge to visit with the animals. I might go riding today if the weather holds.'

'Breanne wants to return to Killcobar today,' Styr said to his wife. 'Without Alarr.'

Caragh's smile faded. 'So you've changed your mind, then.'

Breanne nodded. 'I cannot be a part of his revenge.' She told Caragh of Alarr's plans and the young woman exchanged a glance with her husband. It was clear that the pair of them were deciding what to do, and in the meantime, Breanne distracted herself by rubbing the ears of a young stallion. The horse nudged her shoulder, wanting more affection, and she gave it.

'Alarr will pursue you the moment he knows

you're gone,' Caragh predicted. 'He cares about you too much, Breanne.'

'I am his property, nothing more.' The words cut into her mood, darkening it. 'I will not go with him. Not if it endangers my family.' Or his own life, she thought. The worst part was that she could not deny that her own feelings for Alarr had gone past friendship. She needed to distance herself and remember that he was an enemy. He would not set aside his vengeance, no matter how she pleaded.

Styr regarded her and answered at last, 'I believe it's too late for me to send men to bring you home—especially now. Alarr would only pursue you and cause harm to my kinsmen.' He shook his head. 'I am sorry, but I cannot.'

'She could go if they leave in the middle of the night,' his wife suggested. 'If they ride swiftly, it may be possible.'

'No.' Styr was adamant in his refusal. 'The only thing I can do is send a messenger to Feann. If he wishes to come and claim her, I will allow it. That is the best I can offer.'

Breanne faced the pair of them and realised that she had no choice but to wait. Though she inclined her head and murmured her thanks, inwardly she feared it would not happen. Feann had sent no one to rescue her thus far. This message might have no effect on him, and she would still be forced to go with Alarr.

It bothered her deeply to know that she was alone, with no one to help her. She had relied on others to save her, and it had come to naught. If she wanted to change her circumstances, she would have to form her own plans.

But she would not allow Alarr to use her—not when it threatened the only family she had left.

Three days later

Rurik's wounds were healing, and Alarr was glad to see his brother walking once again. He needed his brother's advice about attacking Killcobar. During the past two nights, he had spent time apart from Breanne. She hardly spoke to him any more, and he regretted what he'd said. He had let himself get too close, and that was his own fault. Better to cut his ties now than to watch her anguish when he took Feann's life.

'How are you faring this morn?' he asked Rurik.

'Well enough.' His brother exposed the angry red flesh that was healing from his shoulder wound. 'Would that it had been my left shoulder that was injured. But I can still fight if I must.'

'Good. I will have need of your blade when the time comes.'

Rurik's expression twisted. 'We need to talk.'

He suspected that his brother would try to convince him not to fight Feann. But Alarr nodded and said, 'We should go outside the settlement to speak freely.'

Rurik agreed, and they walked past the outbuildings through the gates. When they were a short distance away from the tribesmen, Alarr said, 'Tell me why you are trying to avoid confronting Feann. You know what he did to our father.'

His half-brother paused a moment. 'I asked myself why Feann would travel so far to plot the murder of Sigurd. Only a man trying to provoke a war would do something like that. Or someone who desired his own vengeance.'

'It doesn't matter why. It only matters that he and his men started the battle. I intend to finish it.' Alarr stopped when they reached the outskirts of the forest.

'My mother was from Éireann, Alarr. It was no coincidence that Feann's men travelled across the sea. There is a connection between Saorla and Feann. I believe that.'

'Possibly.' He conceded that there could have been a reason. 'But Saorla came to Maerr of her own free will. She bore children to Sigurd.'

'Was she truly willing?' Rurik questioned. 'Or was she forced?'

He didn't know, but he understood his brother's questions. 'You want to know about her past.'

Rurik agreed. 'And if you kill Feann, I may never have those answers.'

Alarr shrugged and offered, 'I could take him captive. After he confesses the truth, then I'll kill him.' He ventured a slight smile which Rurik returned.

'You and I both know that holding Feann prisoner won't give us any information at all. He's not a man who would admit anything to us. Especially when it concerns our father.' But Rurik's mood had lifted, none the less. 'I want to know about Saorla's past, if there is a connection. Danr will want to know also.' He hesitated and added, 'It would be better if I went alone, before you arrive, to learn what I can.'

The idea didn't sit well with Alarr, sending his

brother off without anyone to guard him. 'No. We go together or not at all.'

But Rurik stared back at him. 'As you will. But know that I intend to learn Feann's reason for the killings first. And once I have my answers, he is yours for vengeance.'

He clasped his brother's hand in agreement. 'So be it.' Though he doubted if there was any connection between Feann and Saorla, he supposed there was no harm in asking.

They spoke of plans and possible ways to infiltrate the castle. Yet all the while, Alarr felt the sting of guilt for what he'd said to Breanne. He knew it had been necessary, but the sight of her stricken expression haunted him still. He had hurt her feelings, and he wished he could shut off his own response to her.

As they walked back towards the settlement, he caught sight of four riders approaching. They were dressed in the manner of the Irish, each wearing a long saffron *léine* and leather armour. They slowed when they reached Rurik and Alarr, eyeing them for a moment, but the riders did not stop. When they reached the gates, their leader spoke to the guards, and Styr's men allowed them to enter.

'Who are they?' Rurik asked.

Alarr's own suspicions were on alert. 'I don't know. But I intend to find out.'

Breanne followed Caragh towards the gates, after the young woman had told her about the visitors. To her shock, she saw three of her foster father's men. One of them she recognised as Darin MacPherson, captain of Feann's guards. He dismounted, along with the others, and tied his horse near a drinking trough. The moment he saw her, Darin smiled and bowed to her. 'My lady, I am glad to see that you are well.'

A blend of emotions washed over her, for the captain was behaving as if she had only been travelling instead of being brought out of slavery. She nodded to him and managed to greet him, 'It is good to see you once more, Darin.'

'I received word from the Hardrata tribe, a day ago, that you were here.'

He glanced around at the fortress, but Breanne felt numb inside. She wanted to ask, *Why did no one search for me?* But more than that, *Why didn't Feann come with you?*

It dug into her heart that her foster father had not searched for her. Finally, she asked, 'Where is the king?'

'He is travelling,' Darin said. 'He left just before you did. He has not returned yet.'

That lifted her spirits somewhat with the hope that perhaps her foster father *had* tried to find her. But she corrected Darin. 'I didn't leave. I was taken into slavery.'

The captain barely reacted to her words. She might as well have told him that she had gone to visit kinsmen. But he said, 'I am sorry to hear of it. We came at once to bring you home.'

Breanne knew she ought to be grateful, but instead, her thoughts grew guarded. She couldn't let go of her annoyance.

Before she could answer, another voice intruded. 'She is going nowhere with you.' Alarr stood beside Rurik, his hand resting upon the blade at his waist.

The silent threat was unmistakable. And she could almost hear the unspoken words: *She belongs to me.*

Anger flared up within her at his possessive behaviour. He had refused her offer of marriage and had treated her like dirt. Instead, she shot him a defiant look.

You hold no claim on me.

After what he'd said to her, she would not obey him. Her father's men had come for her, and she intended to accompany them home.

She suspected Alarr had heard every word

Darin had said. Likely, he intended to alter his plans now that he knew Feann was not at Kill-cobar.

The captain moved his hand to his own weapon. 'Who is this, my lady? Is he a threat to you?'

Before she could answer, Alarr took a step closer. He placed his hand on the back of her neck in an unmistakable claim. 'I am the man who bought her in the slave market.'

Her face reddened at his words, and her anger rose hotter. His hand tightened upon her nape in a silent warning.

'Then we will repay you for her freedom,' the captain said. To Breanne, he added, 'Gather your belongings, my lady, and we can leave at once.'

Alarr's fury was unmistakable. She suspected that it would take very little to provoke a fight between them. It irritated her that he was treating her like an object.

Caragh came forward to intervene. 'I am certain that you and your men must be weary after your journey. We can discuss Breanne's release after you have had something to eat and drink.' There was a tangible strain in the air, but Caragh met the captain's gaze, saying, 'If you and your men follow me, that will give Breanne a few moments to gather her belongings.'

It was the opening she had been waiting for. Breanne reached back for Alarr's hand and moved it off her neck. He gripped her palm in response and walked with her back to the dwelling they had once shared. The moment they went inside, Alarr spoke a sharp order and the men stood and departed the longhouse, leaving them alone.

Her anger flared once again, and she turned to face him. 'I stayed with you because I believed you were taking me home. After all this time, I never felt like a slave in your presence. Until now.'

She moved towards the partition, but Alarr caught her by the arm. 'I don't trust the guards with you. Or any other man.' There was a note of jealousy in his tone, and she didn't know what to think of that. He had already claimed that she meant nothing to him. He had no right to interfere.

'They are my father's men,' she insisted. 'I know Darin, and he is one of Feann's strongest guards. I have the right to go home with them.'

'No,' Alarr insisted. 'I do not trust them.' He lightened his touch upon her arm and instead of a grip, it felt like a caress. She froze when he rested his palm upon her back, gentling his touch. 'You could be harmed, and I would not be there to protect you.'

She tried to steel herself against the warmth that washed over her with his words. He didn't mean what he was saying, and she had to stop herself from falling prey to idle feelings.

'Why does it matter to you if I leave?' The words came out as a whisper. 'We both know that I mean nothing to you.' She threw his own words back at him. 'I am only your slave. Isn't that what you said?'

But when she stared into his eyes, Alarr made no effort to hide his desire. His blue eyes held the fire of longing, and he looked as if he wanted to mark his claim upon her. Her skin tightened at his gaze, and she was caught up in wanting someone she could never have.

His hands moved up her spine, his hand cradling her nape. 'The truth is, I want you far too much, *søtnos.*'

The heat of his touch evoked a response she had never expected. Her head tried desperately to warn her, but her body savoured his caress. Her skin tightened, yearning for him, even as she knew he would not turn aside from revenge.

Alarr was a *Lochlannach* warrior, a Norseman who would not yield to anyone.

And God help her, she wanted him, too.

The pieces of her heart crumbled when he cupped her face in his hands, leaning in to claim a kiss. His mouth coaxed her to kiss him back, and she melted into him, feeling as if her skin were blazing. Her brain tried to warn her of the danger, but Alarr's mouth silenced any protests.

'I won't let you go.' He spoke against her lips, drawing her body to his.

Breanne could feel the caged strength in his body, and she struggled to find her will power. 'I have to go back. Killcobar is my home.'

'And what if I refuse to let you leave?' he mused aloud. He drew her to their shared pallet and pushed her back against the furs. Gently, he pinned her wrists. 'What if I keep you here, bound to me?'

Alarr leaned down to kiss her again, and she suddenly understood what this was, beyond temptation. He wanted her to stay of her own free will by offering her the pleasure of his touch. A part of her hungered for the affection, as if he could push away the loneliness of the past few years. For so long, she had felt isolated, apart from everyone else at Killcobar. And Alarr was slowly taking apart the invisible walls she had built to shield herself from hurt.

His hands moved to her breasts, stroking them through the rough wool of her gown. Her nipples grew erect, and the sweet torment of his caress made her weak with desire. She wanted him badly, wanted to lose herself in him.

But it was an illusion, wasn't it? Alarr didn't truly want her. Had she not been King Feann's foster daughter, he would have left her in the slave market to become another man's possession. A harsh lump of disappointment pushed back the desire, and she turned her face aside.

'I don't want you to touch me,' she whispered. 'Please stop.'

He did, but the raw need in his expression made her falter. She sat up when he moved away, drawing her knees in. Right now, she wanted to weep, but she would not give Alarr the satisfaction.

'I am going home,' she told him. 'If you try to kill Feann, I will have no choice but to warn him.' She could not stand by and let her foster father be harmed.

Alarr's face turned grave. 'I cannot forget what Feann did to my bride and my family, Breanne. Justice must be served.'

She understood his desire for vengeance, and yet, she intended to confront her foster father first.

'He must have had a reason,' she said. 'Feann is not a murderer. I believe what you say, but he would never act in such a way without purpose.' Though he had a ruthless side, she could not imagine her foster father attacking if there was no cause.

'And what purpose was there in killing my bride? Gilla was an innocent.'

She didn't know what to say to that. Innocent people died in battle all the time. But her foster father was not cruel in that way. She had seen him spare men's lives before. It was not usual for him to threaten a woman, and she had no answer for him.

'Did you love Gilla?' she asked quietly. Not that it mattered, but she wondered whether he grieved for her still.

'We were friends.' He sat beside her and admitted, 'I didn't love her, but we could have made a good marriage between us.'

It should not have made a difference, but she felt a slight sense of relief. As soon as the thought struck her, she pushed it away. Why should it matter if he was in love with his bride? Alarr was her captor and her enemy. He intended to murder the man who had given her a home and a family. She owed him nothing at all.

But she could not deny that he had spared her life and her virtue. It was difficult to reconcile the two sides to the man. And perhaps it was too late to change his mind.

'I should go back,' she murmured. 'The others will be waiting for me.'

'Let them wait.' He caught her hand, tracing the centre of her palm with his thumb. The caress reached beneath her defences, unravelling her senses.

'You will allow me to leave,' she said quietly. 'Because you are a man of honour.'

'Am I?' He reached out to caress her hair, sliding his hand down her spine. 'Because right now, all I want is your body beneath mine.'

A flame of desire took hold, drawing her beneath his spell. She could not deny the raw physical attraction she felt, but she gathered the shreds of her willpower and stepped back.

'Goodbye, Alarr,' she murmured. For a long moment, she stared at him, wondering if he could ever reconsider his revenge.

And then she walked away from him.

* * *

'I never thought you would let her go.' Rurik stood beside Alarr as Breanne rode away with the soldiers.

'I'm not letting her go.' He didn't trust Feann's guards at all. They had not found her until Styr had allowed her to send word to Killcobar. Had they ever intended to search for her? He was beginning to have his doubts, since Styr's settlement was only a day's journey away. It would not have been difficult to find her. Their negligence didn't seem right, and Alarr intended to follow them in secret—not only for his own purpose, but also to ensure that she was protected.

'You want to track them.' Rurik's gaze was knowing, and he crossed his arms.

Alarr didn't deny it. He wanted to ensure that Breanne made it safely home again, and if that meant following at a swift pace, so be it. 'I don't trust them.'

'You wouldn't trust any man with Breanne.'

'Especially not soldiers who would wait so long to search for her. And I have not forgotten what I came here to do.'

That prompted a pained expression from Rurik. 'Feann isn't at Killcobar. You heard him say it. We have no reason to pursue Breanne.'

'We don't know for certain whether Feann is there.' He didn't trust their claims, and it was better to discover the truth for himself. 'Even if he is not, I think we should go and gather information. You were wanting to learn about your mother. I want to know about Feann's defences.'

'We might be recognised,' Rurik said. 'It's dangerous.'

His brother was right, but he still believed it was best to gather information. Someone might have the answers he sought.

'That may be true,' he said. 'But we can say truthfully that you have come in search of answers about your mother. And we may learn more about Feann while we are there.'

Rurik seemed to consider it. 'Has Breanne talked sense into you, then?'

'About killing Feann? No. But I agree that we should learn why he went to Maerr.' He stared out at the horizon to the riders that were no longer visible. Would Breanne be safe while he trailed them? It struck him as strange that the guards had barely questioned what had happened to her. Had Alarr been in their place, he would have demanded answers about how Breanne had been stolen away. He would have spent time ensuring that she was not injured—and never would he have allowed her to go off alone with a man who claimed to be her master.

'When do you want to go to Killcobar?' Rurik asked. 'And do you want escorts?'

Alarr thought about it and shook his head. 'Not at first. It would make us too conspicuous. Better to travel alone and let others believe we are searching for your family.' Only Feann and a handful of men might recognise them. And none of the tribe knew Rurik, since he was not at the wedding.

'I want to leave as soon as our belongings are prepared.' It was a risk to go alone, but he also understood Styr's reluctance to endanger his tribe. Perhaps the leader might be willing to visit Killcobar with his men, a few days from now.

He shielded his eyes against the sun, knowing it had been a mistake to let her go. Then he turned back to his brother. 'We are going to find our answers. No matter how long it takes.'

'And when Feann returns? Do you still intend to sacrifice your life for his? All to avenge a man who never cared about either one of us?'

'It's not only about our father. The king and his men slaughtered Gilla and her family. It was an act of war, and I intend to avenge our family's honour. The other tribes need to know that if they dare to attack, our retribution will be merciless. Already it has taken too long for us to respond.'

His brother fell silent for a time. 'And if you do kill him and lose your life, what will stop Feann from returning to Maerr?' He shook his head. 'Learn the truth if you will, but there are only two of us to fight. It's not enough.'

'It's enough for a slip of a blade between his ribs.' Yet even as he spoke the words, Alarr recognised his brother's truth. He didn't know how to make Rurik understand his reasoning. His brother couldn't understand why he was willing to take such a risk. But in all honesty, he had nothing left to lose.

'Why do you want to die, Alarr?' Rurik asked quietly.

He thought about his brother's question for a time, choosing his words carefully. 'When I fought against Feann, he stole from me the life I was meant to have. I am no longer the fighter I was. No woman wants me the way I am. Hardly able to walk…barely able to wield a sword.'

'You survived wounds that would have killed most men. I am glad you are alive,' Rurik said. 'But I came with you to Éireann because I wanted answers. And because I wanted to stop you from doing something foolish, like murdering a king.'

'You cannot stop me, Rurik. I have chosen my path.'

'And what of Breanne? It will destroy her if you kill her foster father. He is all she has left.'

Alarr knew that, and yet, he could not turn from this path. Only after he had slain Feann would he believe that he had any worth as a man. Breanne might feel pity towards him, but that was all. If he somehow survived the fight, it would change naught. The thought of having to leave her filled him with regret. But there was nothing to be done for it.

'We will go to Killcobar and follow Breanne,' Alarr said. 'Until Feann returns, we will learn what we can and wait.' And in the meantime, he would protect her from harm.

Rurik met his gaze steadily and gave a nod. 'So be it.'

Breanne rode with the soldiers towards her father's lands, but inwardly, she could not shake the premonition that something was wrong. When they stopped to make camp for the night, Darin came to help her down from the horse.

She smiled at the captain. 'Thank you.'

He guided her towards a clearing where one of the men was attempting to build a fire. 'Come and warm yourself,' he offered. The night air was cool, and she was eager to rest. Her thoughts remained troubled, and although she knew she had made the right choice to go with them, she could not stop thinking of Alarr. He was handsome, and his dark hair and fierce fighting skills allured her. She had loved sleeping beside him at night, feeling his hard body nestled against hers. And his kiss haunted her still.

He was a man living in darkness, bound to vengeance. She didn't understand how he was willing to sacrifice his life in a fight with Feann. Did he really believe he had so little value? Even Rurik had tried to stop him from this path towards death.

An ache settled within her at the thought. She knew what it was to feel as if no one wanted you. The solitude held an oppressive weight, and she understood the feeling of isolation. But for a brief moment it had seemed as if there was a connection between them before he'd pushed her away.

You made the right choice, her brain reminded her. *He was only intending to betray you.*

And yet, she somehow didn't believe that. When she had ridden away from the Hardrata settlement, she had caught Alarr staring at her with longing. Despite his cruel words, it seemed as if he didn't want to let her go. Her own feelings had been torn and confused, for it seemed as if his words and actions were in conflict. He had claimed she meant nothing at all to him… but she sensed that it was a lie.

'Are you hungry?' the captain asked.

'A little.' She held out her hands to the fire, trying to warm herself. He went to his saddle bag and withdrew some dried meat. He gave her the venison, but it was tough to gnaw. She struggled with the meagre food, and he gave her a sip of ale from a drinking horn.

Darin sat nearby, and she waited for him to ask questions. Surely, he would want to know what had happened to her. But instead, he said nothing, only staring into the fire. For a time, Breanne thought she should begin a conversation or at least try to talk to him. But there was only silence.

It felt as if she had been forgotten by everyone…as if her disappearance meant nothing. She had wanted to believe that she was Feann's adopted daughter, to feel as if she belonged at

Killcobar. All these years, she had tried to shape herself into the woman he wanted her to be. She had remained passive and obedient, quiet in the shadows. But now, it was clear that she had always been an outsider. No one had even noticed when she'd gone.

Breanne forced back the self-pity as her frustration rose higher. Though she wanted answers, did it even matter what they thought any more? They had abandoned her, and it was time to stop living her life to please others. No longer would she allow them to shape her destiny. This time, any decisions made would be her own.

At last, she spoke. 'Why did no one come for me during the past few weeks?'

The captain tossed a brick of peat into the fire and shrugged. Which was no answer at all. She waited again in disbelief, her anger rising. 'Am I worth so little to everyone?'

He hesitated and admitted, 'I know it must have seemed like this.'

'Then tell me what happened,' she demanded. 'Where is Feann now?'

Darin glanced over at his men, who quietly excused themselves to give them privacy. He stared into the fire for a long while, as if searching for the right words. 'He travelled to the west.

King Cerball asked for his help with an escaped prisoner. We sent word to him after you were gone, but I know not if he received our messages.'

She stared hard at him. 'And you didn't think you should send other men to search for me?' Her irritation heightened at his lack of effort, though she realised that it was possible Feann hadn't known she was a captive—especially if he had been travelling. The flames flared against the peat bricks, a bright orange colour against the night sky.

'We should have,' he confessed. 'But then, Styr Hardrata sent word to Killcobar that you were at the *Lochlannach* settlement.' His expression turned guilty, and he said, 'I am sorry you felt abandoned, my lady. That was never our intention.'

She supposed she ought to feel relieved that soldiers had come to bring her home at last. But instead, she was starting to question all that had happened. Alarr had openly admitted that he didn't trust Feann's men, so why should she? Moreover, was it possible that one or more of them had conspired with the man who had sold her into slavery? For what purpose? She didn't believe Darin would do such a thing, but it made her wonder whom she could trust.

She had once believed she could trust Alarr. And yet, he had let her go.

Her heart gave a curious ache at the thought, and it made her suddenly think of his desire for revenge. Where was Alarr now, and was he still searching for Feann? She was afraid to imagine his intentions, and no matter what she said or did, she could not stop him. There was no choice but to warn her foster father.

Darin's face was shadowed, and he seemed preoccupied by something. He stood, walking towards the edge of the forest. Once again, his attention seemed to be elsewhere, and she could not guess why. It was almost as if he were waiting for something. Or that he had sensed someone approaching. Soon enough, Breanne heard the sound of a horse, and Darin went towards the clearing, reaching for his sword. He spoke quietly to his men, and all went on alert. Breanne couldn't say whether there was truly a threat, but her instincts warned her to hide. She backed away into the shadow of the trees, wondering if she was foolish for doing so.

A twig snapped from behind her, and she spun.

'Are you well?' came a low voice from the shadows.

Breanne bit back her surprise and suppressed a curse. 'Alarr?' He moved closer, and her mood tensed at the sight of him. 'What are you doing here?'

'I followed you to ensure that you were safe. I don't trust these men.'

'You don't trust anyone,' she pointed out. Though she ought to be irritated that he had tracked her, another part of her was startled that he would care. And despite her better judgement, she warmed to it.

He didn't argue with her but reached for her hand. His palm was warm, callused from fighting. She remembered the sensation of those fingers trailing over her skin, and she could not deny the thrill of memory.

When she walked back towards the campsite, he kept her hand in his, and she saw Rurik holding a sword and shield, staring at the captain and his men. Though he hadn't provoked a fight, it was clear that he was diverting their attention.

'Darin,' Breanne said.

He kept his weapon in hand as he turned back to her. When she saw her holding Alarr's hand, he froze and waited for her command. 'My lady, do you want me to send them away or let them stay?'

'It wouldn't matter, even if I did want them to go. Alarr would not leave.' Even so, her heart gave a sudden thrill of anticipation. She was unaccustomed to being followed, and she didn't know whether to be flattered or frustrated. 'They can stay.' To Rurik, she said, 'You may set up your camp over there.'

She wanted to maintain a distance between them to guard her wayward feelings. Alarr kept her hand in his, and his thumb was drawing lazy circles over her palm. The simple touch went deeper than she'd imagined, and she could feel the echo of the caress in other places.

'You didn't just follow me to ensure my safety,' she murmured. 'There was another reason.' Her brain warned her to strengthen the walls around her feelings. *He is using you.* It wasn't wise to imagine that he wanted her for anything other than to get close to Feann.

He leaned in close so that she could feel his breath against her ear. 'You are still mine, Breanne.'

Her mouth went dry, and she felt her restlessness brewing. Alarr gazed at her with undisguised interest, and every memory of his touch came back to her. She remembered the feeling of his heavy body pressed above hers, and the way she had melted into him.

But those memories wouldn't change the rift between them. She let go of his hand, rebuilding her self-defences. She could not trust this man, despite how he had already saved her life. Alarr had already admitted that he would not set aside his vengeance for her. And how could she care for a man who wanted to hurt someone she loved? It was impossible. The thoughts burdened her, making her wish she could simply lock her heart away.

The ache of regret weighed upon her, for she had let herself long for someone she couldn't have. *He doesn't want you.* No one did, it seemed. And it was hard to push back the loneliness when she had never had any true family or loved ones. Feann was the only person to show her kindness, and even he had abandoned her.

She needed to find the strength to live her own life without relying on anyone else. Although she would return to Killcobar with Darin and his men, no longer could she live a shadowed life where no one cared if she was there or not. And no matter what feelings she had towards

Alarr, she would cut them off. It was better to be alone than to be used and discarded.

But for now, she would listen and watch.

Alarr led her towards the fire, and she sat on a fallen log. He took a place beside her, and then regarded Darin again. 'Where is Feann now?'

The man hesitated a moment. 'King Cerball wanted him to—'

'I asked where he is. Not what he is doing,' Alarr interrupted.

Darin eyed Breanne as if he didn't want to answer. At last, he said, 'I don't know where Feann is now.'

He wasn't going to tell Alarr anything, and she understood that. But he could tell her the truth if she commanded it. And perhaps she could confront Feann and end the vengeance between Alarr and him.

'But you do know where the escaped prisoner was being held,' she pointed out.

There was tension in his shoulders, as if he didn't want to reveal too much. She understood that he was trying to protect Feann, for her sake. His loyalty was commendable.

At that point, Rurik interrupted. 'Alarr, I can join these men and escort Breanne to Killcobar if you want to go in search of Feann and the prisoner.'

There was a silent glance exchanged between the men, and she wondered why Rurik would want them to split up. She was trying to decide what to say when Alarr's gaze narrowed upon Darin. 'There's something you're hiding from us, and it's not about Feann. It has greater importance, doesn't it? It's the reason why he didn't search for Breanne.'

The captain shifted his gaze back to Breanne but made no denial. 'My duty is to keep Lady Breanne safe.'

'But there is another threat,' Alarr guessed. 'And I suspect it has something to do with the escaped prisoner.'

The captain tried to keep his face expressionless, but Breanne saw the way he averted his gaze. There *was* something Darin was hiding.

'Tell me,' Breanne insisted. 'I have the right to know the truth.' He refused to meet her gaze, so she stood and drew closer. Her senses grew heightened as she waited for him to answer.

At last, he lifted his head and regarded her. 'You do.' With a pause, he added, 'The prisoner that King Cerball exiled was your mother.'

Chapter Six

Breanne's heart was pounding with a blend of anxious nerves. 'They told me she was dead. My father was executed, and I thought Treasa was killed alongside him.' But now, she wondered if Feann had lied to her about everything.

The captain shook his head. 'Your father was executed for treason, and your mother was exiled. King Cerball has command of their lands at Clonagh.'

For a moment, she felt as if she had been turned to stone. Everything she had known in her life was a lie. A tremor of anger took root and slowly kindled into rage. 'And Feann knew she was alive. All this time, he knew.'

Darin nodded. 'Feann was trying to negotiate with King Cerball. He wanted you to reclaim your birthright by wedding a man loyal to Cerball. But Cerball denied him for years.

Feann never told you because he didn't know if he would be able to bring you back again.'

She was already shaking her head. Right now, she felt as if her life had spun out of control, and she was struggling to grasp the truth. How could Feann have lied to her all those years about her family? The thought sickened her. She had believed that he cared for her like his own daughter. And now, it seemed that he had only been using her to solidify his alliance with Cerball and possibly gain command of Clonagh.

One moment, she had planned to leave Killcobar behind and begin anew with her own choices. Now, it seemed that kings were manipulating her life, pulling her in directions she'd never imagined.

There was only one person who could tell her the truth of what had happened. And she needed to understand all of it. She regarded Darin and asked, 'Where is my mother now?'

'If Feann was successful in capturing her, then likely she was returned to her exile at Dún Bolg,' the captain answered.

'What do you want to do, Breanne?' Alarr asked. His voice was quiet, almost gentle. 'You can go back with Rurik. Or if you want to go with me to Dún Bolg, I will escort you there. The choice is yours.'

At first, she didn't know whether to let him accompany her. But if Feann had already brought her mother to Dún Bolog, then likely her foster father was returning to Killcobar. It was better to keep Alarr away from Feann. 'I want to see my mother.'

She had so few memories of her past, and she didn't even know if she would recognise Treasa. Was her mother aware of what had happened to her? Would she care at all? A fervent longing prickled within her with the hope that she did have at least one person to call family.

'We can leave as soon as you are ready,' Alarr offered.

It surprised her that he wanted to travel by nightfall, but perhaps it would be safer. The moon was bright, and most of the journey would be through open fields. Breanne had never been to Dún Bolg, but she had heard that the lands lay towards the west.

She gathered a few belongings, along with some food, while Alarr and Rurik spoke in the Norse language once more. Then the brothers bid one another farewell, embracing before Alarr brought his horse to her. He tied her bundle to the saddle and helped her mount.

To the captain, she said, 'I bid you and your men good fortune.' Then she turned to Rurik. 'Swear to me that you will not harm Feann.'

He nodded. 'I swear it. I only want information about what happened on the day we were attacked.'

She believed he would keep his word. 'I hope you learn the truth. Send word to me after Feann returns to Killcobar.'

'I will.'

Alarr swung up behind her and turned the animal westwards. Breanne leaned back against him as they rode. She said nothing, but during the ride, she was conscious of every line of his body. He was warm, his arms sheltering her from the cold. Her body ached from exhaustion, and in time, the swaying of the horse caused her to grow weary. Alarr seemed to sense her weakness, and he murmured against her ear. 'Sleep, if you wish. I won't let you fall.'

She closed her eyes, grateful for his presence. 'Thank you.'

As she succumbed to her exhaustion, she was confused by the feelings of security. This man had been her captor, and now they were travelling together as equals. No longer did he seem like an enemy—instead, she grew aware that he had protected her at every moment.

His very presence made her want to lower her defences—just for a moment.

Alarr rested his cheek against her hair, and she indulged in the feeling of comfort, no matter that it was wrong. She told herself that it wasn't real, even as her wayward heart softened to his touch.

For the next few hours, they rode through the night along the edge of a winding stream, until the landscape shifted into rolling hills. Breanne slept against him, until at last, he came to a stop. The pale grey light of dawn creased the horizon, and she realised that they were in a part of Éire-ann she had never seen before. The green hills rose into a wooded area, but a road cut through the trees. In the distance, she saw mountains rising up, revealing a cashel atop the hillside.

'Where are we?' she asked.

'A few miles outside of Dún Bolg,' he answered. 'My father spoke of it during his travels, but I've never been there before.' He guided the horse up the hillside, and she then saw rock formations that provided natural shelter from the elements. 'We'll stop and sleep a while before we find your mother.' He didn't speak of Feann, though they both knew there was a chance that her foster father was still here.

Alarr chose a small indentation in the rock, not quite a cave, but surrounded on all sides. He dismounted and helped her down. Breanne started to gather supplies for a fire while he tended the horse and led it to drink at a mountain stream trickling down the hillside.

He chose a grassy place to tether the animal loosely, so the horse could graze. When he returned to their shelter, he nodded in approval at the kindling and wood she'd gathered. Alarr tossed her a flint, and she used her knife to strike a spark. She fed the spark dry grasses, blowing gently, before she added dry twigs and sticks. Eventually, she added wood, and she warmed herself at the flames.

She hardly knew what to think of anything right now. Alarr had escorted her here, but she knew better than to imagine that it was for her sake. He wanted to confront Feann, whereas she wanted to see the mother she had never known. What could she even say to Treasa? Breanne had not seen her since she was two years old. The woman was naught but a stranger. Nerves gathered within her at the thought of seeing her mother.

Alarr spread out a sleeping fur on the ground and stretched out beside the fire. She knew he was tired from all the travelling, but he had not wanted to stop until now. Likely, he didn't want any of the guards at Dún Bolg to be aware of their arrival. It was too easy for them to be seen in an open clearing.

She wondered if she should remain on the other side of the fire, apart from him. Ever since she had left, there had been an unspoken tension between them. There was no question that he desired her…and yet, she knew the danger of drawing too close. Alarr allured her, and she could not deny that she wanted him too. If she lay beside him, all her defences would crumble. And then he would leave her. Whether he returned to Maerr or whether he died fighting Feann, the result was the same. It was not wise to let herself care about this man.

'There's no need to be afraid of me, Breanne,' he said. Alarr leaned back on the fur and regarded her. 'I won't harm you.'

'I remember too well what happened the last time I was close to you,' she admitted. She didn't trust herself around him.

'I won't touch you unless you ask.' His voice was deep and resonant, as if he wouldn't mind it at all.

She drew close to the fire, holding out her hands. It was still cool in the morning, but she knew better than to get too close. For a moment, she gathered her thoughts, wondering if there was any means of dissuading him from his chosen path. She had asked him to give up his plans of vengeance before, and he had refused.

'Alarr,' she began, choosing her words with care, 'is there anything that would satisfy your need for vengeance that would allow my foster father to live?'

He leaned back against the furs, staring at the sky. 'No.'

She had expected this, but she was prepared to argue with him. 'Killing Feann won't bring your father back.'

He rolled to his side to face her. 'This isn't only about Sigurd. It's about me.'

Breanne came to kneel beside him. 'What is it?'

He sat up then and touched his legs. 'Feann took away more than my father's life. He took away the man I used to be.'

She sobered, but she wanted him to understand

that he was not broken in her eyes. 'That's not true. Because of *your* actions, you protected me. Even when Oisin tried to take me.' She reached out to touch his knees. 'You are still a worthy fighter. You've overcome so much.'

Alarr captured her hands, holding them there. 'I have no balance, and I cannot run very far. When it rains, I feel the pain aching deep within. These are wounds that will never heal.'

She understood, then, why he believed he had to die in this battle. He did not believe he was a man of worth any more. His vengeance was not about hurting Feann—it was about ending his own pain of loss.

She leaned in closer and touched her forehead to his. 'Your wounds are not here, Alarr.' She lifted her hands from his legs and moved them to his heart. 'Your wounds are here.'

His face was a breath away from hers, and inwardly, she was trembling. His blue eyes were searing, his hunger burning within them. May the gods forgive her, she wanted him to touch her —even though she knew he would not stay.

She closed her eyes, trying to gather what little control she had. Beneath her palms, his skin was warm, but she did not pull her hands back.

'You are still a man of strength,' she whispered. 'He didn't take that from you.'

'He took away everything that mattered,' he said softly.

Her heart bled for him, for the losses he'd endured, and the dark frustration that shadowed his heart. And despite everything, she wanted him to live. Even if they could not be together, she wanted him to put the past behind him.

'He didn't take away everything,' she whispered. 'There are many who care about you.'

Alarr drew his hands around her waist and lay back on the furs, pulling her body atop his. She could feel the hard ridge of his arousal between her thighs, and it caused her body to ache. Beneath her gown, her breasts tightened, and it was difficult to catch her breath.

'What do you want from me, Breanne?' His voice was hoarse, as if he had no control remaining. The tension stretched between them, and her heartbeat quickened as she sat astride him.

The silence that fell between them was a chasm of unspoken words. He tightened his hold upon her body, and another flicker of heat licked at her skin. She hardly knew how to answer. At last, she said, 'I want you to let him live.'

Before he could refuse, she touched her fingertips to his mouth. 'I don't expect you to let go of your hatred or anger. But I am asking that you do this for my sake.'

He stared at her as if she had asked too much of him. Already she could see the refusal in his eyes. But this was about more than abandoning his vengeance. She didn't want him to die.

At this moment, she could not put a name to her feelings for Alarr, for they were tangled up in invisible knots. She knew he was wrong for her, an enemy. She knew he would leave. And yet, when she was in his arms, she felt alive. He had been both her warrior and her rescuer—a man who tempted her in ways she didn't understand.

But more than that, she wanted to close up Alarr's invisible wounds and make him see that he was more than a fighter. He was a man who deserved a new beginning.

Despite all the reasons why this was wrong… she could not suppress the longing that rose within her. And if she made Alarr believe that there was another way to avoid bloodshed, she could save them both.

'If you let Feann live, I will give you whatever you want.' Her voice was breathless, but she kept her gaze fixed upon him. Slowly, Breanne reached for the laces of her gown and loosened them. She knew it sounded as if she were making the ultimate sacrifice. But the truth was, she wanted Alarr badly. She hadn't lied when she had called him a man of strength. He had shielded her all these weeks, keeping her safe.

Alarr said nothing but distracted her by drawing his hand down the curve of her spine. He moved beneath her, and a shiver of anticipation slid over her. Her breath hitched, and she reached for his shoulders. He pressed against the juncture of her thighs, and a surge of desire prickled within. She grew wet between her legs, wanting something she could not understand.

'Feann must face justice for what he did.' His voice was like iron, rigid and unyielding.

Breanne drew her hands to his chest. 'I agree that he must atone for the attack. But grant me his life, I beg you.'

She leaned in and kissed him, hoping she could change his mind. Her action seemed to ignite his desire, and Alarr answered the kiss, devouring her with his mouth. His tongue slid inside, and she felt an answering ache between her legs. Her breathing grew rough, and she gripped his hair, meeting his needs with her own.

'He isn't worth your innocence, Breanne. Save that for a man worthier than me.'

She understood then, that he was granting her the choice. He wanted her, but he would not claim her body unless she gave her full consent. She could stop her actions now, and he would let her be. But she could not deny that his caress tempted her, making her want to be loved.

There was a strong chance that he would not agree to this bargain. But she didn't want to stand back without fighting for the lives of the men she cared about. 'You *are* a man of worth, Alarr.'

He lifted his hand to her face. 'When you left with those men, all I could think of was bringing you back.' He brought her palm to his heart, resting it there. 'I want more than your innocence, Breanne.'

She didn't understand what he meant. When she studied his face, she saw the man who had come for her, time and again. Alarr had been hardened by battle and the need for revenge. Yet, within him, she saw the same shadow of loneliness. He had lost everything—his father, his bride, and even his strength in battle.

His blue eyes burned into hers. 'If you give yourself to me, I will not let you go. Once you make this choice, we will be bound together by the gods.'

Her emotions softened when she realised what he was offering. This was not a man who was forcing her to bargain her virtue for Feann's life. It was much more than that. 'You want me to stay with you.'

'Of your own free will,' he said.

Her heart quaked at the thought, for she was afraid to ask for how long. He might intend for her to be his concubine…or perhaps his wife. She had never expected this, and it unsettled her. What was his purpose? Why would he ask her to stay?

It went against everything she had believed about him—that he would take what he wanted and then leave. Instead, he was reaching out to her, wanting her to remain with him. Never had she imagined this, and her defences came crashing down.

Of all the people in her life, Alarr was the only man she had come to depend on. He had never forsaken her, and that meant something. He was a man who had endured as much loss as she had. And perhaps they could fill the emptiness in one another.

'If I agree,' she said quietly, 'will you let him live?'

His expression never faltered, and he gave a single nod. Breanne studied him, trying to discern if he was telling her the truth.

In answer, she leaned in to kiss him again. Alarr claimed her mouth relentlessly, letting her know without a doubt how much he wanted her.

With shaking fingers, Breanne lowered her bodice, never taking her eyes from his. Then she took his palm and laid it upon her bare breast.

The scalding heat of his palm aroused her, and Alarr stroked her breast, lightly grazing the hardened nub. A bolt of heat made her moan, and he deepened the pleasure when he lowered his mouth to her nipple. Gently, he suckled the tip, his tongue driving her wild. She arched, unable to stop the surge of pleasure that filled her.

Against her skin, he murmured. 'You belong to me now, Breanne.'

She gripped his hair, his touch arousing her deeply. Then she added, 'And you belong to me.' To emphasise her words, she reached out to unfasten his tunic.

He helped her, stripping it away before he drew his lips back to hers. Against her mouth, he said, 'From now on, you will spend every night in my bed.'

With his hands, he drew back the edges of her gown, exposing her naked body. She felt the heat of the fire against her skin and the fur beneath her body. Alarr removed the rest of his clothing and then pressed her back. 'I hated watching you leave with those men,' he said, trapping her wrists upon the furs. 'I didn't trust them to guard you.'

He lowered his mouth to her other breast, giving it the same attention as the first. She shuddered against him, threading her fingers through his hair. His touch was possessive, and it evoked a fiery pleasure she had never imagined. It was as if the years of loneliness had gathered up within him, and he needed her to fill the void inside.

Breanne framed his face with her hands. His blue eyes stared into hers, and she kissed him again. 'You always kept me safe.' She drew her hands down his muscled torso, feeling the rock-hard muscles beneath her palms. There was no trace of fat upon him, and his abdomen had several ridges. When her fingertips brushed against his ribs, he jolted with a slight laugh.

'You're ticklish,' she accused, and he did not

deny it. Instead, he drew her hand lower, until her palm brushed against his large arousal. For a moment, her apprehension returned, and she closed her eyes. Alarr guided her to his manhood, and demanded, 'Touch me, Breanne.'

She curled her fingers around his shaft, understanding that he meant to empower her. Tentatively, she stroked him, and he hissed.

'Did I hurt you?'

'No.' He showed her how to touch him, and she felt his erection grow harder against her palm as she stroked. She marvelled at the sense of power that rose up and the heady pleasure of caressing him.

Alarr drew his hand between her thighs, and she grew embarrassed by her wetness. He seemed pleased, however. 'Do not be shy, Breanne. Your body knows what it wants. And I intend to learn what you need.'

He began rubbing gentle circles against her intimate opening. A shock of sensation flooded through her, and she gasped when he slipped a finger inside. In answer, she stroked his length, finding what made him groan with arousal. 'Don't stop what you are doing, *søtnos.*' He drew her hand higher, and she felt the answering bead of moisture at his tip.

Slowly, he began to penetrate her with his finger in slow strokes while his thumb moved in light circles. The motion wound her up tightly, and she found herself squeezing him, evoking a stronger sensation. He added another finger, stretching her and making her crave more. As the feelings rose up within, gathering into a fist of desire, he lowered his mouth to her stomach. He kissed her skin, parting her thighs and raising her knees. She did not know what he was planning to do, until she felt his warm breath against her intimate opening.

'Alarr?' she questioned, gripping the furs. Her skin was unbearably sensitive, and when he replaced his fingers with his mouth, she could not stop the cry mingled with a gasp. He was tormenting her, forcing her higher until she was sobbing. Over and over, he stroked her with his tongue, until she felt herself slipping over the edge. A shimmering eruption of release flooded through her, and she trembled hard as the pleasure claimed her.

Only then did he rise up, sliding the edge of his erection to her wet opening. She was still so overcome by the shocking sensations that she was barely aware of him entering her body. There was a slight discomfort as he breached her innocence, and then she welcomed the invasion that brought him deep inside. She tried to move against him, but he imprisoned her wrists again.

'Slowly, *søtnos*.' Alarr ground against her, and she quaked as an aftershock flooded through her.

He took her lips, kissing her as he began to thrust. She felt uncertain at first and a little sore. But gradually she found herself meeting him, lifting her hips as he caressed her deep within.

She arched her back, trying to get closer. Her breathing was hitched, but he kept his lovemaking slow, coaxing her passion higher. When she thought she could bear it no longer, he slid in deep and held himself there, gently stroking her hooded flesh. A shocking coil of desire struck hard, and she moaned as his caress evoked a powerful release that filled every inch of her body.

Her heart pounded, and she gripped the furs, trembling violently with the storm of pleasure. Breanne wrapped her legs around his waist, and he quickened the tempo, gripping her hips as he entered and withdrew. His breathing was harsh, and when she squeezed him with her inner walls, he lost control. Over and over, he took her, until she climaxed again, and he emptied himself inside. His breathing was laboured as he rode out his own release, and he collapsed on top of her.

She held him close, their bodies damp with perspiration. Never had any man made her feel this way. Her heart was thundering, her body alive in ways she'd never imagined. While he slept against her, she pushed back his hair, memorising the lines of his face. He would not let her go now, and she found that she *wanted* to be with him, whatever came next. Her feelings were vulnerable, and though she was wary of loving this man, she could not stop the emotions from gathering inside.

And as he drifted off to sleep, their bodies still joined, she prayed that she had made the right decision to stay with him.

Chapter Seven

Alarr made love to her twice more as the morning waned into afternoon. Though his conscience warned that he should not have taken advantage of her offer, he could not bring himself to hold regrets. The craving for her touch consumed him, and the knowledge that he was the only man who had ever claimed her body made him feel even more protective of Breanne.

She held an inner strength and bravery that he admired. But more than that, she had insisted that he was a man of worth. He didn't really believe her, but she had forced him to consider a decision beyond his thoughts of vengeance. It was still likely that he would die in battle, even if he did keep this vow. And for that reason, he had agreed to Breanne's bargain.

Alarr knew his fate, but before he breathed his last, he wanted to spend his remaining days with her. He wanted her bare skin next to his, just as it was now. And every time he pleasured her, he wanted to watch her tremble with release, welcoming his body inside hers. It was as close to a true marriage as he would ever have. And if somehow she conceived a child, a part of him would live on.

A hollow ache centred inside him at the knowledge that he would not share that with her. All he had were these last few days, and he wanted to savour them, searing them into his memory. He kept their bodies intertwined, feeling content as he had never been before. She was awake, but neither spoke. It was as if words would break the spell between them, bringing reality back. And he didn't want that—not yet.

But soon enough, Breanne's stomach growled, and at her soft laugh, he realised he could not keep her here for the rest of the day, much as he wanted to.

'Do we have anything to eat?' she asked, tracing his bare skin.

'I know what I want,' he answered, rolling her to her back and taking her breast into his mouth. He was rewarded with her slight gasp, before she sighed and moved her hips against him.

'Much as I love having you in my bed, we do need food.'

'Do we?' He reached to touch her and found that she was as aroused as he. Giving in to his desire, he slid inside her welcoming depths.

Breanne's swift intake of breath told him that she wanted him, too. He entered and withdrew slowly, and she raised her knees to take him deeper.

'When we approach Dún Bolg, we will tell them that you are my wife. It's safer to stay together.' But it was about more than protecting her—it was because he wanted no man to even look at Breanne. She was his for these last few days, and he needed her with him.

'I agree.' She pulled his face closer and kissed him. He took her mouth, kissing her deeply as he continued to make love to her. Breanne met his thrusts, digging her fingers into his shoulders until she wrapped her legs around his waist, demanding more.

'If Feann is there—'

'Then I will stay with you and speak with him,' she interrupted. 'As you said, we will let him believe we are married.'

He didn't argue, but continued to love her, driving her close to the edge. If he dared to tell

Feann that he had wed Breanne, the king would demand his life in return. Their battle might be this day. For all he knew, this might be the last time he could be with this woman.

He slowed his pace again, wanting it to last. Her breathing had shifted, and she tried to urge him on, begging, 'Alarr, please.'

But he continued to draw out her pleasure, sliding deep within as he lowered his mouth to her breast, stroking her with his tongue. He was starting to learn what she needed, and when she arched against him, he reached down to stroke her intimately.

She was shuddering against him, but he wanted her to remember this moment between them. Gently, he urged her higher, until she gave a keening cry and shattered in his arms. She was panting as he entered and withdrew. All around his erect length, he could feel her body spasming and embracing him.

By the gods, he needed this woman. And if this was the last time between them, at least he knew he had glimpsed the life he would never have. He penetrated her, grasping her hips as she clenched him, and when he emptied himself inside, he held her close, breathing in the scent of her hair. His heart was racing, and he never wanted to let her go.

But he had no choice in this. She had to face her past, just as he did. With great reluctance, he withdrew and kissed her again before he helped her put on her gown. He got dressed and they put out the fire.

Breanne picked up the furs and folded them, and he brought them over to their horse, binding the coverlet to the saddle. He lifted her on to the animal and then mounted behind her, guiding them back on to the path leading to Dún Bolg. The green fields spread out in the distance, and he took the horse towards the fortress. A high wooden fence surrounded it, and he approached the gates slowly.

His thoughts were troubled, for he was only waiting to learn if Feann was still here. He had made a promise to Breanne not to kill him, and yet, he still wanted justice for his father's death. The question was whether that could happen without bloodshed. He doubted if that was possible.

When they reached the entrance, two guards called out for him to halt. Every sense went on alert as Alarr dismounted, holding the reins of their horse. He kept his hand near his weapon to protect Breanne.

'Who are you, and why are you here?' one guard asked.

'I am here to bring my wife, Breanne Ó Callahan, home to see her mother.'

The guard spoke to the other and answered, 'We have no Ó Callahans here.'

Breanne muttered beneath her breath, 'He's lying.'

Alarr suspected as much, since the woman had gone into hiding. 'May we speak with your king or your chief?'

'Wait here.'

One of the guards departed to ask, and Breanne kept her voice low. 'Why do you think she was exiled in this place?'

'I don't know. But Feann may have the answers if he's here.' Inwardly, the tension was stretched tight within him, making him suspicious of everyone.

A little while later, the guard returned and opened the gates to him. 'Follow me.'

They did, and Alarr saw that the fortress was organised and neat, with the thatched round-houses evenly spaced. Outdoor hearths burned with bricks of peat, and an iron pot hung over another fire, redolent with the succulent aroma of stew. There was an air of peace and contentment here, not one of war or imprisonment. He didn't know what to think of that.

When they reached the largest dwelling, the guard stopped. 'Our chief will speak with your wife alone.'

'I will not leave Breanne alone with a stranger,' Alarr countered. 'I will remain with her at all times.' He pressed his hand to her waist to emphasise it.

'Iasan does not wish to welcome a *Lochlannach* in our midst,' the guard said.

He didn't care what the chief wanted. Breanne's safety came above all else. But then, she turned to him and touched a hand to his shoulder. 'The chief may know something about what happened to my mother. Let us compromise.' She regarded the guard and said, 'Tell Iasan that I will speak with him, but only if my husband can be present at the door or closer.'

The guard inclined his head. 'I will ask.'

Alarr wasn't convinced it was a good idea to let her speak to the chief alone, particularly if Feann was here. But he was starting to believe that his enemy was already gone, for there was no sign of visitors.

Breanne's mother might have answers about Feann, since she had chosen to foster her daughter with him. But when Alarr glanced at his wife, he saw her twisting her fingers together.

'What is it?' he asked gently.

She shook her head. 'Nothing, really. It's just that I'm nervous about seeing my mother for the first time in so long. I haven't seen her since I was a young child.'

Their upbringing had been vastly different, so it seemed. He had been part of a large family with many kinsmen in the tribe whereas she had been more isolated.

'Do you still want to see her, if she is here?' he asked. 'She might not have told them her real name.'

Breanne nodded slowly. 'Even if I don't know her, I would like to speak to her.'

The guard returned and said, 'Our chief has agreed to come and meet you here.'

Alarr understood that the leader wanted to ensure that there was no risk of an attack. He agreed, and within a few minutes, a man emerged from the roundhouse, leaning against a walking stick. His hair was a blend of grey and red, and though he was past his fighting years, there was no doubting the razor-sharp awareness in his eyes. When he studied Breanne, there was a visible discomfort, as if he recognised her somehow. He motioned for the guard to come closer and murmured a command in the man's ear.

'I understand you came in search of a Ó Callahan woman,' the chief said. 'Why?'

Breanne took a step closer. 'I was told that my parents were killed, years ago, and I lived with my foster father ever since. I learned only recently that my mother, Treasa, was exiled here. I was hoping to find her.'

The older warrior stared at her for a time, as if discerning something. Alarr met the man's gaze, and added, 'We mean no harm to her or to anyone of your tribe.'

The chief seemed full of distrust, and he said, 'That remains to be seen.' Then he added, 'You may stay the night with us. A few of our men are going hunting now, and you may join them if you wish. Your wife can stay with the women.'

Alarr was about to refuse, for he didn't like the idea of being separated from her. But then, Breanne leaned in close. 'I think he wants to learn if we truly are a threat. Go with them, and I will stay here. I have your knife, if there is a need.'

He was about to argue with her, when abruptly,

he heard an audible gasp. A woman broke free from the others and hurried towards Breanne. Her hair was reddish gold, like Breanne's, and her face was an older version. There could be no doubt this was her mother.

Breanne stood motionless, in shock. For a moment, the two women stared at one another, until the older woman said, 'Breanne?'

When she gave a nod, the woman embraced her, openly weeping. Though Breanne did not push her away, it was obvious that she knew not what to do. She appeared startled by the woman's presence and could not quite return the affection.

'I think I should remain with my wife,' Alarr said to the chief, 'while she becomes reacquainted with her mother.'

Breanne followed her mother across the fortress to another roundhouse. Treasa gripped her hand as if she never wanted to let go. There was no denying that her joy was real. Her cheeks were wet with tears, and her smile spread across her face.

As for herself, Breanne felt only confusion. She couldn't force herself to be happy at seeing Treasa, for she didn't know her at all. It almost made her feel guilty that she couldn't return her mother's happiness. All she could think of was how Feann had never once spoken of Treasa. Breanne had always believed that she was alone, never knowing that she had a surviving family member. More than anything, she had wanted to have that kinship bond with another person. Instead, she could hardly bring herself to feel anything. There was no sense of connection with her mother, and a slight flare of guilt troubled her. She ought to be overjoyed, instead of mistrustful.

Alarr followed her, and he appeared to be searching for any signs of danger. She was grateful for his presence, for she believed he would keep her safe. His hand remained at her waist in a silent warning to others, and the gentle touch brought her comfort.

Ever since she had given herself to him, he had remained close. Though she wanted to believe that he would keep his promise, she remained cautious. It did not seem that there was any trace of her foster father, and she was grateful that she had more time before the two men confronted one another.

An uneasy feeling settled in her stomach as she wondered if Alarr had been right about Feann.

She had never seen a darker side to the king before. Had he exiled her mother as a means of controlling her lands at Clonagh? Or had he tried to save Treasa's life after her husband was executed? She couldn't understand why her mother would be a threat to anyone. But Feann's purpose remained unclear. Breanne didn't know what to think about a man who would lie about Treasa's existence for so long.

Her mother led her inside and bade her to sit down. Alarr joined them but remained near the doorway to give them a measure of privacy.

She braved a smile. 'I cannot tell you how glad I am that you came to visit me, Breanne. I've been in hiding for so long, I never imagined I would see you again.'

'Feann told me you were dead,' Breanne answered honestly. She hardly knew what to say or where to begin.

Treasa's expression grew pained. 'Sometimes I wished I were dead.' She took a steady breath and admitted, 'I lost everything. My home…my husband…even you.'

Breanne felt as if her emotions were in turmoil right now. She needed to put together the pieces of the past. 'I need to understand what happened to you and my father. Will you tell me how you came to Dún Bolg?'

And why you remained hidden for so long.

Even as a prisoner, someone could have told her that Treasa was still alive. But they didn't want her to know the truth, and she couldn't guess the reasons why.

Treasa rested her hands in her lap and glanced at Alarr. Breanne reassured her, 'Alarr can be trusted.'

Her mother hesitated for a moment as if trying to decide whether to believe it. Finally, she said, 'Your father, Dal, was a good friend and an ally of King Cerball MacDúnlainge. He is a powerful ruler, and there was a time when we thought of marrying you to one of Cerball's sons.'

Then her expression hardened at the memory. 'Dal thought we should send you to him for fostering, but I wasn't so certain. I knew Feann would protect you, and he was not as ambitious as Cerball.'

Against her spine, Breanne felt the light touch of Alarr's hand. Then he spoke, 'Where is Feann now?'

Treasa shrugged. 'He was here a few days ago. I suppose he returned to Killcobar.' Her expression revealed nothing about her failed attempts at escape. In fact, from her demeanour, Breanne questioned whether Darin had been telling the truth. Was she truly a prisoner in exile? Or were there more lies?

From the tension in his hand, Breanne knew that Alarr wanted to ask more, but he held back the questions.

'What happened to my father?' she asked Treasa.

Her mother's face tightened with emotion. 'Dal wanted to raise his own status by fighting Cerball's battles with our own men. I told him we should stay at Clonagh, but he refused. Instead, he went into battle against the *Lochlannach*, time and again, while he left me with Cerball. He believed I would be safe there, as an honoured guest in the household.'

Her face tightened, and she lowered her gaze, gripping her hands together. 'But I was Cerball's prisoner.'

Breanne sensed there was more that her mother did not wish to reveal. She turned to Alarr. 'Will you leave us alone for a moment?'

He drew his hand to her nape and nodded. 'If you feel safe here. I can guard the door.'

She nodded. Before he left, he pulled her close and kissed her. It was likely a mark of possession, to show her mother that they were bound together. But even so, the brief kiss made her savour the light pressure of his mouth. Breanne gathered her composure and after he left, she regarded her mother. 'How long were you his prisoner?'

'For three years,' Treasa answered. There was hatred within her voice, and Breanne suspected what else had happened.

'Were you his prisoner...in all ways?'

Her mother closed her eyes. 'Cerball told me he would send Dal to fight at the front of the battle lines if I did not give myself to him. I despised what he did to me, but I had no choice, if I wanted to keep your father alive. In the end, it didn't matter.'

'I'm so sorry for what you endured,' she whispered to her mother. The thought of being a king's prisoner, and being forced to share his bed, was horrifying. It evoked memories of Oisin and his attempt to take her into captivity. She could not even imagine her mother's pain— even worse because Cerball had still ordered Dal's execution. Breanne could see the suffering in Treasa's face, and she took the woman's hand, squeezing it.

Her mother tightened her lips and took a

breath. 'It's over now, and I've made a new life for myself here.'

'They told me that my father was executed for treason. Was it because the king wanted you?'

Treasa stood and paced across the small dwelling. For several moments, she said nothing. Then she admitted, 'Cerball was a proud man, and he believed that I would love him more than my husband. He wanted me to set Dal aside and become his queen.' Her eyes gleamed with unshed tears, and she rested her hand upon one of the beams supporting the roof. 'When I refused, he grew enraged. He accused Dal of conspiring against him.'

'Do you think my father knew what was happening?'

Treasa nodded. 'Once Dal realised I was Cerball's captive, he did everything in his power to get me out.' She wiped a tear away and said, 'He helped me escape with one of his men but paid the price with his life. Cerball executed him and stole our lands.' She took a moment to gather control of her emotions.

'And you left me with Feann,' Breanne finished.

Her mother nodded. 'I was grateful that he

promised to protect you until you came of age. Even if I was not allowed to see you.'

Breanne frowned, not truly understanding the reason why Feann had not wanted her to know that her mother was alive. Was it for Treasa's protection, or was it for his own reasons? She wanted to ask questions, but something held her back. Someone was lying, and she knew not if it was Feann or Treasa.

'Are you still a prisoner here?' she asked her mother.

Treasa gave a weak smile and nodded. 'This is where I have been exiled. After Cerball no longer desired me, he has kept me here all these years.' She added, 'I tried to visit Clonagh a time or two. Feann heard of it, and he brought me back.' Regret tinged Treasa's voice, but she could understand her mother's reasons for wanting to go home.

'What of our people?' Breanne asked quietly. 'What became of them?'

'They are under Cerball's rule. Feann was trying to arrange for you to reclaim Clonagh by wedding a man loyal to Cerball. I had hoped he would manage it.' Her mother's expression grew tense. 'But you are already wedded to this *Loch-*

lannach.' She appeared displeased by it. 'I don't know what can be done about an alliance now.'

Breanne thought about admitting to her mother that they were not truly married but decided against it. Instead, she rose from her seated position and went to the door to bring Alarr back inside. She had never thought about Clonagh in the past, always believing it was lost. But now, she wondered what to do.

Alarr came to sit beside her, and she took strength from his presence. Treasa eyed him and asked, 'Tell me how you came to be with my daughter.'

'I am Alarr Sigurdsson of the kingdom of Maerr,' Alarr replied. 'Breanne was in danger, and I wed her as a means of protecting her.' His tone remained neutral, the lie flowing easily. He slid his arm around her waist in a silent gesture to emphasise his claim.

Treasa's expression grew strained. 'Was it your wish to wed him, Breanne?' She appeared disconcerted by the idea of a union between her daughter and a *Lochlannach*.

Breanne caught his gaze and recognised that Alarr was trying to gain more information for both of them. She would say nothing to dispute his claim. 'It was my choice, yes.'

Inwardly, she wondered if it had been the right decision to offer herself to him. She didn't know if Alarr would keep his vow not to kill Feann. But beyond her foster father's life, she could not bear the thought of Alarr's death. She wanted him to live, to recognise that he had a life beyond fighting. Would he truly set aside his plans for revenge? Or was he only saying words she wanted to hear?

His hand moved over her waist in a slight caress of reassurance. She glanced at Alarr, and in his eyes, she saw a man who would not let her go. His gaze was steadfast, and she wondered if the sudden intimacy between them would bring him out of his shadows and into a life where there was hope. For the first time in her life, it felt as if she had someone she could love. And though she was afraid to trust him, she wanted to believe that he would not betray her.

'How did you learn I was at Dún Bolg?' Treasa asked. 'Did Feann tell you?'

'No, it was another man,' Alarr responded. 'Breanne wanted to see you, and I agreed to bring her here.' He said nothing of Feann, and she knew it was a deliberate omission.

But Treasa would not be deterred. 'What other

man? Was it Oisin MacLogan?' Her demeanour tensed, and Breanne stared in shock.

'Why would you speak of Oisin?' The very memory of the man made her skin crawl. Were it not for Alarr's rescue, she had no doubt that Oisin would have raped her or forced her to wed him.

'Oisin is one of Cerball's bastard sons. He was the man Cerball chose for you to wed.'

Breanne shuddered at the thought. But she was starting to realise that Feann had done all that he could to keep her from the alliance.

'Oisin was angry when I did not agree to wed him,' Breanne confessed to her mother. 'He tried to take me by force.' She explained how the man had tried to hunt her down, and Treasa's face blanched.

'Oisin had no lands of his own. He wanted to wed you, in order to claim Clonagh as his own.'

'But now, he cannot.' Breanne eyed Alarr, re-alising that they had destroyed Oisin's plans.It made her wonder about her future. Did Alarr intend to wed her in truth one day? Or was he only intending to keep her as his lover? Both possibilities made her uneasy. If she married him, he would want her to leave Éireann and return to Maerr. But if she was only his concubine, he might one day abandon her. The thought left an icy chill sinking within her mood. She didn't like the thought of being powerless to command her own future or being left behind.

Her mother reached out and touched his shoulder. 'Alarr, might I have another moment alone with my daughter?'

He hesitated, but Breanne nodded. 'I don't think there's any danger, and it's just the two of us.' She suspected that Treasa wanted to discuss her 'marriage' to Alarr.

'If you wish.' He rose and went to the door. Before he left, he glanced at Treasa and then back at Breanne. He was still wary, but she was glad for his overprotective nature. It had helped her to survive more than once.

When he had gone, Treasa sat closer, lowering her voice. 'Breanne, I must ask you this, in all seriousness. Would you consider setting aside Alarr as your husband? You could keep him as your consort instead.'

Her mother's question took her aback. 'Why would you say this?' She had no desire for a different man. She preferred to remain with Alarr, for he was a man of honour and strength.

'For the sake of our tribe,' Treasa continued. 'They are under Cerball's rule, and I know they are suffering. You need a husband who can help you take back our lands at Clonagh.' She glanced at the doorway. 'But we can never do this if you have a foreigner at your side. He is the enemy, Breanne.'

'Alarr protected me when no one else would,' she argued. And she saw no need to reclaim lands she barely remembered.

'I am not saying you must give him up,' Treasa insisted. 'Keep him as your lover, if you will.' She took both of Breanne's hands in hers. 'I do not ask you for a decision now. I ask only that you think about it. But we need an alliance with another Irish tribe if we are to reclaim Clonagh.'

We? Breanne thought. They had gone from being strangers, and now her mother expected her to tear apart her life for a birthright she didn't want? Her initial reaction was to refuse, but something made her hold her tongue.

Treasa seemed relieved by her silence. She squeezed her daughter's palms and added, 'I cannot tell you how glad I am that you are here now. I've not seen you since you were a child. It means everything to see you all grown up.' Her eyes gleamed with tears, though she smiled.

Breanne didn't know how to respond, for her thoughts were in turmoil. It had been years since she'd seen Treasa, and her mother had never attempted to contact her. She had not even sent word that she was alive. It was possible that the leader at Dún Bolg had refused to allow it, or possibly Feann had not wanted contact between them. But it seemed that only now, when she was of use to Treasa, did her mother appear to have feelings towards her. Though Breanne tried to suppress her suspicions, she couldn't bring herself to have any emotions of her own. There was a distance between them, a tangible rift that she could not quite bridge.

But Treasa did not appear to notice her discomfort. 'Let us go and join the others,' her mother suggested. 'The men may have brought back fresh meat from the hunt, and we can help them cook the evening meal.'

She followed Treasa outside and found Alarr standing at the doorway. He sent her a questioning look, and she nodded to reassure him that all was well. His gaze transformed as he watched over her. In his blue eyes, she saw the promise of another night in his arms. The thought only deepened her confusion, for she could not deny that she cared for this man. If she was not careful, she might grow to love him.

But her heart ached at the thought of leaving

Éireann behind if Alarr wanted her to journey to Maerr. She wasn't ready to leave her home for a man who might one day set her aside. She didn't know what his feelings were towards her, beyond desire. She had indulged in a forbidden liaison, and she knew not what the future held.

Her mother had spoken of the suffering at Clonagh—suffering Breanne held the power to end, if she chose a proper alliance. It was what Feann had wanted, but she couldn't imagine taking another man as her husband or, sharing his bed. She wanted Alarr, despite all else.

As if in answer to her idle dreaming, he returned to her side. He drew his arm around her waist and leaned down to kiss her. Though she knew it meant to show his claim upon her, the heat of his lips rekindled her desires. She welcomed the embrace, bittersweet though it was.

When he pulled back, she fumbled for something to say. On the far end of the ringfort, she saw a group of hunters returning with a deer.

'It's good that they brought back venison,' she said. 'I am hungry tonight.'

'So am I,' he breathed, kissing her again. And there was no doubt what kind of hunger he was feeling.

Breanne answered his embrace, but it was still

difficult to push back the uncertain emotions mingled with guilt. There were still so many unanswered questions. And she didn't know if Alarr truly wanted her—or if he was still using her for his own gain.

That night, they made their bed in a small storage chamber amid bags of grain. Alarr closed the door behind them and drew her close. He had held back his desire for most of the day and night, and he craved the touch of her hands on his body.

He had seen her apprehension around Treasa and the worry in her eyes. And although Feann was not here, he knew that the fight between them would happen soon enough. Alarr intended to make the most of whatever days he had left.

'Come here, *søtnos.* I've been waiting to touch you all day.' He kissed her roughly, and she met his lips with her own, winding her arms around his neck. At her sweet response, his desire grew hotter.

'Treasa wanted me to set you aside,' she confessed.

He wasn't surprised to hear it, but he tensed none the less. 'And what do you want, Breanne?'

She stood on tiptoe and drew his face down

to hers. 'I don't want to think about her. Or anyone else.'

There was a desperate rush for both of them. He tore at the laces of her gown while she reached to pull his tunic off. He dragged her gown from her shoulders, below her breasts, baring them to his sight. By the gods, he needed her. The urge to mark her, to make her his, was burning through him. He took her nipple into his mouth and was rewarded by her groan.

Her hands gripped his face, and she gasped when he suckled her hard. There was no time for gentleness now. He lifted her up against a stack of grain sacks, and she pulled him close.

'Alarr,' she breathed. Her eyes were heavy with desire, her lips soft. He wanted nothing more than to take her now, but first, he wanted her to feel the bond between them. For whatever time they had left, he wanted her beside him. And he wanted her to know that he was hers, just as she was his.

He reached to touch her inner thigh, moving his hand higher. She arched against him, and at the touch of her opening, he could feel her wetness coating his fingers. He bent to take her other breast in his mouth, and he caressed her intimately, ensuring that she was ready.

'Do you want me inside you?' he murmured against her skin.

In answer, she lifted her knees to offer herself. He pressed her skirts to her waist and cupped her hips. In one swift thrust, he filled her deeply, and she cried out at the pleasure. There was no resistance, only her silken wetness surrounding him.

She met him as he plunged deep inside, her body shuddering at his invasion. He lost himself in her, revelling as she squeezed him within her depths. 'There will be no other for you but me,' he demanded. At least, not while he lived. The thought of any other man touching her sent a roar of jealousy within him. With her body pressed against the grain, he thrust inside her, over and over.

But it was more than the need to claim her. He wanted her to remember him after he was gone. Breanne had somehow pushed away the all-consuming anger that fuelled his vengeance. In these moments with her, he forgot about the rest of the world. She made him feel something, and she didn't care that he was no longer the warrior he'd been. When she welcomed him into her body, he saw a faith in her eyes that he didn't deserve. And may the gods help him, he wanted to spend every last moment at her side.

Abruptly, she shattered in his arms, her body spasming around his length. The sensation of her pleasured response aroused him harder, and he kissed her to muffle a scream. Her legs tightened around his waist and he continued to grind against her, his own breathing harsh. But he slowed his pace, wanting to know more.

'What did you tell your mother after she asked you to set me aside?' he asked, tracing his fingertips over her bare back. Her hands dug into his skin in response, and she moved her hips beneath him.

'I said nothing.' Her voice was hitched as she tried to make him continue the lovemaking.

Her answer was a blow to his mood, for he'd wanted her to refuse. Yet, he had no right to demand that of her. She was free to make her own choices, even if she did not choose him.

With reluctance, he withdrew from her body and picked up the fallen furs they had brought with them. He arranged them on the ground and drew her to lie down beside him. He covered her with one fur, and drew her to her side, her backside pressed against him. His body was still rigid, but he held himself back.

Breanne remained still, sensing his anger. 'Treasa said that I owed it to our people to marry a man who could overthrow Cerball's rule. And she implied that I should not put my own personal desires above the needs of our family.'

The woman's proposition wasn't unexpected. Breanne was of noble birth. Her choice to stay with him was a decision born from her desire to save her father's life. She was never meant to be bound to a man like him.

He waited for her to say that she would not consider her mother's assertion, but her silence made him uneasy.

Breanne turned to face him, and her expression was troubled. 'She told me to keep you as my consort, and not to give her a decision about the marriage yet.'

Which meant that she *had* considered it. A tension rose up within him, that she would turn against him.

'No. I will not remain your consort on the side,' he said darkly. He would never allow another man to come between them.

'Isn't that what I am to you?' she countered. 'Your consort? Or am I a concubine?' To emphasise her words, she rolled to her back, pulling him on top of her. And he felt the need to possess her, to prove that she was more.

'You are mine,' he answered, leaning down to kiss her throat. He drew her so close, their bodies were skin to skin. He didn't want to put a name to their relationship, for in his eyes, they belonged to each other.

And yet, he knew that Breanne had not given up her innocence because she cared. It had been a negotiation to save Feann. A vain part of him had wanted to believe that she had enjoyed sharing his bed, for she had given herself willingly.

Breanne cupped his cheek with one hand and said, 'I feel as if I'm being blown around in a storm. Everyone wants to make decisions for my life. And I don't know what the answers are.'

He rested his hand upon her bare hip, and gooseflesh rose upon her skin beneath his touch. 'You already made your choice, *søtnos*. From the moment you surrendered yourself, I swore I would not let you go. You will never share another man's bed. Not while I live.'

His body was still aroused, and he needed her to know that she belonged to him. He wanted to claim her, to drive away all thoughts of anyone else.

'I don't want another man,' she whispered.

'But I feel as if my life isn't my own any more. I feel as if the chains are still there, though I cannot see them.'

He drew his hand over her bare breast, and she inhaled as the nipple grew erect. 'In what way?'

'I thought I was Feann's foster daughter with no living family. Now I find out that my mother is alive, but she's in exile. And she wants me to take back a homeland I don't even know.' She covered his hand with hers, straining at his touch.

Though he understood her dilemma, he wanted her to recognise that she did have control of her choices. 'You have the power to say no.'

She turned to meet his gaze. 'A woman holds no power at all. She is at the mercy of others.'

Alarr thought of his mother Hilda and his aunt Kolga, both of whom held a great deal of power in Maerr. 'The women of my tribe are equal to men. If anyone tried to tell my mother Hilda that she was at the mercy of others, she would strike them down.' A faint smile caught his mouth at the thought. Then he turned serious. 'You can make whatever choices you want, Breanne. So long as you stay with me.'

Alarr bent down and suckled her breast, moving his hand lower. She inhaled sharply, as he was learning just how to touch her, to draw out her pleasure.

'I want to stay with you,' she whispered.

He guided his shaft to her damp opening. Although she tried to welcome him inside once again, he held back, resting his body weight on his arms. 'Your life. Your body. Your very soul is mine, Breanne.'

He thrust deep inside her, marking her as his own. She gave a cry and gripped his hair, embracing him. As he took her, she rose to meet his hips with her own.

'If that is true,' she whispered, her face revealing her desire, 'then you belong to me as well. Your life.' She squeezed his length within her depths, and he hissed at the dark pleasure that filled him.

'Your body.' She kissed him hard, lifting her mouth to his. He returned the kiss, claiming her lips, welcoming the soft intrusion of her tongue.

'Your soul.' She moved him until he was on his back, buried deep inside her. Breanne rose up on her knees, riding him. He let her take her pleasure, watching her face tighten with rising desire. Her breathing rhythm shifted, and he sat up, lifting her hips and plunging inside hard.

This was no longer simple lovemaking. Instead, it was a battle for control—and he gave it to her.

She met him, thrust for thrust, until her face transformed with raw desire, and she shattered around him. Alarr could feel the pulse of her release, but he would not stop. The sight of her coming apart was his own undoing. He penetrated her, over and over, until he erupted deep inside and his own shout joined hers. It was brutal, passionate, and his heart would not stop racing.

He remained inside her, bringing her gently to the side. 'Did I hurt you, *søtnos*?' He had been so caught up in the moment, he had lost control.

'No,' she breathed, smiling at him. 'I liked it.'

He kissed her, sliding his hands over her body. He could not stop touching her, marvelling that this woman was his. But then came the clouded reality that she would only be his until he faced Feann. He knew not if they would have any life together afterwards, especially if he kept his vow not to kill Feann.

He had never promised not to seek revenge—only to grant the king his life. But a gnawing suspicion took root that he could still die in battle. His time with Breanne might only be brief, though he would savour every moment.

It was sobering to think of losing this woman, and he pushed away the thought. Or worse, the idea of betraying her.

Chapter Eight

'Have you thought about what I said?' Treasa asked. Her mother had an expectant look upon her face, along with a slight smile. Undoubtedly, she believed Breanne would follow her wishes and wed a different man.

'I have,' Breanne answered. 'And I have decided to remain with Alarr.' After the night she'd spent in his arms, she believed that he would let her make her own choices. But more than that, she believed that he cared about her. This morn, they had lain in each other's arms, and he could not stop himself from touching her. The light caresses were an unconscious gesture, and she warmed to the affection. She didn't want to be with another man—not now.

Her mother sighed. 'I was hoping you would understand, Breanne. This is about more than your personal needs. It's about our home and our people.'

Treasa's unspoken message was: *You're being selfish.*

But Breanne refused to be manipulated by guilt. 'You cannot expect me to sacrifice myself for a home I do not remember and people I have never seen.'

'It is your duty,' Treasa said. 'You are all we have, Breanne. It must fall upon your shoulders.'

Frustration and irritation brimmed inside her at the woman's expectation. 'That isn't true. Why don't *you* marry an ally and restore our lands?'

'I am too old, and no man would have me.' Treasa's voice grew weary. 'I am sorry if I have asked too much of you. I had hoped that you would agree, knowing that you could keep Alarr with you.'

'No. I would never use him in that way.' She understood his pride, and Alarr would not allow her to go from another man's bed back into his. Nor would she consider such a thing. She had honour and loyalty.

Treasa's gaze narrowed. 'Was it Alarr's intent to take command of Clonagh? Is that why he wed you?'

He never wed me, she thought to herself, but sidestepped the question instead. 'Of course not. Why would you think that?' It was as if her mother believed Alarr intended to conquer their lands. 'He wanted to protect me. And he has his own lands in Maerr.'

She spoke with confidence, but the truth was, she knew little about Alarr's lands or even his family. They had hardly spoken about his life back in his homeland.

Treasa drew her hands together and sat down. 'I do not know your *Lochlannach* well enough to understand his intentions. But you are my only child, Breanne. I love you, and I want to ensure that you have a home. I cannot let Clonagh remain part of Cerball's kingdom.'

Though her mother's words sounded sympathetic, something did not ring true. She understood her mother feeling responsible for the fate of her people, but Breanne was unwilling to become Treasa's pawn. 'Then ask Feann to help you take it back.' She squared her shoulders and faced Treasa. 'Clonagh is not mine.' She had no memory of their lands, and Killcobar was the only home she'd known. She felt no obligation towards Treasa.

Her mother took a deep breath. 'I am sorry,

Breanne. I suppose I should not have put so many of my hopes on you. But… I think you should see Clonagh before you make your decision. It has been a long time since you've been there. I could make arrangements for your travel.'

'No, thank you,' she said. She saw no reason to create ties with her past. Clonagh had never been her home, and she doubted if it ever would be. The true question was where would she live now? Alarr had sworn that he would stay by her side; yet, they had never spoken about what they would do next. She knew he had planned to remain here for a short time and then go back to Killcobar to confront Feann. But after that? She didn't know. Did he want to return to Maerr, after Feann paid the *corp-dire* for his father's death? She decided to ask him when they were alone.

To her mother, she said, 'I hope you find a way to win back Clonagh.'

'So do I,' Treasa answered.

There was a bitter tone to her voice, but Breanne refused to feel guilty about it. She would not sacrifice her life for strangers. She'd made her choice, and it was enough. She excused herself and walked outside.

She found Alarr among the men who had returned from fishing that morn. They had baskets filled with fish, and when he saw her, he set his own basket down.

'You look pale,' he said. 'Are you well?'

'I'm just restless,' she said. 'Will you walk with me a moment?'

He did, and she told him of her conversation with Treasa. 'I refused to submit to my mother's wishes,' she admitted. 'I see no reason to give myself up for land I've never seen and people I do not know.'

Alarr took her hand in his, leading her back to the privacy of their shelter. Inside, it was dark, with only a few rays of sunlight piercing through the crevices in the wood. 'I would not have let you go to another man, Breanne. You know this.'

He leaned down to kiss her, and she felt the familiar ache of longing. When had this happened? The thought of being parted from this man was a physical pain, and it confused her. She had given herself as part of a bargain, but with each moment she spent at his side, she wanted more.

'What will we do now?' she asked.

He cupped her cheek, tilting it up to meet her gaze. 'We have unfinished business with Feann.'

'You swore an oath,' she reminded him.

'I swore not to kill him. That does not mean he will not face justice.'

'You will do nothing to endanger yourself,' she insisted. 'We must consult the *brehons.* They will pass judgement, and Feann will accept their wisdom.'

'Will he?' He leaned down to kiss her throat, and she threaded her hands in his hair. 'You seem convinced that all will go according to your plans.'

'It will,' she answered. She saw no choice but to believe it. She knew Feann would be angry with her for choosing Alarr, but she didn't care. Her *Lochlannach* had captured more than her body—he had stolen her heart.

He kissed her deeply, his hands moving over her. He laid her back against one of the large piles of grain sacks, so that he would not have to lean down. She welcomed the familiar rush of need and the rise of desire. Somehow, he knew exactly how to touch her until she craved his lovemaking.

'I will have my answers from Feann, Breanne.'

'You will.' She trembled as he caressed her, and whispered, 'Then we will go back to your lands in Maerr.'

Though she was afraid of leaving Éireann, she

realised that if she stayed, she would be pressured into obeying the commands of Feann or Treasa. Here, she had hardly any freedom. The idea of starting over was a welcome thought, to travel with Alarr to a place where no one would use her for their own gain. Her life would be her own again. And while she was afraid of the unknown, she knew she would be happier with him than if she were left behind.

He kept his eyes locked upon her. 'You would give up your home for me?'

She lifted her hips to meet him, cupping his face between her hands. 'I will go wherever you go.' Her emotions grew heavy as he kissed her again, his tongue tangled with hers. She was starting to love this man. And though it made her vulnerable, she realised that she wanted a home with him and children.

Alarr murmured against her mouth, 'We will travel back to Killcobar in a few more days. Then we will take our ship back from Styr and return to Maerr.'

A tremor caught her as he continued to stroke her with his fingers. She came apart, her breathing a sharp moan as her body embraced him. Liquid desire pulsed in a fierce eruption that made her shake, crying out as the pleasure climbed higher. His tenderness was her undoing, and she could hardly breathe from the sudden release.

'You've bewitched me,' he admitted, a lazy smile coming over his mouth. 'I cannot stop touching you.'

'I don't want you to stop,' she whispered, pulling his mouth to hers and kissing him deeply. He invaded her mouth, his tongue tangling with hers until she felt the delicious echo in her womb.

Alarr remained within her for a few more moments before he said, 'While I would love to stay here with you, we need to rejoin the others.'

'At least until tonight,' she promised, stroking back his hair. She intended to give him the same pleasure he had given to her, until he could no longer bear it.

When they emerged from the shelter, she saw her mother staring at them. The look in Treasa's eyes held regret, as if her plans had shattered apart. And though Breanne understood her mother's desires, it was not her task to fulfil them. She had made the decision to leave her old life behind and begin anew.

And no one would stand in her way.

* * *

Alarr rode back towards Killcobar with Breanne and the six escorts sent by Iasan, the chief of Dún Bolg. Along the way, he thought of the older woman's discontent and her last words to him. 'Breanne is giving up her birthright and her kingdom for you. What kind of a life will she have in Maerr? Will she be queen there, as she would have been in Clonagh?'

'I will provide everything she needs,' he'd said. 'It will be enough.' But in truth, he didn't know if he could keep that vow. After he and his brothers had been declared outlaws and sent away, he knew not if he had a home, much less if he would survive the fight with Feann. If he died in battle, Breanne would be forced to remain with her foster father. It bothered him, for she didn't deserve a life where Feann would tell her who to marry. She was fighting for her freedom, and she deserved to choose her own path.

Were it possible, and if his life were different, he might have asked Breanne to marry him. The thought of waking beside her and watching her grow round with an unborn child was a welcome vision.

You cannot wed her, a voice inside him warned. *You don't deserve happiness with her.*

As one of the survivors of the massacre, he owed it to Gilla and Sigurd to seek vengeance. He could not set aside the past or even dream of a future until he had settled that promise.

Although he had decided to keep his vow to Breanne, he fully intended to wound Feann— even at the risk to his own life. He knew that the moment he struck down the king, the soldiers would attack. While they would not harm Breanne, Alarr knew better than to believe he could escape unscathed. And if Rurik was still there, his brother would face the same threat. More likely, his brother would fight at his side and die at the hands of their enemy.

He needed to send Rurik away. His brother would not stand by and let him face the battle alone. But Alarr didn't want him to die because of the choices he'd made. Somehow, he had to convince Rurik to go, in order to protect him.

They would reach Killcobar in the early evening. Breanne had guided them there throughout the morning and afternoon, and as they neared the fortress, he saw the sudden worry in her eyes.

'It's going to be all right,' she said quietly. 'I will speak to my father and see what can be done. But keep your face hidden for now.'

Although he knew she wanted to try, he knew better than to believe that this confrontation would result in peace between himself and Feann. The Irish king would never admit to wrongdoing, and Alarr fully intended to seek restitution. He raised his hood in the hopes that no one would recognise him.

'Wait here,' she said, dismounting from her horse. She walked to the gates and spoke with the guards for a few moments. Then she returned and took the reins of her mount. 'I told them that you are my escorts. Stay behind me when we go inside.'

The guards held their spears as Breanne led the way, allowing them to enter the fortress. She guided them towards the stables, and Alarr dismounted, ordering Iasan's escorts to take the horses and remain apart from them. Breanne took his hand in hers, and said, 'I could meet with Feann alone first, if you wish.'

'No.' He wanted her at his side at all times. 'We remain together.' Alarr glanced around and asked, 'Do you think he's here?'

'I don't know.' She continued walking towards the largest dwelling. It was rectangular in structure, and the roof was made of thatch. Breanne pushed the door open and brought him inside.

Several stone oil lamps were set out, providing a dim light. On the far end, he saw a dais with wooden chairs, but no one was seated in them.

'Alarr!' came a man's voice.

He turned and saw his brother Rurik. He removed his hood and embraced his brother. 'Are you well?'

Rurik nodded. 'Come and join me. I have much to tell you.'

'Where is Feann?' he asked.

'He has not yet returned, but he sent word that he will be back within a few days.'

'So, you've not seen him yet.'

His brother shook his head. 'But I learned a great deal about my mother from the men here.' He beckoned for Alarr and Breanne to sit at a low table. They did, and Rurik poured them cups of mead. 'She was Feann's sister.'

His brother's revelation was not entirely a surprise. Saorla had always carried herself like a noblewoman. Alarr barely remembered her, since she had died years ago, but he knew she'd been angry with Sigurd.

'Sigurd led her to believe that they would be married. She went away with him when she learned she was with child, and he brought her to Maerr. Then she discovered that he already had a wife.'

Alarr eyed his brother and said, 'So you and Danr are Feann's nephews.'

'We are. Though I doubt if it means anything to him.' Rurik took a long drink of mead. 'Feann travelled to Maerr after he learned of Saorla's death. He intended to avenge her by killing Sigurd.'

'And they did,' Alarr said.

But Rurik surprised him by saying, 'No. Sigurd was already dead before Feann could reach the longhouse. There were other enemies there.' His blue eyes were serious when he said, 'Feann was furious that he was unable to kill him. The men told me of his plans, but he was unable to achieve them.'

'Who else was there?'

Rurik shrugged. 'They didn't know the men. But one was from Glannoventa in Northumbria. They heard his men call him Wilfrid.'

'Why would Feann's men tell you anything?' He wouldn't trust them at all. They were strangers with no reason to confess the truth.

'I never told them who I was,' Rurik said. 'Remember, I speak the Irish tongue better than you. I asked questions, but I gave them no information about me.'

'Will you tell Feann the truth about your mother?' Alarr questioned whether it was wise to reveal it, since the king might not believe him.

His brother inclined his head. 'If the moment is right.' He paused a moment and said, 'Alarr, we will have our answers. But Feann was not the cause of his death.'

'He intended to kill Sigurd.'

'But he didn't. And neither did his men. We need to find out who our other enemies were. Feann may be able to help us with more information.'

A soft touch on his arm caught his attention, and Alarr turned back to Breanne. She ventured, 'Let me talk with my foster father after he returns. He may trust me more than both of you.'

Rurik's gaze fixed upon her and then he turned back to Alarr. From the knowing look in his eyes, it was clear that he was aware of their connection. 'What happened after I left?'

Alarr knew exactly what his brother was asking, but he feigned ignorance. 'We found Breanne's mother. She was exiled after her husband turned traitor. She wanted Breanne to reclaim their lands at Clonagh by wedding a man loyal to King Cerball.'

His brother's eyebrows raised, and he straightened. 'And what does Breanne think of that?' He turned to hear her answer.

She squared her shoulders. 'I care not what Treasa or Feann think I should do. This is my life, and I intend to remain with Alarr.'

'That wasn't what you said a few days ago when your father's men arrived to take you home.' Rurik refilled their cups, and Alarr distracted himself by drinking.

'Leave her alone, Rurik.' He sent his brother a hard look, warning him not to question her further. For a long moment, they stared at one another. He knew that Rurik was only trying to protect him, but he wanted his brother to back down.

'It's all right,' Breanne intervened. 'He can ask me his questions. I will answer.'

At that, Rurik's expression grew tense. 'What agreement did you make with my brother?'

'We made a bargain between us,' Breanne answered. 'He promised not to kill Feann.' She kept her tone even, but Rurik was not fooled by it.

'And what did you receive in return?'

Alarr did not want to dishonour Breanne by implying that she had traded herself. Instead, he said, 'She swore that she would seek justice on our behalf.'

His brother did not appear convinced. He took a step closer and his gaze hardened. 'If you betray my brother to Feann, you will answer to me.'

Before he could say a word, Breanne released his hand and stepped forward. 'I will never betray Alarr. After everything I faced, he is the only man who ever fought for me.' The iron in her voice was unyielding, and her fierce tone made his brother smile.

'Good.'

Alarr moved to her side, resting his hand upon her waist. 'Breanne will return to Maerr with us, after this is all over.'

Rurik hesitated and said, 'I do not think Feann will allow her to go. It would be safer if you do not tell him your plans.'

'You may be right,' she agreed. 'While I don't think he will seek to harm Alarr, we should all be careful.' To Rurik, she asked, 'Who do the clansmen believe you are?'

'I told them I was from the Ó Callahan clan.'

At that, she smiled. 'They think you are one of my kinsmen?'

Rurik shrugged. 'It seemed like a good idea at the time.'

Breanne thought a moment and then said, 'Do you think anyone will recognise you, Alarr?'

He wasn't certain. 'I don't think so, since it was over a year ago. But it is likely that the king might remember me.' As for himself, he could never forget the man who had caused his injuries. His legs would never be the same again because of it.

Breanne eyed them both and then said, 'I do not wish to lie to Feann. But if he does not remember you, that might be for the best. I could tell him that Alarr rescued me and brought me home again.'

Alarr exchanged a look with his brother but said nothing to ruin her dreams. Feann would never believe such a thing. But he only squeezed her hand and silently warned his brother not to speak. 'We will make that decision when the time comes.'

Breanne immersed herself in the familiar tasks of Killcobar. The activity filled her days, but she was aware that her people were wary of her friendliness with Alarr and Rurik. She and Alarr had decided not to avoid raising suspicions until Feann returned, and for the past week, she had not shared his bed. The strain was growing between them, and she knew he craved her body as much as she longed for him.

A few days ago, she had tried to send her mother's escorts back to Dún Bolg, but all had refused. She couldn't understand why. There was no need for them now, but each time she asked, they declined. She was beginning to believe that the men were spying on her with the intent of bringing back news to Treasa.

This morning, she had gone to meet with the captain of the guards. Darin had informed her about Feann's imminent return and the talk of invasion.

'Our men train each day,' he said. 'They are prepared for any battle or raid.'

'Good,' she said. She believed him from what she had seen thus far. And yet, another question abraded her mind. 'Has there been a recent threat that called Feann away? I thought he intended to return to Killcobar sooner than this.'

'There have been many threats,' Darin answered. 'Not only from other kings, but also from our alliances.'

A sense of foreboding caught her, and she wondered if he meant a threat from Oisin. More and more, she wondered if it had been a mistake to leave him alive. She tried to push back her apprehensions, and she thanked him quietly.

The captain returned to the other soldiers who were training outside. Among them were Alarr and Rurik, though they remained apart from the others. They sparred against one another, using dulled swords. Both men had stripped away their tunics, bared from the waist up. Though it was not a warm summer day, their bodies gleamed with sweat from exertion. Breanne stopped to watch, and she was not alone. Several women found reasons to stop their tasks and observe the sword fight.

Alarr swung his weapon hard, and Rurik blocked it with his shield. Over and over, he struck, and his brother met each blow. Then Rurik took the lead and wielded his weapon against his older brother. Their movements were smooth, like a dance, and their expertise was evident. But after a while longer, she saw Alarr's movement beginning to change. No longer was it an easy deflection, but instead, she saw the slight limp in his step. His brother seized the advantage and struck harder, forcing Alarr to retreat. His limp grew more pronounced, and Rurik continued to wield punishing blows against him.

Abruptly, Alarr stumbled and dropped to the ground. Rurik moved in for the kill, but before he could do anything, his brother tripped him and sent him sprawling. A moment later, he stood over Rurik with his sword against his brother's throat.

With a wry grin, he offered his arm and pulled Rurik to stand, while some of the men applauded. Some exchanged coins, revealing that they had gambled on the fight. Alarr waited until the others returned to their sparring, before he walked towards her. Though he tried to disguise it, she could still see his limp.

His gaze was heated, and Breanne stood her ground, watching him. Other women eyed him with interest, but he strode past them until he reached her side. Without a word, he took her hand in his and led her away. She knew his leg was bothering him, but he continued walking towards the stables.

'Are we going somewhere?' she asked, but he didn't answer.

The moment they were inside the stable, he pressed her up against a horse stall and kissed her hard. She wound her arms around his neck, answering his kiss with her own. His tongue threaded with hers, and she felt the answering pull deep inside her.

'I've been needing to touch you,' he said. 'This has gone on long enough.'

'I agree,' she said. His mouth moved to her throat, and she touched his bare chest, tracing the ridged muscles.

'I want you,' he growled. 'Here and now.'

'Anyone could see us,' she whispered. 'It's not safe.' But the idea of being taken like this was arousing in a way she hadn't expected. Alarr was already reaching beneath her skirts when she felt a warm tongue against her ear. She started laughing when she realised that the horse was peering over the stall, licking the salt from her skin.

'Ugh.' She started to pull away, and the horse whinnied, shaking its head.

Alarr was grinning, and he drew her away from the stall. 'This wasn't my intention, *søtnos*. It was an impulse.'

She stood on tiptoe to kiss him again. 'Impulse or not, I promise you this night you may have me in any way you wish. Wait for me in your tent, and I will come to you.'

He took her lips, gripping her hips so she could feel his rigid staff. Then he lifted her up, and she drew her legs around his waist. 'Or I could have you now.'

'I'd rather have hours with you,' she murmured. 'I don't want to stop. And the others will wonder where I've gone.'

He cupped her breast, toying with her erect nipple. 'Swear it, Breanne.'

'I will find a way. I swear it.' She ground herself against him, and he inhaled sharply at the contact. He held her there a moment, until at last, he let her down. She drew her hands over his chest, loving the feeling of his body beneath her palms.

No sooner had they left the stable, when there was a commotion from the gates. Breanne released his hand when she saw the horses approaching. Behind the first two riders, she spied Feann. His gaze narrowed when he saw her, but it was not the look of a man who was happy to have her home. There was tension there, and it sharpened when he stared at them. Alarr rested his palm upon her spine in a possessive manner, raising his chin in defiance.

Although she ought to be overjoyed at the sight of Feann, her heartbeat began to quicken.

For she suspected that he would not approve of them being together. It was more likely that he would attempt to sever their relationship entirely.

Feann dismounted and crossed past the others to stand before her. His face was a hard mask asserting his dominance.

'You've returned, I see. And brought enemies among us.'

Chapter Nine

Alarr met Feann's gaze, and there was no doubt that the man remembered him. Fury brewed in the king's eyes, especially when he saw their joined hands. His own anger was barely in check, for the very sight of his enemy evoked the memory of the swordfight. He recalled Feann's fury when the blade sliced through skin and muscle, nearly ending Alarr's ability to walk. The past rose up between them, and were it not for his promise to Breanne, he would have claimed his vengeance this very moment. The man's life meant nothing to him.

'Alarr and Rurik are not our enemies,' Breanne said. 'And this isn't a conversation I wish to have outside. Come and join us for food and drink. We will talk about what has happened.'

'I will speak with *you*, Breanne,' Feann said. 'But not them.'

'Come inside,' Breanne repeated. 'We will dine alone, the four of us.' She did not wait for her father's agreement, but instead led the way, holding Alarr's hand in hers while Rurik trailed them.

The interior of her father's home was warm from the heated stones set all around the room. Breanne gave orders for food and busied herself with preparations. Alarr stood with Rurik, noting the number of guards who joined them. The king was not a fool, and he spaced out his guards in a circle all around the room.

Feann took his place at table, in the centre of the dais. He motioned for Breanne to come and sit beside him, but she hesitated. With a look towards Alarr, she picked up another stool and brought it with her, nodding for Rurik to do the same.

It took an effort to hide his smile. Breanne was eliminating any chance of Feann presiding over them. After she set down the stool, she stood before her foster father, but he noticed that she did not embrace the man. 'Did you have a good journey?'

Feann only grunted and sat. Breanne joined him, and Alarr chose the seat on her opposite side. Rurik also sat, but he kept a wise distance from the king.

'Why have you brought them here, Breanne?'

Alarr felt her fingers reaching beneath the table for his hand, as if she wanted the security. He squeezed her palm in reassurance.

She straightened, raising her chin. 'A better question might be, why didn't you send men to find me when I was taken away into slavery? Alarr saved me and brought me home. And yet, you treat him like an enemy.'

'His father *was* my enemy,' Feann said. 'After what Sigurd did to my sister, Saorla, he deserved to die. Why should Sigurd's sons be any different?' His eyes blazed with fury, as if he already suspected the intimacy between them.

'Because they did nothing to you,' Breanne argued. 'And yet, your men attacked on Alarr's wedding day. What you did was wrong.'

'You have no right to judge my actions, Breanne. What I did was justice.'

'Many innocents died that day,' Alarr said. He could not hide the rage in his voice. 'Your men killed dozens of my kinsmen. And my bride.'

'So you came here to kill me, is that it?' Feann's rigid stare held no empathy. 'You used Breanne for your own purpose.'

'At first, that was my intent,' he admitted. 'But she bargained for your life.'

There was a faint surprise in the man's face, as if he'd not expected Alarr to confess the truth. 'Is that supposed to make me feel better about dining with you?'

'We need to talk about what should be done,' Breanne started to say, but Feann cut her off.

'Do you really think I would believe any words spoken by a *Lochlannach*?' He shook his head in disgust. 'My men will escort you out. I give you the gift of your lives, for Breanne's sake. Go now, before I order my men to cut you down.'

'No.' Breanne stood, her face pale. 'Alarr will remain at my side.'

At her declaration, Feann's face grew thunderous. 'Why would you dare such a thing, Breanne?'

Alarr stood beside her, still holding her hand. He didn't trust the man's rage, and he intended to guard Breanne from all harm.

'Because Alarr took care of me when I needed help. He rescued me from the slave market, and he protected me from Oisin.' Her voice was tremulous, but she slid her arm around his waist to emphasise her words. Alarr pulled her close, watching as Feann's mood darkened. Against his body, he could feel the tremor of her fear.

'I will not let you remain with a *Lochlannach*,' the king insisted. 'Especially one who wants me dead.'

She faced him boldly, and admitted, 'I would rather have a man willing to fight for me than one who treats me as if I am worth nothing at all.'

Feann's face turned stony. 'I knew nothing of your captivity until recently. And by then, my men had found you.' There was no sympathy in his tone, and Alarr sensed that the man was holding something back. There were secrets the king was keeping, though he could not guess what they were.

'I want you to leave Killcobar,' Feann commanded Alarr. 'Take your brother with you, and do not return. Breanne, you will remain here.'

Her face turned scarlet with her own anger, and she levelled a stare at Feann. 'I brought these men here because Alarr deserves justice for the murder of his bride and his father. I told him that the *brehons* would treat them fairly. But I never imagined you would behave in this way. I believed that you were a man of honour.'

'I owe nothing to these men,' Feann countered. 'They are lucky I didn't kill them that day.'

Before Breanne could respond, Rurik stepped forward. 'There is more you should know about your sister, Feann. I believe you will want to hear my tale.' He paused a moment, then added, 'Or perhaps I should call you Uncle.'

At that, Feann froze. He stared hard at Rurik, but his emotions were unreadable. It was a risky move, but Alarr understood why his brother had spoken. The question was whether the king would recognise Rurik as his nephew.

'Saorla was my mother,' Rurik continued. 'She gave birth to my twin brother Danr and me after she reached Maerr.'

'You have no proof of that,' Feann started to say. 'Why would I believe this?'

'She told me stories about you,' Rurik continued. 'Though she refused to speak any names from her past, she told me that the two of you were close. And that you gave her a blade when she was young.' He unsheathed the knife and held it out hilt-first.

At that, Feann's expression transformed. He took the blade and examined it, running his thumb along the curved antler handle. He glanced back at Rurik for a long moment, his gaze passing over him. There was an unread-able emotion in his eyes, a flare of grief min-gled with distrust.

Rurik asked, 'Why did you come to Maerr to attack my father? It was twenty years since Saorla left. If you wanted to kill our father, why wait that long?'

'I did not know that Sigurd had set her aside,' Feann said. 'I believed Saorla made the choice for her own happiness, to wed a man she loved.' He shook his head in disgust. 'But I was wrong to let her go with him. Once I learned the truth, I sailed across the sea to kill Sigurd for what he did to my sister.'

It made Alarr wonder who had informed Feann about his sister and why. Saorla had died years ago, and no one had known that she was a king's daughter, save Sigurd. After all these years, why would anyone bother to send word across the sea to Éireann? His first thoughts went to his mother. He wouldn't put it past Hilda to do such a thing. Or perhaps his aunt Kolga.

'Saorla sailed to Maerr of her own free will,' Rurik reminded him. 'When she learned she was with child, she remained there.'

'Likely she was ashamed,' Feann answered. 'She fought everyone for the right to abandon her responsibilities and run away with him. But I don't understand why she didn't come home after he set her aside.'

'I heard them fighting, years ago,' Rurik answered. 'Sigurd would not let her go unless she left my brother and me behind. She refused.' He turned sombre at the revelation, as if he blamed his father for imprisoning her.

Feann's expression tightened with unspoken emotion. 'Our father was furious with her for leaving her responsibilities and our kingdom. But Sigurd was only using her, wasn't he?' While he spoke, he kept his eyes fixed upon Alarr. There was no doubt of the hidden meaning in his words.

'Sigurd was already married,' Rurik answered. 'And while his actions lacked honour, he did give Saorla a home of her own, and he provided for Danr and me.'

'My sister deserved better than to be treated like a whore,' Feann shot back.

'Then why did you not come earlier to see her for yourself?' Rurik asked. 'If you cared about her welfare so much, why did you never visit while she was alive?'

'Because we argued the day she left. Saorla swore she would never speak to me again. I was angry with her for choosing a *Lochlannach* instead of obeying our father. I told her she was welcome to return, but I would never set foot in Maerr.'

Breanne took a steadying breath before she turned to look at him. 'I think it would be best if I spoke with my foster father alone now. Will you leave us for a moment?'

Alarr touched her face, understanding that she wanted a private conversation with Feann. She was more likely to gain what she wanted if he allowed it. 'So long as you are safe.' He beckoned for Rurik to join him. Then he leaned down to kiss her, knowing it would irritate the king. She embraced him, and then he stepped back. 'We will await you near the stables.'

Breanne waited until they were gone, and the soldiers followed. Her foster father paced across the dais without speaking, but she could read his frustration in every step. Her mood matched his own, but she waited for him to speak.

'You cannot give yourself to a *Lochlannach* enemy.' He faced her, his expression forged in anger. 'He cannot be trusted any more than Sigurd could. He will use you and set you aside.'

She took a breath and chose her words carefully. 'I trust him.' Her answer was a silent defiance, and she stood her ground.

He looked as if he wanted to fly into a rage, but he gathered his control and regarded her. 'What is it you want, Breanne?'

'I want justice for what was done to Alarr and his family. You must pay the *corp-dire* for your vengeance. You killed his *bride*,' she shot back. 'An innocent woman died at the hands of your men, as well as his father.'

A thin smile stretched across his face. 'But I did not have the honour of killing Sigurd. When I reached the longhouse, he was already slain.'

'You caused Alarr's injuries,' she continued. 'It took him over a year before he could walk again.'

'I could have taken his life,' Feann answered. 'Instead I allowed him to live. Which was a mistake, now that I look back on it.' Her foster father steepled his hands. 'Had I cut him down, you would not believe yourself bound to him.'

Breanne fell silent, wondering what to say to him now. He would not listen to reason, and he was behaving like an overprotective father.

But he had lied to her, letting her believe her mother was dead. Treasa was her only living blood relative, and he had kept that knowledge from her, all these years. She wanted to confront him over it, but something held her back. Right now, she didn't trust him, and she decided it was better not to reveal that she had met with her mother.

Feann stood, his face a mask of stiff rage. 'Breanne, let him go. You can never wed a *Lochlannach.*'

'Why not? Because then I cannot wed a man of your choosing?' A look of guilt flashed in his eyes at her accusation, and she pressed again.

'Or is it because your only claim to Clonagh is through me?' she ventured. Perhaps Feann wanted to choose a weak man as her husband, one whom he could control. She was beginning to wonder if greed had played a role in his secrets. If so, he would not want a *Lochlannach* on the throne beside her.

'Clonagh is under King Cerball's rule,' Feann said. 'The lands became his by right of conquest, after your parents' treason. I have only governed them on his behalf.'

'Treason according to whom?' she demanded. 'It sounds as if King Cerball accused them of treason in order to gain possession of my father's kingdom.'

Feann sighed and sat down once again. 'You're

wrong, Breanne. Cerball did not seize the land with the intend of keeping it. I was asked to protect Clonagh until you came of age. You were to marry a man loyal to Cerball. But now, your actions have changed that. What man will want to claim you now?'

She was beginning to realise the far-reaching implications of staying with Alarr. Both Feann and Treasa wanted to use her for their own gains.

'You must leave him,' her foster father said. 'If you do, it is possible that you may regain all that was lost.'

'And what of Alarr? He will never regain all that he lost.' Her voice cracked, revealing her own frustration. 'But that doesn't matter to you, does it?'

'No.' Feann drew closer to her, his eyes hardened into stone. 'His fate means nothing to me.'

Breanne was beginning to realise the depths of his hatred. Once, she had believed that Feann had held affection for her, that he had thought of her as his true daughter. She had done everything to please him, trying to shape herself into the person he wanted. But now, she could no longer deny the truth.

'I don't matter to you either, do I?' It broke her heart to realise that all these years, he had never thought much of her. He truly didn't care that she had been sold into slavery. Her only use to him was for a marriage alliance.

For a moment, his steel gaze seemed to relent, but he said only, 'Think of your duty, Breanne.'

'I have,' she whispered. And duty be damned. She would no longer allow her life to be twisted as everyone else wanted. This time, she would make her own decisions and be herself, not the woman others wanted her to be. 'I only wish I had seen you for what you are sooner.'

With that, she walked away, tears filling up in her eyes. She crossed past familiar faces, people she had once believed were her friends. But they, too, were controlled by Feann. A true friend would have greeted her, welcomed her home. And although she had worked among them during the past few days, she realised that there would always be a distance between them. She was not a MacPherson and never would be.

When she reached Alarr, he seemed to sense what she wanted—an escape before she released the hold on her emotions. Without asking he led her mount forward and helped her atop the saddle.

'Where are we going?' Rurik asked.

'*You* are staying here,' Alarr answered. 'I am

taking Breanne away so we can speak alone. We will return later.'

She was grateful, for he seemed to understand that her feelings were hanging by a single thread. The tears and anger were so tightly intertwined, she didn't know if she wanted to weep or rage at the world.

'If you have need of protection,' one of the guards offered, 'we can join you.'

'No.' Alarr swung up behind her and said, 'I can defend Breanne on my own. We won't go far.'

With that, he nudged the animal forward and outside the gates. She took comfort from his arms around her and let the tears fall freely. No one would see them, and no one would judge her for them. But it hurt so deeply to recognise that Feann had never loved her as a daughter.

Alarr took the horse into a hard gallop, and the wind caused her hair to stream behind her. They rode for several minutes, until he found a small outcropping of limestone. Then he slowed the mare's pace to a stop and dismounted, helping her down.

Breanne dried her tears, grateful to be away from Feann and the others. Her heart ached with the sadness of loss. And through it all, Alarr had been steadfast.

'You kept your word,' she said at last. 'Though I know you wanted to kill him.'

His face tensed. 'I did.' Then he paused and added, 'I still do.'

Breanne couldn't stop herself from pacing from one stone to another. Restlessness pulsed in her veins. She wanted to rage at Feann and at herself for believing that he had ever cared about her. To his credit, Alarr said nothing but let her be.

At last, she stopped to face him. 'I know I promised you justice. But I do not know what I can do now.' The thought of Feann made her stomach clench. She had defended him for so long, but he had only wanted to use her.

'Do you still want him to live?' Alarr asked.

Breanne closed her eyes, pushing back the pain. Even though she despised the king right now, it wasn't possible to push away the years of memories. He had cared for her, and when she was a little girl, there were nights when he had comforted her after bad dreams. In spite of everything, she didn't want him to die.

'Yes, he should live,' she answered. 'But I don't want to stand by and let him get away with what he did to your family. It isn't right.' Her cheeks were still wet from her tears, but she needed his arms around her. She went to Alarr and pressed both hands against his chest. His arms came around her, and she drew comfort from his embrace.

'Then we must take away something that has value to him. Does Feann have sons?'

'He does, but they are still being fostered elsewhere. They are not yet of age.' She drew back and said, 'I know what you are thinking, but I don't want to harm my foster brothers. I would rather take away his power.' She thought a moment, an idea starting to form in her mind. There was nothing that would irritate Feann more than to have a *Lochlannach* claim the Irish throne he was protecting.

'We should go to Clonagh together,' she suggested. 'And…if we married, you could take possession of the land as my husband.' It was a risk to mention it to him, for she had already agreed to travel to his homeland. Even more, she did not know if he wanted her to become his bride after all that had happened.

Alarr was already shaking his head. 'I cannot stay here in Éireann. I belong in Maerr. You know this.' He traced the edge of her jaw, and her skin tightened at his touch.

She covered his hand with her own and stared back. Did he feel the same as she did, this sense of longing? Or was it only her loneliness that made her crave a deeper connection with Alarr? She closed her eyes, forcing her attention back to the problem at hand.

'I wanted Feann to grant you compensation for your losses. But silver is not enough to bring your loved ones back, is it?'

He shook his head. His expression was stoic, devoid of emotion. She wanted to reassure him, to somehow make him see that she would find a way to grant him justice.

'Feann will face the consequences for his choices,' Alarr said. 'I promise you that.' The coldness in his voice unnerved her. 'And then I will find the man who murdered Sigurd and avenge my father's death.'

Breanne studied him closely, and then wondered aloud, 'Why do you think it was a man?'

Alarr paused, wondering what she meant by that. 'There were no female fighters at that battle, Breanne.'

'A woman does not need to swing a sword to

be responsible for a man's death.' She squeezed his hands and prompted, 'What of your mother? I imagine that she was not pleased about Sigurd's infidelity. Or his bastard sons.'

Alarr had considered this, for Hilda's jealousy and resentment of Saorla had been no secret. But would she truly go that far? 'I don't know.' But he could not deny the possibility.

A coldness settled inside him at the thought. His mother had sent Brandt away on the morning of his wedding, claiming that there was a raid. Was that true? Or had she known something about the impending attack? She might have been trying to protect her eldest son.

Hilda had forbidden them to carry weapons that day, which had left them unarmed in the presence of enemies. Alarr had been fortunate to have two ceremonial swords, but others had no means of defending themselves. He didn't want to imagine that his mother had enacted such a brutal attack...but she had played a role in it, whether or not she had intended to do so.

'What do you think we should do now?'

Alarr hesitated, considering it. Breanne had given him the chance to confront Feann, and in return, she had asked him to spare her foster father's life. But he had no intention of sparing the king from his retribution. 'Feann stole my ability to fight. The wounds he left will always be there. I want him to suffer as I did.' He intended to attack the king, even knowing the risk to his own life.

Her face held a flicker of fear. 'And what of our agreement? Do you intend to go back on your word?'

'I will spare his life,' Alarr answered. 'But after all he has done, he must face the consequences.' At the very least, he wanted to wound Feann, to make him understand how he had suffered. His anger rose hotter, and in this he would not yield.

Her face grew troubled. 'Anything you do will not change the past. And while I will ensure that he pays you *corp-dire*, that is all we can do.'

'I don't want blood money for what he did.' He didn't bother to hide the edge of his rage. And Breanne took a step backwards, wary of his mood. She could never understand his anger, and there was nothing he could say to change that.

'Alarr, there are better ways to gain your vengeance,' she said softly. 'I don't want you to endanger yourself.'

Though he supposed she was trying to show

him that she cared, it made him realise that she had no faith in his fighting skills. And why should she? He had nearly failed her once before. Though he tried to push away his resentment, he was starting to see the truth. Though he desired this woman and wanted to be with her, she deserved better. One day, she might face a threat, and if he were unable to defend her, he could never forgive himself.

She had spoken of sailing away from her homeland, never to return. But she didn't belong in Maerr any more than he belonged in Éireann. It was wrong to ask her to stay with him. And when she rested her cheek upon his heart and embraced him, the guilt only deepened.

If you truly cared for her, you would let her go, his conscience warned.

And though the very idea caused a wrenching ache inside, he knew it was the right thing to do.

'Breanne, I think you should know the truth about what happened when you were taken from Feann as a slave. I owe you that much.'

'Go on.' In her green eyes, he saw compassion. She would despise him afterwards, but he could not keep it from her. Breanne deserved to know everything. And so, he started at the beginning.

'I travelled to Killcobar and watched Feann

for a time. I realised that I could never get into the fortress without a good reason. And when I saw you, I saw an opportunity.' He stood and turned away from her, gathering his thoughts. 'I bribed one of your father's men to take you from Killcobar. I wanted him to imprison you and bring you to me. Then I planned to use you to get close to Feann.'

'But Feann had already left in secret.'

He nodded. 'I didn't realise it at the time.' Which was fortunate for the king, since it would have been a simple matter to end Feann's life, if he had caught him.

Breanne's expression grew clouded. 'I never saw the soldier's face. He blindfolded me and gagged me on the night I was taken. It was in the middle of the night, and he sold me to the traders before dawn. I don't even know who it was.' Her mouth pressed into a tight line when she confronted him. 'If you paid him to take me, why didn't you rescue me from the slavers sooner? Why would you allow them to hold me captive for so long?'

Her accusation only deepened the burden of guilt. He knew he should have kept a closer eye upon her. 'It took some time before I discovered your whereabouts,' Alarr admitted. 'I didn't know he'd sold you. I thought he was holding you somewhere for ransom.'

Her gaze never wavered, the resentment filling up her expression. 'How did you find him?'

'He went hunting boar with a group of men. I separated him from the others and…questioned him.' After he'd learned of the man's betrayal, Alarr had shown no mercy. 'It took another day to track where the slavers had taken you.'

Her face winced when she realised what he was implying. 'Is he dead now?'

Alarr gave a nod. 'The others thought he was hurt by the boar. I made certain his injuries appeared accidental.' He held no regret for what he'd done. Any man who would sell the king's foster daughter into slavery deserved to die.

Then he continued. 'We tracked you to Áth Cliath, and I intended to outbid any man who tried to buy you. But then, you tried to escape.' He crossed his arms and said, 'You already know the rest.'

For a time, she remained quiet. 'So, *you* were the reason I was taken from Killcobar.'

'Yes.' He refused to deny the role he had played. 'I don't want you to think of me as the man who saved you. I was the man who caused your suffering.' He remained apart from her and confessed, 'It was my fault.'

She didn't move but clenched her hands together. Her expression held doubts. 'I need time to think, Alarr.'

He could see the uncertainty in her eyes, but he said, 'You deserve the truth, Breanne. I cannot pretend to be a good man. I'm not.'

'And you told me this, because you want me to hate you,' she finished. 'So you can walk away from me and it will be easier for you to end what is between us.' Her green eyes turned stormy. 'You don't want me to go back to your homeland.'

He didn't argue with her. It was better to break the fragile bond between them and let her go. Then she could be free to love a man who would give her the life she deserved.

'You should hate me,' he agreed. 'I paid to have you taken from your home, and I stole your innocence.'

'No.' She crossed her arms as if to ward off his words. 'I gave you my innocence.' A flush suffused her cheeks, and she confessed, 'I am glad it was you.'

He didn't know how to respond to that, so he

answered, 'You were trying to save Feann's life. I had no right to claim you.'

Her anger rose up higher, her face scarlet with anger. 'Do you truly believe that was the reason? Do you deny that there are feelings between us?'

Her words stopped him cold, for he hadn't wanted to believe it. He didn't want ties that bound him to this life. He had sailed this far for vengeance, fully intending to sacrifice himself. As a scarred, wounded man, he had no value as a warrior.

But Breanne was undermining his plans. When he looked upon her face, he saw a woman who captivated him. She had woven her way into his life without him realising it. And when he made love to her, she made him feel as if there was nowhere else he'd rather be, save in her arms. He craved her, and it was killing him to be apart from her at night.

Yet he knew he could not give her the life she needed. He *did* care about her, and for that reason, it was best to let her go.

'We don't belong together,' he answered. 'Once I have settled the matter of my father's death, I will return to Maerr alone.'

Tears rose up in her eyes, and he felt like an utter bastard for hurting her. 'So you'll just avenge yourself against my foster father and leave me behind.'

He avoided answering her, but admitted, 'I intend to question him first. Feann claims that he did not kill Sigurd. I need to know who did. Whether it was Wilfrid or someone else.'

She took a breath, shielding her emotions. 'And once you have your answers, you will go.'

'If I survive the fight, yes.'

She waited for a time, choosing her words carefully. 'I think you're afraid to stay. You always planned to end your life while bringing Feann down. You would rather die than face a life where you are not the man you once were.' She shook her head in disbelief. 'But you are so much more. Your wounds made you into the man I care about.'

Her words were a sharp blade, cutting into his heart. She was right, that he had never intended to survive the fight against Feann. Nor had he intended to intertwine his days with Breanne. For the first time in years, he found that he had someone to live for—and yet, he didn't feel that he had earned that right.

Even so, he wanted her. From the moment he awakened with her beside him, to the moment he lay down to sleep, she filled the emptiness inside him. But if he admitted his feelings, it weakened him. He had sailed across the sea for vengeance—not to fall in love and allow Feann to escape with no consequences. He had no right to seek his own happiness, especially when he had not achieved his goal of punishing Feann.

Breanne moved in closer, regarding him. She rested her hands upon his heart, and the touch of her fingers blazed through him. 'Look into my eyes and tell me you want to leave. That you don't care about me.'

He knew she wanted a life he couldn't give to her, but he took her hands in his. 'I cannot stay here, Breanne.'

She released his hands, and he could see her trying to regain her composure. 'Then I don't have a choice any more.' Her voice grew softer, more vulnerable. 'I'm not going to stand aside and let others decide my fate.'

'What are you going to do?'

Her green eyes were filled with tears, but she said, 'I'm going to return to my mother. And then I won't have to watch you fight the only father I've ever known.'

Chapter Ten

They did not dine with Feann that night, as Rurik did, but instead took food to share in Alarr's shelter. Rurik had wisely left them alone, and Breanne had been careful to slip into the shelter unnoticed. Her heart was raw with unspoken pain. A part of her had hoped that Alarr would argue with her and try to stop her from leaving. But he had said nothing at all.

Now, more than ever, it was clear that his vengeance meant more than his feelings for her. And there was nothing she could do to change his mind.

'When will you go?' he asked.

'At dawn. I will take my mother's guards back with me.' She now understood why Treasa had insisted that the men remain with her. It gave her a means of protection on the journey back to Dún Bolg.

'Good.' Alarr's tone was dull, devoid of emotion. 'It's better this way, Breanne. I will fight Feann on the morrow, after you're gone. He consented to the match.'

His statement took her by surprise. 'Alarr, why would Feann agree to this? What could he hope to gain?' She knew his guards could cut Alarr down in moments, without warning. There was no reason for her foster father to seek one-on-one combat.

'Because he wanted to defend your honour.'

She winced, for it meant Feann was fully aware that she had given her body to Alarr. 'You told him about us?' These past few days, she had been careful to sleep alone to suppress idle tongues.

'He guessed the truth. I didn't deny it.'

A sudden fear took hold of her at the thought of them battling against one another. She couldn't bear to be caught in the middle any more. 'And you think this will somehow grant you the vengeance you seek? Will you hurt him?'

'If he doesn't defend himself, then yes. I won't hesitate to wound him. We will fight until the other can no longer fight.' He stared at her, and she saw only distance and ice in his gaze. 'My honour will be satisfied.'

She didn't know what to say, but it bothered her deeply that Feann had agreed to fight Alarr. 'I am glad I won't be there to see it.'

He reached out to cup her face between his hands. 'No matter what happens to me, I hope you find the life you deserve, Breanne.' She memorised the lines of his face, the dark hair that fell to his shoulders, and the piercing blue eyes that were watching her. Never had she felt like this before with any man, as if the rest of the world could fall away.

But until he set aside his revenge, there could be no life for them.

'I wanted a life with you,' she confessed. 'I wanted a husband and a home. Perhaps one day a child.'

His face softened, and he stroked back her hair. 'You will have that one day. I believe it.'

'But not with you,' she finished. She closed her eyes, holding back the rising anguish. Though she did not want to think of it, one of the men she loved would be injured on the morrow. One might die. And yet, both were too stubborn to stand down.

Alarr leaned in and murmured, 'Will you kiss me goodbye, Breanne? Give me a memory before I fight Feann.'

She didn't want to, for it would only remind her of the nights they had shared in each other's arms. Her body ached for his, but she held herself back. In the end, he ignored her silence and claimed her lips.

It was a gentle kiss, coaxing her to respond. His mouth was warm and seductive, his tongue sliding against the seam of her lips. Her body responded with heat and desire, and between her legs, she grew damp. Alarr continued kissing her while he drew her down. He sat upon a low stool and pulled her to straddle his waist. Against her womanhood she could feel his hard length.

Though he did naught but kiss her, she craved more. She ached to have his body inside hers, and she wanted to remember every part of this moment.

He pulled back, and her lips felt numb and swollen. She needed him badly, and her heart raced within her chest.

'Breanne,' he said quietly. 'I want you to know that I never wanted any woman as much as I want you.'

'Then let go of your vengeance,' she offered. 'Leave with me, and turn your back on the past.'

He held her waist, and answered, 'You know I cannot.'

'Will not,' she corrected. 'You're making a choice.'

'I can't let it go,' he said. 'Feann changed me. He took away my ability to fight, and I will have to live with this weakness for the rest of my life. He must pay for what he did to me.'

'You are still the same man as before.' She reached out to touch his heart. 'Your strength of will is greater than any man I've ever met.'

'It does me no good if I lack balance or the ability to run.' He tightened his grip around her waist. 'Because of him, I cannot defend you the way I once could. I would never forgive myself if someone hurt you.'

And she sensed that this was the true reason. No matter what she said, he did not believe he could protect her. Rather than try to make the best of his skills, he had chosen to walk away. There was nothing she could do to change his mind.

Instead, she extricated herself from his embrace and stood. 'You may not believe you are the same man as before. But I believe you are stronger now. I pray that you will abandon this vengeance and leave with me at dawn.' She bent down and kissed him. 'Goodbye, Alarr.'

As she left his shelter, her heart broke. But she

had no other choice than to walk away from a man trapped by the past, unable to look towards his own future.

Alarr hadn't slept at all that night. His furs had felt empty without Breanne in his arms. And though he'd told himself that he had done the right thing, a part of him didn't believe it.

Breanne had left at dawn, as promised, with the guards her mother had sent. She'd spoken no farewell to him or even to Feann. But as she'd ridden away, it had torn a piece of himself away. The emptiness flowed through him, and he realised that she had given him a gift by leaving. There would be no distractions during the battle, nothing to stop him from fighting with everything he had.

Feann had arranged for the battle to take place at sundown. Alarr had spent the day with Rurik, sparring and preparing for the fight. His brother had said little about the upcoming contest, but there was no doubt that he did not approve.

At twilight, Alarr walked towards the inner part of the fortress. His emotions were calm, and no longer did he fear death. Breanne was gone, and it made it easier to face her foster father. This was the day he had been waiting for, the moment when he would face his enemy and prove that his fighting skills were not lost. Vengeance belonged to him.

In one hand, he held a wooden shield and in the other, his uncle's sword. Rurik had given him the weapon, and when he held it, the weapon brought back a flood of memories. He remembered training alongside his uncle, watching as Hafr had taught him how to lunge and parry a blow. And he remembered the clang of iron and how his arm had gone numb from the force of each strike.

Watch over me, he prayed to the gods. *Let my sword be strong. Let me give honour to my ancestors.*

He walked closer, and the memories shifted to the memory of the wedding massacre. He remembered offering the sword to Gilla and her smile as she had handed him another weapon. Her face had been filled with hope, and yet, it had all ended in death.

But the ache in his heart at this moment was not about losing her, he realised. It was about losing Breanne.

She had made a wise choice not to witness the fight. But her absence was a chasm in his chest, an emptiness that filled him with doubts. He knew that he might never see her again, might never hold her. And it bothered him more than he'd ever imagined it would. She was unlike any woman he'd ever met. Brave and kind, she saw past his physical scars to the man he was inside. When he was with her, he felt as if he were the man he used to be.

Feann was donning leather armour, and his servant held a large wooden shield with an elaborately wrought-iron boss in the centre. The tangled iron reminded him of serpents, and Alarr was eager to begin the fight. At last, this was the moment he had anticipated, and he intended to win.

The clansmen and women of Killcobar were lined up in a circle, surrounding the fighting arena. Alarr approached, and Feann stared hard at him. 'Where is Breanne?'

'She had no desire to watch.' He gripped his shield and took his position opposite Feann. She had not wanted anyone to know of her departure, but he was confident in her safety. Her mother's guards would let nothing happen to her.

Feann reached for an iron helm. He held it a moment and asked, 'What is it you hope to accomplish with this fight, Alarr?'

'Justice,' he answered. He knew that wounding Feann would not eradicate the past. It would not bring back his loved ones. But it would make him feel as if he'd done *something* to fight for them.

Feann's face remained rigid and unyielding. 'And I fight for Breanne's honour. She deserved far better than you.'

Alarr did not argue with the man over that. It was why he had let Breanne go. Feann donned the helm, which covered his forehead and nose, leaving his eyes, cheeks, and mouth visible.

His brother offered him a helm of his own, but Alarr declined. He wanted nothing to hinder his view of the enemy.

He kept his shield up, his sword at the ready while Feann circled. The older man was wiry, his dark hair greying. A thin scar on his cheek had whitened over time. Alarr waited, never taking his eyes from the enemy.

Without warning, Feann struck, and Alarr deflected the blow with his shield, slicing his blade towards the king's head. His enemy sidestepped, and the sword met only air. A slight smile tightened Feann's mouth.

Once again Alarr charged forward and struck, only to come again at a different angle. The king kept circling him, slashing at all different points. He was trying to make him lose his balance.

It was a strategic tactic, but Alarr was careful to keep his footing. The longer he lasted, the more the king would tire.

'For someone who wanted vengeance, you're not fighting much,' Feann taunted. 'Are your legs bothering you?'

He countered by swinging his sword hard and slashing at his opponent. It felt good to fight, to unleash his raw frustration. Not only because of the wounds Feann had inflicted years ago, but also to avenge the deaths of Gilla and his father. Over and over, he swung. When his sword struck Feann's shield, he let his mind go empty. The weapon became an extension of his arm, and he poured all his rage into the fight.

Feann renewed his attack, and this time, he used his shield to shove him back. Alarr stumbled, and the king swung his weapon lower. He dived to avoid the blade and rolled through the dirt. Alarr caught the flash of the weapon and raised his shield, scrambling to rise from the ground.

But then Feann's sword plunged downwards.

He tried to avoid the slice, but pain ripped through him as the blade met flesh.

Breanne dismounted from her horse and trudged towards her mother's dwelling. She had ridden at a swift pace all morning and afternoon. Her body ached, but she was glad to have reached Dún Bolg. More than anything else, she wanted to fall asleep and forget about Alarr.

She pushed the door open, ducking into the small hut. 'Treasa?' she murmured. It was dark inside, save for the faint light of an oil lamp.

'Breanne?' Her mother rose and approached with a smile. 'I never expected to see you. Are you all right? What happened to the *Lochlannach* with you?'

'We decided to part ways,' was all Breanne could say. Her heart was still battered from the loss of Alarr. The ache of loneliness weighed upon her, and she struggled to let him go.

Her mother came to embrace her. She gave no judgement, but only held her in sympathy. For a moment, it felt good to forget about the loss and take comfort in Treasa's arms. The kindness made it hard to fight back the tears, but she did not want to reveal her feelings.

'I am sorry,' her mother murmured. 'I know how you cared for him.'

I fell in love with him, she wanted to say, but didn't.

'It's hard,' was all she could manage.

'Well, I am glad you came back to me,' Treasa said, embracing her hard. 'Are you hungry? Have you eaten?'

She was, but the thought of food turned her stomach. When her mother offered a piece of dense, fresh bread, Breanne took it. Though she didn't truly want to eat, she tried a little, and it did seem to help.

'I still would like you to visit Clonagh with me, if you will think about it,' Treasa said. 'You could see the place where you were born. There are some things that belonged to your father that he would want you to have.'

A sudden tightness caught her suspicions. 'I thought you were in exile and were not allowed to leave.'

Treasa's face softened in the lamplight. 'What I am supposed to do and what I choose to do are not always the same. If I travel with only a guard or two, I can usually visit my people in secret. They are usually glad, because I bring them supplies or do what I can to help. Iasan does not mind, so long as I return within a day, and King Cerball has no need to know. I am only a woman, so what harm is there?'

Breanne thought it was a risk, but if Treasa was only bringing small gifts and then leaving, perhaps it was not so dangerous. 'I will think about it.'

'Good.' Her mother held out her hand. 'Why don't you rest for a while? You must be weary from the journey, and there's time enough to talk about it in the morning.' She led her to a pile of sleeping furs near the heated stones that provided warmth within the hut. Breanne curled up and closed her eyes. But it did nothing to diminish the longing within her. The familiar scent of wood and straw conjured up the memories of lying in Alarr's arms.

Had he fought with Feann this night? Was he alive? Silently, her tears fell, dampening her cheeks. Why couldn't he give up his plans to fight her foster father? It tore her apart to imagine either one of them hurt.

She wanted to believe that he had spared her father's life, but she didn't know what he had done. Silently, she wept, wishing she could push aside the raw feelings.

She heard her mother get up and walk outside. Dimly, she heard Treasa speaking to someone in a low voice before she returned inside.

'I am sending one of my men ahead to Clonagh at dawn, so that our kinsmen will know of our arrival, Breanne,' she whispered. 'They will make a place for us to sleep where no one will know we are there.'

Breanne didn't answer, feigning sleep. Perhaps it was best to return to Clonagh and see for herself what had happened there. She was not about to let Feann arrange a marriage for her—that is, if he had survived the fight with Alarr. Her mood turned bleak as she wondered what had happened to them.

She loved both men, and neither would stand down. And choosing one meant abandoning the other. Because of it, she would have to give up both. It broke her heart, being caught in the middle.

Breanne shifted her thoughts back to Clonagh, and she tried to imagine making a home there. It wasn't the life she had envisioned, but it was time to make her own choices.

Even if that meant being alone.

* * *

Alarr gasped as the blade cut into his shoulder, but he managed to shield himself before Feann could strike again.

He pushed back against the king's blows, rising to his feet. Blood dripped down his arm, but he didn't care. Instead, he poured himself into the fight. His mind blurred, and he used his strength to strike his hardest blows. It was time to end this.

He released a battle cry, using all his strength to catch his enemy off guard. But Feann was a skilled warrior, despite his age. He met Alarr's blows with his own force. They circled one another, and despite it all, there was no doubting that they were equally matched.

Feann lunged, striking a low blow. But as Alarr sidestepped the attack, he brought his blade to the king's throat.

Then, beneath his own neck, he felt the cold kiss of metal. Across from him, he saw his brother staring. Rurik shook his head slowly, as if in warning.

'Enough,' Feann said. 'This fight is over.' To one of his men, he ordered, 'Bring Breanne to me.'

'She's gone,' Alarr admitted. 'She left this morn to go back to her mother.'

At that, Feann pressed the blade against Alarr's throat until blood welled. Alarr answered with his own pressure, never taking the blade from the king's neck.

'You let her go back to Treasa?' Feann said with incredulity. 'Why would you send her there?' He drew his blade back, and Alarr did the same. Feann cursed and swung his sword again. 'She is a conniving viper who will only betray her.'

Alarr didn't know what the king meant by that. Treasa had appeared harmless, hardly any threat at all. But now, the king's emotions caused him to fight recklessly, and Alarr seized the advantage. He allowed Feann to rail with his anger, waiting until the right moment to strike. Iron struck iron, and he kept his patience, until the moment the king crossed his sword, leaning in.

At that, Alarr reached for Feann's wrist and twisted the sword away, disarming him. With both weapons in his hands, he drew the blades on either side of the king's neck. It would take only a single blow to behead him.

'Kneel,' he ordered.

The king's men started to surround Alarr, but

Feann commanded, 'Stand down. This is between us.'

The soldiers took a step back, though they appeared ready to fight. Then Feann met Alarr's gaze. 'Swear to me you will go after Breanne. Her mother is not to be trusted.'

He ignored the man's warning and pressed the blades into his neck. 'I said, "Kneel".'

'Swear it first. You must find her and protect her from Treasa.' The king's eyes met his, and he said, 'Breanne is all that matters. You know this.'

There was true fear in Feann's expression, but it was for his foster daughter, not himself. Alarr didn't understand why the man had abandoned her, if he truly wanted her safe. Something didn't ring true. 'If you care more for her than your own life, why did you not save her when she needed you?'

'Because I thought Treasa had taken her!' the king retorted. 'After I heard she had escaped from Dún Bolg, I searched for them, only to discover that I was wrong.' He took a breath and knelt. 'Seize your vengeance and end my life, if that is what you want. I thought avenging Saorla would heal the guilt I felt over her death. But I know it won't ever bring her back. And it won't mend the past.'

The king's words resonated within him. It was true that killing the man would never bring back Gilla or Sigurd. Feann wasn't even the one who had struck the blow to end their lives. Nor had he begun the fire.

'If you care for Breanne, then you must save her,' Feann insisted. 'Treasa will stop at nothing to get Clonagh—even putting her own daughter in danger.'

He hesitated, and the king met his gaze. 'Please.'

In his heart, Alarr tried to summon up the resentment and rage he'd felt after losing the ability to walk. He thought about striking Feann down, wounding him so he would know the same pain.

But hurting Feann would do nothing. This man was on his knees, not begging for his own life, but pleading for him to save Breanne.

What would she think of him now? He could imagine the fragile hurt in her eyes, the worry and the fear. Breanne was a woman who put others before herself, despite having been abandoned by so many. And he had told her he would leave her too, after he'd avenged himself against

Feann. At the time, he had thought it was the right choice, to let her go.

Now, he realised that he could no more give her up than he could cut off his own arm. He wanted her eyes filled with love and faith, not the pain that he had caused. He wanted to spend each day with her, loving her.

Hurting Feann wouldn't make him a stronger man, but it would break Breanne's heart. He had promised to let her foster father live. And now that he had proven his strength, it was time to keep that vow.

'Alarr,' came Rurik's voice. He saw his brother's gaze and understood the unspoken message.

He lowered his swords and sheathed one, keeping the other in his hand. 'I swore to Breanne that I would not end your life. And I will keep that promise.'

The king stared at Alarr, and he never took his gaze from Feann. For a long moment, the tension remained between them. Although he had won this fight, it was too soon to smooth the sharp edges of their distrust.

But if Breanne was in danger from Treasa, he would need an ally—someone who would put her safety first. Though it was a grave risk, Alarr extended his hand. 'If I'm going to find

Breanne and protect her, I will need help.' With an army of men, they could easily defend her. And despite the years of hatred, they shared a common bond in wanting Breanne to be safe.

The king hesitated a moment but then clasped Alarr's palm and stood. 'So be it.'

He handed Feann his sword back, hilt first. Though he didn't trust the man, it was the first step towards mending the breach.

The king called out to his men to gather nearby. He chose a dozen men to go to Dún Bolg, and he asked Rurik to remain at Killcobar. Another dozen men would accompany Feann and Alarr.

'Aren't we returning to Dún Bolg with the others?' Alarr asked.

Feann shook his head. 'There is only one place Treasa will bring Breanne. She wants dominion over Clonagh. That's where she will go, and that's where we will find them.'

Chapter Eleven

Two days later

It was afternoon by the time they arrived at Clonagh. Breanne and her mother had travelled north-east with only two men to guard them. As they drew near, she glimpsed a small fortress enclosed by a wicker fence. It surprised her, for her mother had spoken of Clonagh as if it were a vast ringfort. She frowned, wondering what else Treasa had exaggerated.

They left their horses with their two guards, and Treasa said, 'It is safe to go through the gates.'

Breanne was still wary of walking alone, but her mother remained cheerful, as if she was delighted to be home. They walked uphill, and Treasa smiled at the guards standing at the entrance. They opened the gates without question, and Breanne followed her mother inside. Inside the ringfort, she saw very few people. As Treasa had said, there was a sense of hopelessness and loss.

Her mother took her by the hand and led her to an old man standing outside one of the round-houses. He wore a long grey *léine*, and his expression was sombre. When they reached his side, Treasa said, 'This is Father Bain.'

She didn't know quite what to say, except, 'I am glad to meet you, Father.' She was surprised to find a priest here, for they were nowhere near a monastery.

The priest ventured a smile that didn't quite meet his eyes. 'And you, my child.' He glanced towards the gates, and it was then that Breanne became aware of more guards gathering at the entrance.

Treasa's face grew uneasy. 'I think we should go inside, Breanne. It might be best to remain hidden, in case there is a threat.'

'I thought they were our kinsmen,' she replied.

Her mother shook her head. 'We have a few men loyal to us, like those who met us when we first arrived. But King Cerball has his own forces here, mingled with ours. They know I am only a woman and there is no harm by my presence. But it doesn't mean they will let me come and go freely.'

'Are we prisoners now?' Breanne asked. She was aghast at the idea, wishing she had heeded her instincts. Without knowing King Cerball, she had no idea what she had done by coming here.

'No, no. Nothing like that,' Treasa reassured her. 'But, let us say, we are well guarded.' Her mother took her arm in hers and bid the priest farewell. She guided her to the far end of the ringfort where there was a smaller roundhouse. 'Let us go somewhere we can talk freely.'

With no other choice, she followed her mother. Even so, she grew aware that several soldiers were watching. An older woman risked a gaze at Breanne and shook her head.

What did that mean? Something was very wrong at Clonagh, and already she was regretting her decision to come here. She could not make her home in a place like this, heavily guarded by a neighbouring king who had executed her father for treason.

Her mother pushed open the doorway and

waited at the entrance. 'Come inside. There is someone else I've been wanting you to meet.'

Breanne risked a glance back at the soldiers and the old woman. Every part of her felt the invisible threat. She knew it wasn't safe here, but no longer did she have strong *Lochlannach* warriors to guard her. Instead, she would have to defend herself.

You've done nothing wrong, she reminded herself.

These men had no reason to harm her. Unless they did not want her or her mother to dwell here. Clonagh felt like a graveyard, filled with spirits haunting the air.

'Breanne?' her mother prompted. 'Go inside. It's warmer there, and we can talk.'

With a sigh, she decided to obey. There was no reason not to. She ducked her head inside the low opening and stepped inside the space. The ceiling was tall, supported by heavy beams, and the roof was made of thatch.

The door closed behind her, and she turned to where her mother had been standing. But Treasa was gone.

'Mother?' she asked. She tried to open the

door, and when she did, she saw the face of Oisin.

'Hello, Breanne,' he said. His smile held malice as he pushed his way inside. 'I've been waiting a long time for this.'

They journeyed with all haste, for which Alarr was grateful. He had never imagined that Treasa was a threat to Breanne, and he cursed himself for letting her go. Feann had insisted that they take his fastest horses, and when night fell, they stopped briefly to let the horses drink. Alarr held the reins of his mount. 'Why do you think she brought Breanne to Clonagh? Why not Dún Bolg?'

'Because Treasa wants to rule over Clonagh. She won't hesitate to use Breanne for that purpose. Whether that means another arranged marriage to a weaker man or she'll choose a man who will die sooner, leaving Treasa in command.' Feann rubbed his horse down, tending to the animal.

'What happened to Breanne's father?' Alarr asked. He had heard murmurings about treason, but it made him wonder what the truth really was.

'Treasa lied to Cerball. She tried to seduce him and failed. Then she told him that Dal was cruel and beat her. She claimed that Dal was raising an army against Cerball. But the men Dal brought to the gates were men who had planned to swear an oath of fealty to Cerball. Dal was trying to bring their families together.' Feann let out a breath and lowered his gaze. 'Treasa betrayed him, and he was executed before anyone recognised the truth.

'When Cerball learned that he had killed an innocent man, he had Treasa exiled. Were it me, I would have executed *her* for what she did to Dal.'

Alarr had never suspected that the matron had caused so much trouble, and he hoped they could reach Breanne in time. 'What will Treasa do to her daughter?'

'I don't know,' Feann admitted. 'But we're going to find Breanne and bring her home.'

Alarr nodded in agreement. But this time, he wanted to offer her a different choice. She had begged him to set aside his vengeance, and now, he had come to an understanding with Feann. No longer did the bitterness of revenge burn within his veins. Instead, he saw a man who loved his foster daughter as his own blood, who would stop at nothing to save her. Alarr had found a grudging respect for the king, in the way he had gathered his forces and planned their strategy.

'Do you need to rest?' Feann asked.

'Only when we have her back,' Alarr answered.

At that, the king's face relaxed somewhat. 'If you were not a *Lochlannach* who tried to kill me, I might like you, Alarr Sigurdsson.' He mounted his horse once again and led the animal back to the pathway.

Alarr climbed on to his own horse. 'If you were not the man who took away my ability to walk for a year, I might like you, Feann.' He shrugged, making it clear that it was still unlikely. Though he had bandaged his shoulder, the cut still burned from their earlier fight.

There was a slight lift in the older man's mouth, as if he were suppressing a smile. They rode in silence for a time, and finally Feann asked, 'Why did you let Breanne leave that night? Especially with so few men to guard her?'

Guilt pressed upon his conscience, for Alarr regretted it. But a part of him had known that if he didn't let her go, she would talk him into giving up his vengeance. She held a power over him that he didn't understand. And the only way to overcome it was with distance.

'She wanted to go, and I don't believe in imprisoning women. Since I hold no command over your men, I couldn't send them with her, could I?'

'You should have told me of her plans to leave.'

'It was her decision to make. And she wanted to leave quietly.'

Feann tightened his grip on the reins, his expression a harsh mask of anger. 'You wanted her to go, didn't you?'

He didn't answer the king. Because both answers were true. He'd wanted Breanne to leave because he didn't want her to witness the fight. He had needed the chance to fight Feann, to drive out the demons of his past and strike back. In the end, the battle hadn't given him the resolution he'd wanted—but he held no regrets.

'I didn't want her to watch our fight,' he admitted. 'And I knew I wasn't worthy of her.' But he'd missed waking up and seeing her each day. He missed the warmth of her mouth and the touch of her hands upon him. She had healed a part of him he hadn't known was broken. For so long, he had lived for his vengeance, never daring to imagine a life after his injuries. He'd believed that he didn't deserve to live after he'd failed his family.

Before Feann could speak, Alarr added, 'But I will find her and protect her from all harm. And I will do everything I can to be the man she needs.' The loss of her was an emptiness he needed to fill. And if she would have him, this time he would not let her go.

Feann studied him for a time, as if discerning the truth. Then he shrugged. 'That remains to be seen.'

Alarr wasn't surprised at the man's reluctance and he turned the conversation to their plans. 'What do you want to do when we arrive?'

'I don't want Treasa to know you are here,' the king answered. 'It's better if you remain hidden. Then if there is trouble, you can get Breanne out.'

Alarr understood that they needed an alternative plan, in case there was an unforeseen danger. And yet, he wasn't about to let Feann go in alone. 'I will disguise myself among your men, if that is what you want. But I won't remain outside the fortress.'

Feann met his gaze steadily. 'Do not let her see you.'

Alarr privately agreed with the king. He was there to ensure Breanne's safety, and he did not want to alert Treasa's suspicions. He would support Feann's quest to bring her to safety, but he would not reveal his presence unless it was necessary.

It was early morning, and Breanne jerked to a seated position when she heard footsteps approaching. She had spent the night locked inside one of the dwellings, hardly able to sleep at all. Her mother had left her alone after she'd refused to speak with Oisin.

When they started to lift the bar that held the door shut, she stood, searching for some sort of weapon—but there was nothing. Instead, she stared at the door, squaring her shoulders in preparation for the fight to come.

Her mother entered first and smiled at her. Oisin followed behind her, and the knowing look on his face made her stomach clench. Fury blazed through her that her mother would dare to invite Oisin into their ringfort. He was an enemy whom she had barely escaped the last time.

'Why would you bring him here?' Breanne demanded.

Though his injuries were somewhat healed, she noticed that his shoulder was still bandaged. Even so, she could feel the threat of his presence.

He was standing tall, his expression filled with gloating. 'I came for you, Breanne,' he answered. 'Your mother was kind enough to make the wedding arrangements.' He turned to Treasa and added, 'Go now, and leave me with my bride.'

Her mother only nodded and closed the door behind her.

'I will never wed you,' she told Oisin. But worse than this situation was the clarity of her mother's betrayal. Though she had known Treasa wanted Clonagh, she had never imagined the woman would stoop to such depths for her own ambitions. Her own daughter was nothing but a pawn, just as Breanne had feared.

She had no intention of obeying Treasa's wishes. She would fight back against a forced marriage, even if there was no one to come to her aid now. The bleak feeling of isolation threatened to drown her, but she tried to steel her courage. If no one could save her, then she would have to save herself.

Oisin drew closer, and she took a step back, trying to keep distance between them. He smiled at her. 'King Cerball ordered that you should wed a man loyal to him. Who better than his own bastard son?'

'The only loyalty you hold is fealty to yourself,' she countered. 'You do not want to wed me.' Oisin only wanted to control her, to mould her into his imagined wife.

'You're wrong,' he answered. 'I wouldn't care if you had the face and temperament of a shrew. Marriage to you will bring Clonagh under my dominion.' He took another step, and when Breanne tried to move away, he seized her arm and pressed her against the wall. 'But as it is, I do desire you, Breanne.' He leaned in, and his hot breath fanned her cheek. She was repulsed by him, for he appeared to delight in her inability to fight him. When she tried to shove him back, he pinned her with one arm.

'I am going to enjoy claiming you with my body,' he said. 'I'll enjoy it more if you fight me.' To underscore his words, he pinched her nipple roughly.

This time, she used all her strength to push

against Oisin, but he only laughed. Panic flooded through her at the realisation that he could easily subdue her, and she could do nothing to stop him. She struggled against him, fighting to break free, but it was like trying to push back a stone wall.

'Do you see how weak you are? You cannot fight me.' Oisin reached for the hem of her gown and lifted it while he continued to hold her against the wall with his arm and shoulder. He started to reach between her legs, and fear shot through her. He intended to claim her now, to assert his body over hers.

She had to fight back, to protect herself somehow. But there was nothing she could use as a weapon, and she lacked the strength. Breanne screamed as loudly as she could, but he seemed to delight in her terror.

'I'm going to enjoy taming you,' he said. To emphasise his words, he kissed her roughly, biting her lower lip until he drew blood.

Her heart pounded, and she realised she was in a state of shock. Her mind went blank, her limbs frozen as she trembled.

Don't surrender, she warned herself. *You have to fight. There is always a way.*

Her gaze fixed upon his bandaged shoulder,

and when he tried to touch her intimately, she rammed her head against his wound. Oisin roared at the sudden pain and released her. Breanne raced for the door, but before she could reach it, he grabbed the length of her hair and pulled her back. With his fist, he backhanded her, and the pain exploded against her mouth. 'You're going to regret what you did,' he swore. 'And you'll stay here until you willingly agree to wed me.'

Breanne tasted blood, but before she could run again, he closed the door and secured it behind him. She was alone in the darkness, imprisoned within the dwelling.

Her teeth chattered, and it was only then that she realised how badly she was shaking. Slowly, she sank against the wall until she was sitting on the ground. Silent tears ran down her face, and she realised just how dangerous Oisin was. He was not a man who would listen to reason. He delighted in hurting her, and marriage to him would be horrifying.

But you're not going to wed him, she reminded herself.

No one could force the vows from her lips. She might be at the mercy of her mother and a man she despised, but that didn't mean she was powerless.

She could try to send someone from Clonagh back to Killcobar. Or seek help from the people here. Though she lacked the physical strength, she had intelligence. There had to be a way to free herself from this prison.

She lay down upon the furs, wishing she had not left Alarr. If he were here, he would hold her until she stopped trembling. She would draw strength from him, and he would break down the door, freeing them both. The thoughts brought her comfort, though she knew they were only an illusion.

She loved him, in spite of everything. Though she could not bear to watch him fight Feann, it cut her deeply to be without him. Whether he was dead or whether he had returned to Maerr, the aching emptiness was consuming. She could hardly bear it.

In her heart, she believed that he had kept his vow not to kill Feann. The only question was whether her foster father had granted him the same mercy.

Breanne swiped at the tears, gathering her emotions and pushing back against her fear.

You're going to escape, she told herself. *No matter what happens, you will find a way out.*

And once she did, she would find out what had happened to Alarr and learn whether they could be together.

Hours passed, and afternoon faded into evening. Breanne had calmed her terror, forming a plan, despite her earlier fears. A knock sounded at the door, and a woman's voice said, 'May I come in?'

Breanne rose to her feet, and an older woman came inside, holding a loaf of bread, a small flagon, and a bundle of clothing. 'I brought you food and wine.' The matron set it down, but before she could leave, Breanne ran to the door.

'Wait. Please.' She blocked the woman's exit. 'I need your help.'

'I can do nothing,' she insisted. 'Do not ask me to let you go. They will hurt my family.'

Breanne didn't bother to ask who *they* were. Instead, she said, 'How many guards are outside this shelter?'

The matron glanced at the doorway as if uncertain whether to answer. But at last, she mumbled, 'Six.'

Then any attempts to flee would be futile.

There was no means of escaping six men. She needed to find a different way, perhaps a hidden way out of the shelter. But there were no windows and no other exits from the dwelling.

She redirected her question. 'What are they planning to do with me?'

The woman bit her lip, as if wondering whether to answer. She looked down at the bundle of food. 'They will come for you on the morrow. The priest will hear your vows, and you are to marry Oisin MacLogan.'

So she had only one day left. Breanne sat down with the bread, her mind turning over the problem. She drew up her knees against her chest and closed her eyes. 'Do I have until sunset for the wedding?'

'No. They have planned it a few hours after dawn,' she answered. With a glance at the door, the older woman withdrew a small eating knife from her waist. Without a word, she hid the dagger inside the bundle of clothing. It was an unexpected gift—and a chance to free herself. For a moment, the older woman met her gaze with understanding before she departed.

Breanne didn't know how she would use the weapon, but it offered a slight glimmer of hope.

You can save yourself, she told herself. *Be strong and use your wits.*

But even so, she was afraid that her time was running out.

Chapter Twelve

It was late at night when they arrived at Clonagh. Rain pounded against them, soaking Alarr to the skin. The harsh weather offered an advantage, for it meant that no one would leave their shelter unless commanded to do so.

'Are you certain you won't remain outside?' Feann questioned. 'We need someone beyond the gates.'

'Let it be one of your men,' Alarr countered. He had no intention of being left behind—not while Breanne was in danger.

The king eyed him with annoyance but relented after a time. 'Fine. But you must remain hidden.'

They approached the gate with stealth where one man guarded the entrance with a spear. To his surprise, Feann signalled to the guard. For a brief moment Alarr wondered if the king would betray him. He wouldn't put it past Feann, for neither of them fully trusted the other. Instead, the king spoke quietly to the soldier, and they were allowed to enter.

'Let no one see you,' the guard warned. He pointed towards a grain storage shed. 'When the next guard comes to take my place, I will come to you.'

The rain continued to pour in punishing sheets, but they made their way to the shed. Though it was cold, Alarr was grateful to be out of the harsh weather. He found a place to sit, and he wondered if Breanne was safe. It tempted him to leave the shelter and find her, for he knew not what Treasa had done.

'We will make our plans tonight,' Feann said in a low voice. 'Nevin is one of my men. I sent him to Clonagh years ago, and no one knows of his loyalty to me.'

Alarr gave a nod, recognising it as a sound strategy. Yet, he questioned what the king would do now. 'What is Breanne to you? A political pawn for your own alliances?'

Feann leaned back against the shed. 'She is a daughter to me, in all but blood. I have cared for her since she was two years of age.' There was a softness in his voice as he spoke of her.

'But you intended to wed her to one of Cerball's men,' Alarr ventured.

'It would have kept her safe from Treasa. I needed a strong man to marry her, one who would protect her and ensure that she would not be killed for her lands. A warrior.'

In the darkness, Alarr could not see Feann's expression. He knew that the king had no wish to see Breanne with a man like him, though he didn't say it. Even so, the thought of giving Breanne to another warrior filled him with a surge of possessive anger.

Another man would not understand that despite her façade of bravery, she had a tender heart and a fierce loyalty to her family. One day, when she bore children, he had no doubt she would fight to protect them. She was a strong woman, and she had faced threats that would have made others weep. Instead, she had risen up to meet those challenges.

Yet, he had turned her away for the sake of vengeance.

He closed his eyes, recognising what a mistake he had made. Although Feann wanted her to wed an Irish nobleman, Alarr knew he could not give her up a second time. She belonged to him and he was hers. Somehow, he would find a way to be with her.

The door swung open, and both of them unsheathed their weapons. 'It's me,' came the voice of the guard, Nevin.

'What can you tell us about Breanne?' Feann asked.

The guard answered, 'She is being held captive in the shelter at the far end of the ringfort. In the morning, Oisin plans to wed her and seize command of Clonagh.' From the man's tone, it was clear that he did not support Oisin's leadership.

Alarr's mood darkened, and he regretted not killing the man when he'd first had the opportunity. He would not hesitate a second time. He gritted his teeth and asked the guard, 'Did he harm her?'

The guard's silence weighed heavily. Then, after a time, he admitted, 'Everyone heard her screams.'

Alarr felt his rage gather into a tight ball of hatred. He never should have let her leave. 'I will see Oisin dead for this.'

Feann caught his arm. 'Take your vengeance upon him. And I will see to Breanne's safety first.' In a low voice, he ordered the guard to leave.

At first, Alarr wanted to be the one to save Breanne. He blamed himself for what had happened, and he should be there for her.

And yet, he remembered how Breanne had felt abandoned by her father. She had gone into slavery, believing that Feann had left her, when the truth was, her father had tried to search for her. Moreover, if he sent the king to fight Oisin, Feann might not survive.

The decision weighed up on him as he tried to decide what was best. Breanne had left him, not wanting to witness their fight. She might not want to see him again, and he knew he would not be able to stop himself from embracing her.

Gods help him, he was in love with her. And he didn't know if he had the strength to let her go. He could not force her to stay with him, nor was it right. She deserved the choice.

'As you will,' he told the king. 'Go and save Breanne. I will face Oisin.' If he placed his focus on killing his enemy, it would be a strong distraction.

The thought of being without Breanne was a physical ache inside him. If she did not want to see him again, it was best to leave Éireann and never look back.

There was a slight ease in the man's tension. 'And after he is dead? What then?'

'I don't know the answer to that yet.' It depended entirely on Breanne's wishes. But after she had left him once, he doubted if she would change her mind.

The king's expression darkened. 'I was right about you. You were only using her for your own gains. Breanne never meant anything to you.'

At that, his temper exploded. He took Feann by the throat and shoved him against the wall. 'Breanne meant *everything* to me. But I know I'm not the man she needs. I cannot ask her to turn her back on her homeland. I will do the right thing by her, even if it means walking away.'

He released Feann and stepped back. The king appeared startled by his outburst, but his demeanour turned thoughtful. 'And what is it you think she needs?'

'A powerful warrior who can love her and protect her. One who is whole.' He hadn't meant to voice the last part, but it was true. He had let her go, fearing he couldn't fight for Breanne the way he wanted to. He never wanted to see her broken or hurt because of him.

'You defeated me,' Feann pointed out. 'But I agree with you. Breanne should not wed a *Loch-lannach* and abandon her kingdom. They need her now, more than ever.'

Alarr said nothing, though he was startled at Feann's reminder. He *had* defeated a strong fighter, in the end. He might not have the speed or balance that he'd once had, but he had been a warrior all his life. Perhaps it was time to stop dwelling on the possibility of failure and live his life for her. Breanne had wanted him to leave the past behind, and he'd refused.

But now, he realised that he didn't want any future without her in it. He would sacrifice everything to save her and give her the choice of becoming his wife. He wanted that, more than all else. If she refused, then after he killed Oisin, he would accompany Rurik to Northumbria. There, they could search for the other fighters who had slaughtered his kinsmen in Maerr.

For now, he hoped he could convince her to stay. In the meantime, he needed to find Breanne and free her from captivity.

'What should we do about Treasa?' Alarr asked.

'She is dangerous,' Feann admitted. 'Ambitious, and I blame her for bringing this threat to Breanne.' With a slight laugh, he suggested, 'You could take her back to Maerr with you where she could do no harm.'

There was a slight lift in the tension between them, but Alarr shook his head. 'Her fate should rest in Cerball's hands.'

'I agree.' The king paused again as he regarded him. 'What will you do afterwards?'

'What I want to do and what I will do are not the same,' he admitted. 'I want to take Breanne back with me to Maerr. I want to wed her and keep her at my side.' He saw the grim look of fury in Feann's expression. 'But it is her choice to make.'

'You cannot ask her to surrender her kingdom. It's better if you leave her behind, even if she grieves.'

He met the king's gaze. 'We both know she is worth more than any kingdom. I will do what is right.'

Breanne had spent most of the night making her plans. It was far better to feign surrender, for then, the others might let their guard down. She had tied the blade and sheath to her thigh beneath her shift. Though she didn't truly know how she would use the weapon yet, she intended to leave Clonagh by any means necessary. A knock sounded at the door, and a woman's voice called out, 'Breanne, may I come inside?' It was her mother.

She bit her tongue to keep from stating the obvious, that she was heavily guarded, and the door was locked. Instead, she answered, 'Yes.' This might be a chance to seize her escape, especially if her mother left the door unlocked.

Treasa lifted the bar and came inside. She was dressed in a crimson gown, and her hair was neatly braided and concealed within a cap. 'I brought this for you to wear.' In her arms, she held out a gown of soft yellow, the colour of morning sunshine. It was beautiful, and for a moment, Breanne imagined herself wearing the *léine* while marrying Alarr instead. The thought made her throat close up with emotion, for he was gone. She had left him of her own free will, and there was no one to save her now.

Her mother helped her change into the *léine*, and when she finished lacing up the gown, Treasa turned to look at her. 'You are so beautiful, Breanne. I could not be prouder.'

'And yet, you are handing me to the enemy,'

she countered. 'You brought me here under the pretence of seeing my homeland. But all along, you intended to force this marriage.'

Treasa's face turned pained. 'Sometimes sacrifices must be made for the greater good.'

'But you are not the one making the sacrifice, are you?' She crossed her arms. 'Oisin is not a kind man. He is not one you can manipulate to do your will.'

The expression on Treasa's face never changed. 'Oh, my sweet girl. You are so very young. Did you believe I would choose a man like Oisin without ensuring that you would be safe from him?'

Breanne didn't understand. 'What do you mean?'

Her mother drew close and lowered her voice. 'Oisin is Cerball's bastard son, but he is not a favourite. We will make the marital alliance and prove our loyalty to Cerball. But Oisin will not live long enough to be a threat.'

Treasa spoke of murder as if she were discussing food to prepare for an evening meal. 'Wed him willingly, and I will see to it that he does not survive the wedding night.'

Breanne said nothing but only stared at her

mother. Treasa folded her hands together. 'Unless you want to lie with him?'

The thought made bile rise to her throat. 'No.'

'Good. Then I will bring you a potion to slip into his wine. He will fall asleep and never awaken.'

Breanne still could not bring herself to speak. Not only was her mother planning a murder, but she intended her daughter to carry out her plans. No matter that she despised Oisin, she was not a killer.

Treasa continued, 'Let everyone believe that the marriage is consummated. I will bring your *Lochlannach* to you later, and you can attempt to conceive a child. We will claim it is Oisin's, and the alliance will be finished.' It was clear that her mother had no qualms about taking another man's life if it served her purpose. And her lack of emotion was utterly chilling.

Breanne decided it was better to behave as if she were ignorant. She lowered her head, wondering how much time she had remaining.

Her unspoken question was answered when her mother asked, 'Are you ready?'

No, she wasn't. But it was far better to leave this chamber than to remain a prisoner. Before she could say anything, she heard the sound of a battle cry outside. Treasa pushed the door closed and blocked her path. Breanne peered through a crack in the door, and outside she saw a group of armed men charging forward. One of them was Alarr.

He was here. And from the looks of it, so was her foster father. Her emotions gathered up and spilled over as she could not stop her smile of joy. They had come for her, and both were alive.

When she glanced at Treasa, her mother's face had turned furious. 'Wait here,' she said. After she closed the door, Breanne heard the sound of the wooden bar locking her inside.

Damn her for this.

She tried to stare through the cracks in the doorway and saw Oisin facing off against Alarr. Feann barked a command and then left with a group of his men. He was stopped by other soldiers, and she watched as the men fought one another. Fear pulsed inside her veins, but she forced herself to watch. Her gaze fixed upon Alarr. His sword moved with speed, and he struck Oisin hard. In his left hand he held a shield, and he used it to protect himself from his enemy's punishing blows.

Over and over he attacked, and she found herself breathless, watching her warrior. He moved with confidence, and she knew he was fighting for her. She didn't know how he had learned of the threat, but at the sight of him, she felt a surge of love.

No matter what had happened, he had always been there for her. She had complete faith that he would protect her. And she would fight alongside him.

A shadow crossed her door, and she heard Feann's voice. 'Breanne, are you there?'

She called out, 'I'm here.' There was a noise of him lifting the wooden bar, and he threw the door open.

'Are you all right?' he asked. His face was creased with worry, and her emotions welled up at the sight of him. 'Did anyone hurt you?'

'I'm fine,' Breanne murmured. She was in his arms a moment later, and he stroked her hair back, gripping her in a fierce embrace.

'We will get you out of here,' he assured her. 'I swear it.'

'What about Alarr?'

'He is fighting Oisin.'

Breanne clung to him, and her foster father escorted her from the shelter. They walked outside, and she froze at the sight of six guards surrounding them. Feann unsheathed his sword and faced them. 'Go back inside, Breanne.'

She hesitated, for her foster father was badly outnumbered. With six men, they could easily kill him, and she could do nothing to stop it.

Don't be a coward, she warned herself.

If she stood back and did nothing, he would die. And despite the danger, she didn't believe they would kill her. She took a breath and stepped forward. 'Stop!' she called out to the soldiers. 'Leave him. I will surrender without a fight.'

'Breanne, no,' Feann insisted. He appeared furious that she would refuse his protection. But she knew better than to let him face so many men. There was a greater chance that Alarr could help her, with her father's support.

She moved another step, standing between them. One of the men seized her arm, while another kept his sword pointed at Feann. Her foster father glared at her. 'Don't do this. I can defend you long enough for you to escape.'

But she would not let him make the sacrifice. 'I'm not going to stand aside and watch you die. Not when I can stop it from happening.'

Two of the men pressed her father back while the others surrounded her. She pushed back the rising fear and forced herself to leave with the men as they retreated.

But as they escorted her to the far end of the ringfort where Oisin was fighting Alarr, she was afraid to wonder what would happen now.

Alarr's arm was numb from the sword fight, but he ignored the pain and continued to strike hard at his enemy. He could see the sweat running down Oisin's face. The man was growing weary, and that gave Alarr an advantage. He lunged with his blade and nicked Oisin's side before the man could dodge the blow.

This was about more than winning a sword fight. It was about protecting Breanne from a man who wanted to possess her. Never would he allow her to marry a man like Oisin, who would subjugate her to his will.

Without warning, Oisin changed his pace. He struck hard, swinging the sword at Alarr's knees. He had to leap to get out of the way, and when his feet landed, he was off balance. Oisin took advantage and shoved his wounded shoulder, causing Alarr to gasp at the pain before he fell to the ground. He rolled out of the way and raised his shield just as his enemy struck a downward blow.

His pulse thundered, and he forced himself to centre his rage. He needed to remain calm and not allow his body's weakness to betray him. But he struggled to push back the frustration of his lack of balance. He could not doubt himself, or it would only lead to failure.

'You cannot win this fight,' Oisin taunted. 'And when you're dead, I'm going to claim her body. You'll die, knowing that she will be mine to do with as I choose.' A thin smile curved at Oisin's mouth.

Not if I can help it.

Alarr knew the man was trying to incite his rage, to make him careless. He used all his strength to push back with his shield and managed to stand up from the ground. His legs were still unsteady, but he feigned a strength he didn't feel.

Oisin pressed back, and when Alarr stared into the man's eyes, he saw no mercy. He had no doubt that his enemy would hurt Breanne, given the opportunity. This time, he would not stop until Oisin was dead and could no longer threaten Breanne.

With a surge of strength, he shoved Oisin back and swung his sword. He saw a slight smile as his enemy dodged the blow, but Alarr ignored the mocking stare and continued to fight.

Out of nowhere, a searing pain struck the back of his knees, and he crumpled to the ground. He spied another man attacking from behind, and Alarr barely avoided the killing blow. It was dishonourable, and he should have expected it from Oisin. The second man struck him with a club, and Alarr bit back a roar of pain as he tried to defend himself from both fighters.

A soft exclamation caught his attention, and he saw Breanne being held by two men, with two others nearby. She wore a yellow gown, and when she caught sight of him on the ground, he saw the fear in her eyes.

'Alarr,' she called out, struggling to free herself from their grasp.

It burned his pride that she had seen him like this, crouched on the ground like a wounded animal. The second man struck again, and his shield reverberated from the vicious blow as he deflected it. But Breanne's presence renewed his resolution to win. He would do anything to defeat his enemies.

Oisin was gloating, and he held his sword aloft. 'Would you like to witness his death, Breanne? I could make you watch while I sink this blade into his heart.'

Alarr struggled and nearly managed to break away. But at a signal from Oisin, two more soldiers came to restrain him. They bore their full weight upon him, and he fought to free himself from the men.

'No,' Breanne said. 'Let him live.' Her tone was quiet, tinged with fear. 'I will do as you command.'

Alarr was about to voice a protest, but he saw her give a slight shake of her head. She had done this on purpose as a distraction. And he needed to take advantage.

Oisin seemed pleased by her response. 'Good.' He reached for her wrist and pulled her closer. 'Look at him.'

Alarr knew that his enemy was trying to demean him in her eyes. Although he ought to feel humiliated, instead he was determined to save her. At that moment, Oisin leaned in and kissed her hard. His mouth was bruising, possessive, and there was no doubt of the message he was sending. The man intended to claim Breanne, forcing her to do his will.

At that moment, Alarr wanted nothing more than to bury his blade in the man's heart. But first, he had to free himself from his captors to reach his weapon.

'Oisin!' came a man's voice. It was Feann. His face was swollen, his lip bleeding as he held out his sword. 'Let her go.'

Oisin turned, and Alarr used the moment to push back against the men holding him down. He rolled away and managed to rise to his feet, though his knees were burning from the pain. He refused to give up and would willingly sacrifice his life for hers. Never would he allow Oisin to claim her.

Despite the pain, Alarr held his weapon and charged forwards, heedless of the soldiers. His only concern was reaching her before his enemy could harm her. Before he got very far, the other fighters flanked him. King Feann rushed forward with his sword and joined at Alarr's side. It was strange to realise that the man he'd tried to kill was now defending him and fighting alongside him. The clanging sound of iron resounded as the king blocked an enemy's sword. They moved back to back, facing off against their common foes. Breanne's face still held worry, yet she appeared startled by the sight of them together.

Oisin's mouth tightened, and he gripped her

arm, moving towards the back of the ringfort. Alarr doubled his efforts against his opponents. He wasn't about to let him take Breanne.

'Go after her,' Feann commanded. 'I'll hold them off with our men.' Just as he'd predicted, several of the Killcobar soldiers joined in. And then, to his surprise, some of the Clonagh men joined at Feann's side.

Alarr didn't argue but hurried towards Breanne. Oisin stopped in the centre of the ringfort in a silent challenge. He held Breanne around the waist, and with his left hand, he reached under her skirt.

No. He would not stand by and let his enemy defile Breanne. Alarr raced towards them, but Oisin withdrew a hidden blade that had been strapped to Breanne's thigh. He held it against her throat and gave a mocking smile. 'Let her go, *Lochlannach*. And I might let you live.'

He pressed the blade against Breanne's skin until blood welled. The sight of her suffering ignited Alarr's fury, but he didn't dare move again for fear that Oisin would cut her throat.

'I don't think you want to come any closer,' his enemy continued. 'Or it will be your fault she died. Just like your first wife, wasn't it?'

Alarr didn't know how Oisin had any knowledge of Gilla, but he remained motionless. His mind tried to think of another way to save her, and he glanced back at Feann. The king and their men had pushed back the other fighters, but he held his sword and shield in readiness.

'If you harm Breanne, you will lose Clonagh,' Alarr warned. 'Her people will defend her.' He had already witnessed that, when the men of Clonagh had joined Feann in the fight.

'These people have never seen her before,' Oisin scoffed. 'They care nothing for her fate.'

'And what of me?' came a voice. Treasa emerged from one of the dwellings, and she pulled her hood back to reveal her face. 'Do you not think my people would defend me?'

Oisin's gaze turned mocking. 'If they cared, they would have brought you out of exile.' He surveyed the lands and added, 'They need a strong leader to guide them.'

'They don't need a tyrant,' Breanne countered. She stared at Alarr in a silent message of her own. She appeared poised and courageous in the face of danger. But he worried that she would fight back. He didn't want to risk her being hurt.

'Oisin, do not do this,' Treasa pleaded. 'There is no need for fighting.' She stepped between them and pleaded, 'Put down the blade. Breanne has already agreed to wed you.'

Alarr tightened his grip on his weapon. He knew the woman was lying, but he couldn't guess what she was trying to accomplish.

Yet Oisin did not lower the knife. Instead, he addressed the crowd. 'I want everyone to know that I will always guard Clonagh from outsiders.' He stared at the people, and many looked away, out of fear. 'No one will threaten me or those I protect.'

'This isn't protection,' Breanne said quietly. 'This is cowardice. You are using me as a shield because you know this is a fight you cannot win.' She tried to pull his hand back, but his grip remained firm.

Alarr studied the man closely, wondering if he could somehow disarm him without hurting Breanne.

Oisin called out to his men and ordered them, 'Take her to my dwelling and bind her. I will come to her later.'

Breanne met Alarr's gaze with a quiet steadiness. He didn't know what her plan was, but it was clear that she had no intention of behaving like a meek woman. There was an aura of determination about her, and he questioned what she would do now.

Without warning, Breanne slumped forward, her body going slack.

It was easy to behave like a helpless woman, for Breanne had behaved as such for all her life. But she'd had her fill of being a man's victim. It was time to act, time to free herself from this prison. The blade was still pressed close to her throat, but Oisin had lightened the pressure after she had let herself fall into a dead weight. Distraction was her aim, and the moment he pulled back the weapon, she shoved him backwards. She regained her footing and ran hard towards Alarr. He caught her in his arms and asked, 'Are you all right?'

She nodded, and he pressed her back. 'Go to Feann. He will get you out.'

'I'm not leaving you.' She knew, without a doubt, that he would stay and fight—even at the cost of his life. But this time, she had no intention of running away. Not any more. She would rather stand by his side and face the worst than abandon him to his enemies.

'Breanne, no.'

Before he could stop her, she turned and addressed the people of Clonagh. 'These men do not belong in your fortress. They have no right to lay claim to your land or your homes.'

She saw her mother take a step forward, as if she wanted to say something. But then, she faltered. Breanne stood at Alarr's back, heedless of the danger. There were dozens of men surrounding her father's meagre forces. Yet, she didn't believe that they wanted to live like this.

'Oisin is not your ruler. Stand together, and drive him out.'

The men of Clonagh appeared uncertain. It was a grave risk, but one worth taking if it meant saving the man she loved.

'These men are not fighters,' Treasa intervened. 'They know they cannot succeed against his forces. They know what will happen if they betray King Cerball and his son.' She returned to the centre of the ringfort and faced all of them. 'Is it not better to be protected by Oisin than to be his enemy? He will guard you and defend you.'

'He will imprison you,' Breanne countered. 'And I have no intention of wedding him.' She turned to stare at Oisin. 'You have no place here. I want you to leave.'

'You may want to reconsider that,' Oisin responded. Then he looked up towards the guard tower and gave a signal.

Within an instant, arrows descended upon Alarr and Feann.

Chapter Thirteen

Alarr barely reacted in time. He pushed Breanne out of range and raised his shield. 'Stay back!' he warned. One arrow grazed his leg, leaving a line of blood on his calf. Feann took an arrow in his shoulder and grunted with pain.

But in that moment, Alarr's rage erupted. Oisin had threatened the woman he loved, and intended to kill anyone who stood in his way. He moved back from his enemy, out of range of the arrows. But instead of running away, Breanne joined him.

'This isn't your fight,' he cautioned. 'It's not safe.'

'It is my fight more than yours,' she shot back. 'Oisin threatened me, my foster father, and the man I love.'

He reached out to take her hand and squeezed

it in silent reassurance. 'I will not let anything happen to you, Breanne.'

'No,' she agreed. 'But Oisin is not going to live.' Her tone was hardened, as if she had nothing to lose. But she had no experience in fighting, and if she tried to face Oisin, she could die.

'Let me fight this battle on your behalf,' he said. 'Let me be your champion and defend your honour.'

She hesitated, as if she did not want to risk his life. Her eyes gleamed with unshed tears, and she squeezed his hand again. 'All right. But after you win, I am staying at your side. Wherever you go, I will go.'

Alarr leaned in and kissed her hard. 'So be it.'

The battle wounds of the past might have weakened his strength, but he would not stand down in this fight. She was his reason for fighting, but more than that, she was his reason to live.

No longer was his life shadowed by the need for revenge. Instead, he would fight to protect the woman he loved.

He moved back towards Oisin, and two of Feann's men joined Breanne to bring her to her father's side. The others were with the king, tending his injury. He embraced his foster daughter and spoke quietly to her.

When Alarr glanced back at the archers, he saw that the men of Clonagh had disarmed them, tossing the weapons aside. It surprised him, for it revealed that the people had no interest in Oisin winning this fight.

Then he turned back to face his enemy. 'Only a coward would send a man to attack from behind or use archers at a distance. You're afraid to fight me. Because you know you will lose.'

Oisin raised his own shield and sword. 'I am not afraid of a crippled warrior. You're going to die, *Lochlannach*.'

'Not by your hand.' He swung his weapon hard, and it struck Oisin's wooden shield. Alarr knew this was about more than defeating an enemy. It was about protecting Breanne and earning the right to wed her.

As he circled Oisin, more of the people gathered around to watch. They appeared intrigued by the battle, and their presence kept Oisin's men from joining in. Alarr centred his focus on his opponent. He knew not to trust Oisin if he revealed any sort of vulnerability, for it was always a trap meant to lure him closer. But the warrior's weakness was pride. If he could somehow humiliate Oisin, his temper might erupt and bring about carelessness.

His enemy fought like a man who had spent his entire life trying to be perfect…like one trying to please his father. And Alarr knew how to press that weakness.

'Your father never noticed you, did he?' he asked. 'Because you were only a bastard.'

He understood that emotion, for his father hadn't noticed him either. He was the second-born son, hardly worthy of notice. Sigurd had given Brandt his full attention, while Alarr was an afterthought, often forgotten.

When Oisin gave no answer, Alarr continued. 'I suppose you thought that by wedding Treasa's daughter, you would have your own lands and become chief.'

'I *will* be their chief,' Oisin answered. 'We will become one of the strongest fortresses in Eireann.'

Alarr lunged and tried to find a weak point, but Oisin only parried the blow. He circled again. 'Your father never believed you would become anything, did he?'

'He will soon think differently. And one day, I will have his lands as well.' The arrogance of the statement revealed his illusions of victory. But they would never come true.

From his peripheral vision, Alarr saw Treasa drawing nearer. She was gripping her hands together and muttering to herself. Worry creased her forehead, and he warned her, 'Stay back, Treasa. This is our fight, not yours.'

'It shouldn't be,' she mumbled. 'I arranged all of it. The priest, the wedding. Breanne is supposed to marry him.'

'Oisin will never be her husband,' Alarr insisted. 'Do as you will for Clonagh, but Breanne is coming with me.'

He continued to strike out at his opponent, but Treasa's hysteria was rising. 'No,' she moaned. 'My daughter must wed the son of a king. She must restore our lands. And I will be the one to guide her. I will be queen here until I have breathed my last.'

She took another step forward, and Alarr cursed under his breath. 'Stay back, Treasa.'

He increased his speed, their swords clashing again and again. Oisin was growing tired, and Alarr saw the perspiration on the man's forehead. He continued to fight, but Oisin barely avoided a death blow when he aimed for Alarr's legs.

The time to finish the fight was now. Alarr

moved with swiftness, and all around him, he heard the sounds of encouragement from the people. It was unnerving to feel their support, but it aided him in a way he had never expected.

And then Treasa bolted between them, her knife raised high. 'She will never wed a *Lochlannach*.'

Alarr barely stopped his sword's motion, but Oisin's never ceased. It sliced through Treasa's flesh and bone, and he stumbled backwards. The people around him inhaled with shock as Treasa fell forward, knocking Oisin to the ground. Her body lay in a pool of blood, and beneath her was Oisin. His expression held shock, and when Alarr pulled Treasa back, he realised that her blade had pierced Oisin's heart when she had collapsed atop him. His enemy was grasping at the weapon, but he could do nothing. He was choking, blood spilling from his mouth. Within moments, both of them were dead.

Breanne came running to him, and Alarr embraced her hard, heedless of the blood. He was dimly aware that one of the blades had cut him, but he cared not. All that mattered was being in her arms.

'I love you,' she whispered, kissing him. 'Thank the gods you are all right.'

Alarr held her close, and in that moment, all that mattered was holding her in his arms. It didn't matter about the people of Clonagh or the bodies of the fallen. All that mattered was her.

'I love you, Breanne,' he said. 'And I want you to be my wife.'

He hadn't meant to blurt out the words so suddenly, but it was the truth. He didn't want to awaken without her by his side. She had never perceived him as less than a man, and with her, he was whole. He didn't care where they lived, so long as they were together.

Breanne's face transformed with a blend of relief and joy. 'Yes,' she wept. 'I promise.'

He buried his face in her hair, feeling gratitude that she would share her life with him. When he pulled back, he saw Feann watching, and a look of understanding passed between them. The king knew that he would guard her with his life and defend her.

For so long, he had lived for vengeance, never realising that it was a hollow emotion. In the end, death would not heal the wounds of loss. Only love could do that.

When he took Breanne's hands in his and faced the people, one of the men approached. The man had dark hair with threads of silver, and he regarded both of them. With a glance at the others, he spoke only a few words. 'Our council of *brehons* would like to speak with you both to discuss the future of Clonagh.'

Alarr didn't answer at first, though he knew it was a grave concern for them. King Cerball wanted Breanne to govern her own lands with a loyal man at her side. But Alarr would never let anyone take her from him now. And that left him questioning what was right.

'I would like to speak to them as well,' came the voice of Feann. 'And I would like to propose that Breanne should become your queen.'

She was already shaking her head in refusal. 'I know nothing about ruling over a clan. And I will not wed another man for an alliance of your choosing. The only one I will take as my husband is Alarr.'

He held her close, feeling her tension rise higher. But the older clansman surprised him by nodding in agreement. 'Having a *Lochlannach* as your husband may prove to be of value. There are several settlements nearby. It would be an advantage to have someone who could intercede on our behalf and prevent raids.'

Alarr sobered as he realised what they were asking. They wanted him to stay at Clonagh with

Breanne. Only a man of honour and strength could rule over a small kingdom. He held Breanne close, and though he had never imagined such a life would be possible, he would do anything to remain at her side.

Four days later

Breanne stood beside her father, the immense joy swelling up within her. Feann's expression held a tight emotion and he ventured, 'You're certain that wedding this man is what you want.'

She nodded, and smiled, feeling as if her heart would soar out from her chest. 'It is.' Her only regret was that Alarr's brother Rurik was not here, though she had sent a message to Killcobar. Likely, he was on a ship already, journeying to Northumbria, in search of answers. But she hoped he would return to visit.

Breanne wore a gown of deep green with a golden torque around her throat. Her hair was braided back with flowers, and the thought of her wedding brought a surge of emotions brimming up within her. Alarr meant everything to her, and she could hardly believe that they would be married this day.

'King Cerball will not like this union,' her

father warned. 'He wanted you to wed an Irish ally.'

'But you will intercede for me, won't you?' She met his gaze with her own fervent hope.

'I will speak with him,' Feann promised. 'But I cannot say that Cerball will approve. If you allow his soldiers to stay for a time, he may relent and call them back, once he is certain there is no threat.'

Breanne didn't like the thought of the ringfort remaining occupied by Cerball's guards. And yet, she also understood that it was a means towards peace and a compromise was necessary. In time, perhaps she could convince the king to send them away.

'I hope that will not take long. The people feel uneasy with so many outsiders.'

Her father nodded with understanding. 'It will take time for them to accept the changes. But so long as you remain queen and appoint a small council of advisors, it will suffice.' One of the terms of their marriage contract was that Alarr had sworn to let her rule over Clonagh. He had admitted to her privately that he agreed with her father. It was easier for the people to accept an Irish queen than a foreigner. In the meantime,

Alarr intended to oversee their defences and protect the ringfort from harm.

Breanne reached out to take her father's hand. Feann walked with her from the small dwelling and led her outside. Alarr was waiting for her, but she could see the apprehension on his face. Not from the marriage, but likely from memories of his previous wedding ceremony. His gaze shifted around the ringfort as if searching for invisible threats.

He wore his *Lochlannach* attire of a woollen tunic, leather armour and dark leggings. She was not at all displeased, for she was about to marry a warrior. This was his custom, and she was proud of his physical form. His dark hair was wet, and his face held the stubble of a dark beard. Around his throat, he wore a bronze necklace with small hammer pendants. It gave him a wild appearance, and a rush of desire filled her up inside. Later this night, she would welcome the chance to feel his hardened muscular form against hers.

But when Alarr caught sight of her, his expression transformed. There was wonder in his eyes, as if he could not believe she was standing there. She smiled at him, and he gave an answering smile. When he took her hands, she squeezed his in reassurance.

'I love you,' she whispered.

'I love you,' came his answer. 'And Freya herself could not be more beautiful.'

Before the ceremony could begin, there was the sound of an approaching horse. To their surprise, the gates opened, and a single rider drew near.

He dismounted and pushed his hood back. Alarr's face held surprise and happiness when he caught sight of his brother Rurik. The younger man hurried towards them. 'Did I miss the wedding?'

'Not yet,' Breanne answered. 'I am so glad you were able to be here.'

'As am I.' Alarr gripped his brother's forearms and smiled.

'Your bride sent a message, and I could not refuse.' He drew back and nodded. 'I wish you both joy in your marriage.' Then Rurik returned to stand by the other guests.

Happiness overwhelmed her with emotions, and she struggled to hold back happy tears. The priest began the words of the marriage rite, and at last, Alarr spoke his vows. 'In the sight of the gods, I take you as my wife, Breanne. I grant you my protection, and I will provide for you and our children. With Freya's blessing, I swear to honour you.'

The tears did fall, then, although she was smiling in the midst of them. The thought of Alarr becoming her husband brought a tender ache to her heart.

Breanne met his gaze and spoke. 'In the sight of the gods, I take you as my husband, Alarr. I will make a home for you and give you children, with the blessing of your gods and my own.'

He gripped her hands tightly, and when she finished her vow, she could see the intense love in his eyes. He would never abandon her, and she had complete trust in him.

The priest gave his blessing and then instructed Alarr to give her a kiss of peace. He did, and she embraced him fully, so grateful to be wedded to this man. But more than that, she was thankful that he had turned aside his vengeance and had learned to live in peace with Feann. She turned to her foster father, and whispered, 'Thank you.'

Alarr led her to the centre of the ringfort and leaned in to murmur at her ear. 'It is time for you to address the people as their queen.'

She kept his hand in hers and smiled at the

people while they gathered around. 'I invite all
of you to share in our wedding feast and celebration. Know that you are welcome here, and it is
our promise to protect this clan. In time, Clonagh will be yours once more.'

At that, she saw tentative smiles among the
people. Many raised their knees as a gesture of
respect, and several cheered.

Alarr brought her a horn of ale and gave her
the first drink before he drank from the same
place her lips had touched. He covered the horn
and then kissed her in front of everyone. It was
a kiss of promise, and it kindled her desire.

Over the next few hours, there was feasting
and dancing. She lost track of all the people, and
there were so many names she would have to
learn. But her happiness soared until she could
scarcely contain her joy.

The air had turned cooler, and Alarr drew his
cloak around her after he saw her shiver. She
turned to him, pressing her hand against his
heart. His arms tightened around her. 'Are you
afraid, *søtnos*?'

She shook her head. Afraid wasn't the right
word. She felt the deep pull of anticipation, and
she drew her fingers lightly over his face. Alarr's

skin was darker from the sun, and his cheeks were rough with his beard. He took her hand in his and led her to the dwelling that would be theirs. She ducked her head beneath the doorway as she went inside. The air was warmer here, heated by the hot stones around the room. There was a bed of furs in one corner, and someone had laid out food and drink for them to share.

'Is it right to leave the people alone at the feast?' she wondered aloud.

'I care not,' Alarr answered. 'I intend to spend the remainder of this day with you, my bride.' He drew a low table nearby and bade her to sit down. He chose a selection of roasted fowl, boiled goose eggs, honeyed cakes, and almonds for her. He broke off a piece of meat and drew it to her lips. She ate and did the same for him, bringing her fingers to his mouth. He sucked one finger inside, and she felt the answering pull of desire.

'Alarr,' she murmured. 'I find that I'm not very hungry right now.' She drew her arms around his neck, hoping he would understand her meaning.

'That's too bad,' he responded. 'For I am starving.' He lifted her into his arms and carried her to the furs.

After he lowered her to standing, he unlaced her gown, sliding it from her shoulders until it pooled at her feet. He kissed her hard, his callused hands moving to her bare skin beneath her shift. She gasped when he cupped one breast, his thumb caressing the erect nipple.

Alarr leaned in and kissed her, sliding his tongue over the rosy tip while he stripped away the rest of her clothing.

He laid her back against the furs, and she could hardly breathe as he feasted upon her, tonguing one breast and then the other. His mouth was hot and hungry upon her skin, tasting every inch. His warm breath brushed over her navel, and he lifted her knees, spreading her open.

She was trembling at that, feeling utterly vulnerable to him. He cupped her bottom, lifting her until he drew his mouth to her inner thigh. She was already aroused, but the tension of his mouth so close to her womanhood was driving her wild. He slid his tongue so close, and then moved to the opposite thigh, kissing her gently.

She was desperate to have his mouth upon her, and her fingers gripped the furs tightly. 'Alarr,' she moaned. 'I need you so badly.'

In the darkness, she could see his head bent between her legs, and his hands gripped her hips, lifting her to him. With his tongue, he tasted her intimately, and she could not stifle her cry. His mouth tormented her sweetly, and she felt herself rising higher. He invaded her with his tongue, nibbling against her hooded flesh while a white-hot fire of need claimed her. She could barely gather her thoughts while he suckled against her most sensitive place.

When he used his thumb to caress her, she could bear it no longer. Her body was alive, the release gathering tightly inside, and when he slid two fingers inside, she lost control. A thousand shudders broke over her, and she arched hard, gasping as the pleasure flooded through her skin. Alarr entered and withdrew with his fingers, and she reached for him, guiding his hard flesh inside. He invaded her in one swift penetration, and she gloried in the feeling of his body joined with hers. She met him, thrust for thrust, wrapping her legs around him.

He deepened the sensations when he suckled at her breast once more, and she squeezed him within her depths. No longer was he gentle, and she revelled in his claiming.

'Take me,' she whispered. 'I am yours.'

He pinned her wrists to the furs, and she released her grip around his waist. Instead, she bent her knees to allow him a deeper angle. This time, his slick shaft rubbed against her, and she could not stop the release that erupted within her. There was only joy in making love to the man she adored, and she gave herself over completely. In his blue eyes she saw love, and when his face contorted, she watched as he took his pleasure, filling her with his seed. He entered and withdrew a few more times until he drew her legs to tangle with his.

She smiled, feeling the heat of their joined bodies. When she touched his chest, she could feel his heart racing. 'I am glad you captured me that day in the slave market,' she murmured. 'I cannot imagine a life without you.'

He kissed her, tracing the skin of her back. 'There is no life for me, without you.' He hugged her close, and she slid her hands down his back, over the curve of his hip, until she reached the scars on the backs of his knees.

He opened his eyes and stared at her while she traced them. 'I am also grateful that you did not kill Feann. And that you made a truce between you.'

'I did it for your sake,' he admitted. 'You are like a true-born daughter to him. He would do anything to protect you. And that is something I understand.'

She brought her hands back to twine around his neck. 'Will you be happy with me at Clonagh? Or do you wish we would return to Maerr?'

'I want to visit Maerr,' he confessed. 'But that kingdom does not belong to me. It is my brother's, if he can reclaim it once more.' He kissed her mouth, and against her lips, he murmured, 'There was a time when I would never have considered staying here. Éireann is not my home.'

'But you belong with me,' she answered.

He leaned in to kiss her. 'You will be my queen, and I will guard you. Whatever we may face, we face it together.'

'Do you want to be a king one day?'

He shook his head. 'Only if there comes a time when the people ask it of me. Until then, I will be your protector.'

'And my husband,' she added. 'Perhaps one day, you will become a father.'

His expression softened, and she realised that he did want that as much as she. 'I will do my best to make you happy, *søtnos*. In whatever life the gods grant us, with any children we may have.' With a wicked smile, he caressed her sensitive breast once more. 'It may take some time before that happens. We will have to keep trying.'

She laughed and embraced him hard. Never had she imagined it was possible to feel so much happiness or love for a man. With Alarr, she became whole and beloved, and her eyes filled up with tears of joy.

'I love you,' she whispered, welcoming him into her arms. And as the afternoon drifted into twilight, he did indeed try again.

And there was only the sweetest pleasure of knowing that she would awaken in this man's arms for the rest of her life.

Epilogue

Rurik stared out over the dark-grey waves as the village of Glannoventa slowly came into view. The fierce wind rippling the sails of the ship assured him that he would reach it by nightfall. Boats bobbed in the sea along its coast. Further up, a fortress sat back on a hillside, the sinking sun turning the stones shades of orange and red. No doubt Wilfrid sat inside those walls, drinking ale and deceiving himself into thinking that he was safe. The man had no idea that vengeance was coming for him before the night was out.

Rurik did not seek revenge for Sigurd's sake—he had his own reasons. He despised his father for what he had done to Saorla. Sigurd had made promises to her that he had broken, and the past could not be healed of its scars. But Rurik intended to seek his own justice for his mother's sake and his brothers. After speaking to his uncle Feann and the others, piecing together what had happened on the day his father was murdered, Rurik had concluded that Wilfrid was the one responsible for the slaughter—and he would pay the price.

He glanced behind him towards the shores of Éireann that had long since disappeared. Alarr had found his own peace with his new bride and would stay there and guard Clonagh. As for the kingdom of Maerr, they both knew it was not theirs. Now that it was ruled by his uncle Thorfinn, no one knew if Brandt would try to reclaim it. Their oldest brother had gone cold with rage, isolating himself from everyone. Sandulf and Danr had their own demons to battle.

This battle was his.

When Rurik looked back at the approaching village, the setting sun had slid from behind a cloud, casting a glimmer on the sea that reminded him of blood. A fitting prophecy of what was to come.

No one would attack Maerr without retribution—he and his brothers had sworn it. Justice was coming for Wilfrid and anyone who stood in Rurik's way.

* * * * *

LET'S TALK
Romance

For exclusive extracts, competitions
and special offers, find us online:

 f facebook.com/millsandboon

 ⃝ @millsandboonuk

 🐦 @millsandboon

Or get in touch on 0844 844 1351*

For all the latest titles coming soon,
visit millsandboon.co.uk/nextmonth

*Calls cost 7p per minute plus your phone company's price per
minute access charge

Want even more
ROMANCE?

Join our bookclub today!

'Mills & Boon books, the perfect way to escape for an hour or so.'

Miss W. Dyer

'Excellent service, promptly delivered and very good subscription choices.'

Miss A. Pearson

'You get fantastic special offers and the chance to get books before they hit the shops'

Mrs V. Hall

**Visit millsandbook.co.uk/Bookclub
and save on brand new books.**

MILLS & BOON